THREE
hard
LESSONS

NIKKI SLOANE

Adobe Edition

ISBN 978-1-507-58189-6

for my husband

chapter
ONE

Fuck this noise.

Traffic on Lake Shore Drive was the worst I'd ever seen. I should have known better than to try it on Black Friday. Even though I was nowhere near Michigan Avenue, it was a parking lot. I glared out over the lake and turned away from the blinding sun that was sinking in the sky to my left.

My phone chimed with a text and I glanced down at the screen. It was my best friend Evie.

> Logan's sick, we have to cancel. Sorry. :(

Well, that's just great. I texted back that it wasn't a big deal, but I was lying. I'd been looking forward to going out for drinks with them the whole week. Ever since Evie and Logan had gotten engaged, I'd been seeing less and less of my best friend. I was happy for her, though. Logan was a great guy. He was hot, hung, and head-over-heels in love with her.

I drummed my manicured nails on the steering wheel of my Jaguar, stared at the taillights in front of me, and considered my options. No way was I going to spend the night alone at my place.

Joseph answered my call immediately.

"Hey, honey, what's up?" My manager's voice was soft and pleasant. He was always so good at making me feel special and anything but another working girl.

"My plans fell through. Can you put me on the list tonight?"

"Of course." There was a rustle of paper in the background. "Should I call Mr. Red and let him know you're available?"

Ugh, no. "Don't do that."

"Oh? Do we have an issue?"

"Someone else needs to take him on as a client. He's getting attached." Joseph knew I didn't do attachments. Mr. Red had money, and I liked money, but there wasn't enough in the world to allow me to get tied down. Well, figuratively. Money got me tied down at the BDSM club I worked at all the time.

"Mr. Red is particular, Payton," Joseph said. "He'll be difficult to persuade to try something new." There was an unfamiliar weight to his voice. Was it fear? "He's also a powerful man."

That wasn't surprising. I'd figured Mr. Red was a major player when he talked about owning half the city, and this was while I had my lips wrapped around his cock.

"He asks me to come home with him afterward. Every. Single. Time."

"A beautiful woman like you probably hears that a lot."

True, but still. "He says he's in love with me. I'm telling you, he's going to turn ugly when he doesn't get his way. I need distance." He sure the fuck wasn't going to get what he wanted from me. I wasn't capable of loving him. I was fairly certain I was incapable of loving anyone.

"Claudia's a lot like you," Joseph said. "Maybe I can give him some incentive to try her."

"Thanks," I said, sincere. I knew Joseph was in a tough

spot. We'd had plenty of clingy clients before, but not one with serious clout.

"You don't have to thank me, honey. I'm excited you're coming in tonight. But fair warning, it'll probably be slow." This was his subtle way of telling me to take the offer when I got it, because there might not be another client interested.

"It's not slow when I'm around," I said, an evil grin twitching on my lips. Traffic was finally starting to ease and my foot found its home on the accelerator.

"No, Payton." He laughed. "It certainly isn't."

Joseph had chosen Nina to be my sales assistant for this evening. Like Scarlett Johansson, Nina had a husky, deep voice that sharply contrasted her petite and undeniably feminine frame. She was a blonde like ScarJo sometimes is, too.

Pairing Nina with me made us an unstoppable force. Someone was going to blow a lot of money tonight, so at least my evening wouldn't be a total bust.

The silk robe came off my shoulders and I caught it in a hand, then carried it to the hook on the back of the door. Room One looked just like all the others. Black textured fabric stretched across soundproof tiles that covered the walls and ceiling, and the absence of color always drew my eyes up to the elaborate crystal chandelier over the table in the center. The intriguing and reinforced fixture was the only light in the room and also pulled double duty. There were plenty of places to hook handcuffs or leather straps onto the iron arms buried beneath the clear prisms.

Nina waited beside the table for me to join her, a pleasant smile on her face as her gaze washed over me. "God, Payton, what I'd give for your tits."

A soft laugh fell out of my mouth. "Please. I've seen you naked at least a dozen times. What I'd give to have that ass."

"It's easy. Pilates," she said, "until you're so sore you can't move, and when you attempt to, you want to die."

Like Nina, I was a total freak about staying in shape. Joseph had a light hand about our figures. One of his girls would have to lose quite a bit of tone for him to say something, but the truth was we all wanted to look our best. Someone you'd pay top dollar for. And of course, there was healthy competition between us. I'd like to think I had the best rack out of the group, and we were all natural. Maybe I had the best legs, too. I was slightly taller than average and the phrase "legs for days" had been thrown my way a few times.

As I sat down on the leather-cushioned tabletop, I tucked a lock of hair behind an ear. I contrasted nicely with Nina's blonde as I was a brunette. My hair color was too dark to really call auburn, but subtle hints of red came out in sunlight, or now in the low, chandelier glow of the room.

The black leather squealed against my bare skin as I slid down to lie flat on my back. Even though the tables were identical in all six rooms, this twin mattress-sized table felt softer than the others. Nina passed me the black blindfold and I hurried to slip the two elastic straps over the back of my head. A tug brought the blindfold down over my eyes, and I descended into the familiar darkness.

My breath picked up. Not with excitement for whatever the person who came in was going to do to me, but with hope. Hope that the thrill of doing this would return. It'd been at least two months since I'd felt anything more than mild interest during a session. I'd been seeing Mr. Red almost exclusively. Maybe that was the cause.

Nina gently took one of my wrists in her hands and set about securing the satiny straps around it.

"Ready?" her smoky voice asked.

"Yeah."

She took my other wrist by my side and wrapped the Velcro closed, securing me to the table. I tested the restraints, which only allowed a few inches of movement, and Nina must have been satisfied because she spoke into her earpiece.

"Room One is ready, you can send the client in."

Her heels clicked across the floor as she went to the white wingback chair perched in the corner of the room. She probably wouldn't be seated for long, unless one of the girls in another room had an appointment with a member. Joseph didn't allow more than one client in the hall at a time for the client's privacy.

Blindfolded and strapped down, I was left with nothing to do but think and wait.

I was kidding myself about my loss of interest being tied to Mr. Red. I didn't want to admit what had happened when I asked Evie and Logan to share their bed with me two months ago. It had been fucking amazing, and insanely hot, but it had started a slow burn in me that I could *not* put out.

I had no regrets about what happened, and they didn't seem to either, but . . . fuck. I wanted what they had. Their connection to each other. I wanted a bond to another person that was so strong, nothing could break it.

Even as Logan was with me, it had been all about her.

I'd been the appetizer to her main course. I needed someone to look at me the way Logan looked at her. It dominated my thoughts when it should have been the men I was servicing.

So now all I could do was hope the man who walked through the door tonight would make me feel something again, and if not, that he'd distract from the powerful loneliness threatening to consume me.

The door creaked open and there was a sound as Nina rose to stand.

"Good evening, sir." God, her voice was sexy. "Please, come in."

Heavy yet hesitant footsteps approached, but stopped several feet away from the table, followed with a sharp intake of breath.

"This one," Nina continued, "is our club's finest."

"Holy shit," a deep, male voice rang out, filled with appreciation.

"Is this your first visit?"

His hurried breathing was nice to listen to. I liked the power I held, how the sight of my naked flesh had affected him.

"Yes," he uttered on a breath.

"Don't be shy. You're more than welcome to look, and I'm sure she's eager to meet you."

Yes, mystery man with deep pockets. Come closer. Will you challenge me tonight?

One footstep. Another. The heavy breathing was nearby now, and I pictured him standing right beside the table, looming over me.

"How did you hear about this place?" she asked.

"Another customer . . ." He trailed off like he was having difficulty focusing. *Good.* Let him be distracted while we negotiated the purchase price.

"A referral? That's great. Are you originally from Chicago?"

He paused. "Milwaukee."

"Oh, no." Her voice was heavy with fake dread. "Don't tell me you're a Packers fan."

Shit. We had code speak, and talking about sports meant my potential client was attractive. Attractive men shelled out less money on average. Football also meant he was late twenties or early thirties. Wealthy, young, and attractive men didn't need to come to the club. Not unless what they wanted was exceptionally taboo.

"I don't get a chance to watch American football."

His deep voice had a delicious roughness I liked, and for a moment I didn't catch the implication. *American* football. Why would someone who grew up in Milwaukee refer to it that way? He sounded like a foreigner.

"That's too bad. The Bears might make the playoffs this year." The room fell quiet, and tension sprang up, winding tighter in the silence. I knew what she was going to say next. "Would you like a taste?" Nina purred.

"How much?" I couldn't tell for certain, but he sounded nervous. Like someone who wasn't willing to part with his hard-earned money easily.

"The taste is complimentary, sir."

"No, I mean, how much for all of it? For her?"

He was going to skip over the sample and get right to it? I struggled to keep myself indifferent while I silently pleaded with Nina not to start too high. He'd freak and bolt. She hesitated. I'm sure she was trying to find the right balance.

It came out shaky and unsure. "Thirty thousand."

Holy mother of god, Nina! Way too high.

I wasn't supposed to speak, but she was going to blow this sale, so I ignored the house rule. "Wait, sir, she meant–"

"All right," he said in his rough but calm voice. "Thirty grand it is."

Stumbled footsteps in heels rang out, like his words had literally knocked Nina back.

I was grateful to be on the table, but I jolted against the straps in shock. He didn't negotiate. Was he not aware this was like buying a car or jewelry? You don't ever go with sticker price. Well, there was feeling in me now, all right. Terror. What the fuck was this guy going to do to me that he was comfortable dropping that kind of money?

"Thirty grand," Nina's voice rasped as she repeated it, stunned. "Uh, excellent. Great."

I could practically hear the gears in her head churning. Was she trying to find a way to get him to negotiate higher? This unprecedented event had us both scrambling.

"Thirty thousand dollars," she echoed again, and it sounded like she's barely left off the phrase, *"You're sure?"* I had to get her out of here before her babbling brought him to his senses.

"Thank you, Nina," I said. Hopefully my dismissive tone wasn't lost on her. Brisk and sharp footfalls away from me announced it wasn't. I let out a breath when the door shut, leaving me alone with the rough edged voice I liked and the worry I did not.

In the quiet, my trepidation built to a level I couldn't control.

"Are you still there?" I couldn't hear him breathing anymore.

"Yes, sorry. I was looking at this, um . . . menu."

The willing list. The menu was set up on an easel in the back of the room. It was everything I would allow my client to either do to me, or was willing to do to him.

"There's a lot on here." It didn't sound judgmental, which was good. He was the one who just agreed to pay for pussy—or whatever else he wanted—so he had no room to be judging anyone.

I controlled my voice. "Are you looking for something in particular?"

There wasn't anything on the list I was opposed to, obviously, but there were a few things I hadn't tried before. Some were the silly ones like diapering, but some were the scarier ones like autoerotic asphyxiation.

"Kissing?"

Oh. "You won't find that on the menu."

"Because it's a given?"

"It's not allowed."

He exhaled. Was that a sigh of disappointment? "A club rule?"

"No," I said. "Mine, sir."

"What happens if I break your rule?" He asked it plainly, like he was concerned he might do it.

I paused. It had happened before, and I had the fucker thrown out. Breach of our totally illegal contract and all. But thirty grand made things different. I was basically the star of this club and received the highest percentage off my deals. I'd be netting ninety percent of that thirty grand, or ninety percent of zero if I wanted to be inflexible on this.

"I suggest you try very hard not to." I didn't want to have to cross that bridge.

"What if I want to hold your hand?" His voice was casual.

I couldn't wrap my head around that concept. "You want to hold my hand?"

"I noticed that's not on the list either."

Was he fucking with me? "If you want to hold my hand, sir, you can do that." It would be awkward as hell, but whatever.

"Dom," he said.

"What?"

"My name. It's Dom."

Of course it is. "Okay. My name is Sub."

"Sub?" This voice was confused. "Is that short for some– ? Oh, I get it. No, my name really is Dom."

His cold, thick fingers touched my wrist and I startled.

"Sorry, may I touch you?"

He'd just agreed to pay thirty grand to do a helluva lot more than *touch* me. My teasing personality slipped out before I could stop it.

"Anxious to get to the hand holding?"

There was a half-laugh from him as he undid the restraint around my wrist, Velcro peeling open with its scratchy, tearing noise. As soon as it was free, footsteps took him around the table to the other side where he freed this wrist, too.

Okay, now what?

I lay motionless on the table, waiting for his command. I had to remind myself he was new to this, and obviously shy. Most guys were on me the moment the sales assistant walked out of the room, some even before. I wasn't sure I had the patience to deal with a timid client, but the money promptly told me to shut the fuck up.

"Dom? You need to tell me what you'd like to do."

"Oh. Can you, um, sit up?"

As I did, there was a rustle of clothes. Good, he was getting undressed. Once the clothes hit the floor I could get this show on the road. The cool fingers closed on my hand, lifting it off the leather.

Right away I could tell his goal wasn't to hold my hand. Warm fabric lined with silk slipped over the skin of my forearm, traveling upwards. Holy shit. He was putting some sort of suit jacket on me, the one he'd probably just taken off.

"What are you doing?" Again, I wasn't supposed to ask questions, but this was disorienting.

"I'd like to talk, and this is the only way we can do that." The jacket was around my shoulders now, and he urged my other arm into the empty sleeve, pulling the front of the jacket closed. "You are way too distracting when you're naked."

The sleeves of his jacket were well past my fingertips, so he was probably tall. The warm, slippery fabric felt wonderful on my skin, and the manly scent of cologne clung to his jacket. Shit, he smelled good. *Focus,* my brain ordered. He wanted to talk, and that idea was scary. I could do all sorts of things he'd like, but conversation? That wasn't one of them.

We lapsed into silence. For wanting to talk, he was doing a shitty job of it.

"Are you nervous?" I prompted. Maybe he was having a hard time getting it up. "Do you want me to go down on you?"

"No," he said quickly. "I . . ." Breath left him in what sounded like a frustrated burst. "I live in Tokyo."

Um . . . kay? He said it like that could explain what his issue was. Was he Japanese? Was this a culture thing?

"Have you ever been?" he continued.

"To Japan? No, but I'd love to. I lived in the Netherlands for a semester, but I stayed in Europe. That's the farthest east I made it."

"What was that like, living overseas? Did you like it?"

I did. That night in the red light district had shown me not just what I was interested in, but what I was so very good at. "It was fucking awesome."

"Did you ever get lonely?" His voice was low, which intensified the gravel in it. "Did you feel like an outsider?"

I shook my head. "In Amsterdam? Nope. I was staying at an international dorm, though. We were a stoned and drunk version of the UN."

His silence drained the memories of my wildest times away. I turned on the table to face his voice, letting my legs dangle over the side.

"Japan is . . . not welcoming to foreigners." So, he wasn't Japanese after all. My hand not holding his suit jacket closed was flat on the leather beside me, and his fingers brushed up against mine.

What the fuck? What was that? How had this innocent gesture made my heart beat faster? The cushion top shifted as he sat beside me, his fingers now trailing a pattern on the back of my hand.

"You know, Japan has these hostess bars where men pay to have an hour's worth of conversation with a woman who's not their wife or girlfriend."

Tingling warmth was left in the wake of his strokes. Everything was upside-down. What was happening? "Why?" I asked in my disoriented state.

"Everyone's desperate to connect. There are people packed in all around, and yet it's the most isolating place you can imagine." Dom eased his fingers under my palm, turning it so he could lace his fingers with mine. "I can't go into a lot of these bars because I'm an American. Not that it fucking matters. It's unlikely the women speak English. And the ones I can go in are usually Yakuza owned. Not exactly safe."

His once cold hand now scorched on mine. Jesus, when was the last time I held hands with someone? Eighth grade? This was weird, and yet, oddly nice. I tightened my hold on him, and my breathing became uneven.

"You like the sexy hand holding, don't you?" he said.

I choked back the startled, nervous giggle. I wanted to take the blindfold off. I wanted him to order me to lie back down so he could shove himself inside me and the power I was accustomed to would be mine again. Nothing shocked me anymore when I was on this table; I'd seen and done just about everything. But this unfamiliar experience and my reaction to it . . .

"We can do so much more than just this," I whispered. It might have been a plea.

"I know. There's a menu of all the stuff we can do over there on an easel." The knuckles of his free hand brushed over my cheek, turning my head toward him. "Maybe I want to do the stuff that's not on there."

I didn't have time to respond. The hand cradled my face and held me into his kiss. Soft, damp lips grazed mine as if testing the waters, and when I didn't move, he kissed me for real. His mouth moved on mine, gentle yet in control. A hint of possession that was kind of hot.

No. Against the rules, my brain yelled.

I tried to turn away, but his hand holding mine abandoned it so he could grip my face between his palms, denying my halfhearted escape, and shifting me to the best angle. So he could slip his wet, soft tongue into my betraying and welcoming mouth.

Electricity arced through my body. Fuck, it turned me on, which had never happened before. Kissing with men usually did nothing for me. It had always been a weird tangle of probing tongues and noses smashed together, but this kiss wasn't anything like that. It was hot. I wanted more, and I sighed audibly when he was polite enough to give it to me.

He must have figured out I was cool with him breaking the rule, because one hand relaxed and worked its way up onto the back of my head, tugging the elastic bands up. The tension on the blindfold eased away just as he did. He was giving me back my sight as a reward for accepting his kiss. When the blindfold was off, my eyes fluttered open and adjusted to the light.

"Holy shit," I said, echoing back his reaction to me.

Dom was a shade too handsome to call cute. He was more elegant and serious looking than a catalog-model pretty boy. The man beside me, a blindfold in one hand, was out of this world hot. Long lashes framed strikingly aqua-blue eyes. His hair was longer on the top than it was on the sides and fawn colored. Two days' worth of stubble etched his strong, defined jaw. Distinctly male, and sexy as fuck.

His piercing eyes clouded with distrust at my reaction, and for a half-second it looked like he was thinking about how he could get the blindfold back on. So I yanked it from his hand and tossed it aside. I wanted to clear that up right away.

"I said *holy shit* because you're really fucking hot. What

the hell are you doing here?" *Stop talking, Payton.* "You could go into any bar and women would drop their panties for you."

A huge smile spread on his face. "You think so?"

I scrunched brows. "I don't get why you did this."

The warmth in his eyes faded a touch. "I don't have a lot of time. I only came home for Thanksgiving." He straightened, smoothing a hand down the buttons of his gray dress shirt. "I'd rather not waste it shouting over a speaker at some crowded bar, hoping to get . . . to find a connection." His eyes drifted from mine. "This way you have to talk to me."

"Talk," I said. "You don't want to have sex?"

His eyes snapped back to mine, and color warmed over his cheeks. "I didn't say that."

Oh, hell. He *was* cute, when he was embarrassed. He wanted a sure thing, too.

"Can I be honest?" His blue eyes blinked slowly, hypnotizing.

I nodded. "Sure."

"Meeting women in Tokyo is fucking impossible when you're a *Gaijin*. I've been there almost a year." His gaze fell away and he tangled his hand with mine once again. "It's been a long time and I'm way off my game."

Oh my god, really? "You haven't had sex in a year?"

He pressed his lips together for a moment. "Not with someone else."

My eyes raked down his body, noting the delicious build hidden beneath the dress shirt and black suit pants. He probably spent as much time in the gym as I did. A year without someone riding that? What a waste.

"You look like a man who knows how to fuck."

The subdued color flashed on his face again. "I'd like to think so, yeah."

"Show me." It came out before I could stop it, and my hand let go of the lapels of the jacket so it fell open. Cool air rolled over my bare skin, giving me goosebumps.

He frowned and cinched the jacket closed, bringing his face so much closer to mine. "Can we slow down?"

The vibrant blue eyes were wide and gorgeous. Flecks of dark gray scattered among his irises matched his shirt perfectly. My job was to give him what he wanted. My desires were irrelevant, I reminded myself. Since he was already there, it took him no time to close the breath of space between us and attempt to kiss me again.

I leaned away. "Remember my rule."

"You didn't seem to mind last time." His voice was an even mixture of accusation and desperation.

"I'm sure it was an accident, and I believe in second chances." I folded my jacket-clad arms over my chest and crossed my legs that dangled over the side of the table. The bottom of the fabric just covered the naughty bits, but gave him a magnificent view of my inner thigh. The muscles along his jaw tightened.

Hidden high in the corner of the room, there was a closed circuit camera, and up in Joseph's office, Nina and Joseph would be monitoring the feed for security. She had to be wondering what the hell was going on. I glanced at his hunched shoulders and how he had his head cast down.

"Dom, can I be honest, too? I'm terrible at talking. It makes me kind of uncomfortable." The idea took shape and then I blurted it out. "I'll be better at it if I'm distracted."

I put my hand on his thigh, halfway between his knee

and his hip. Not too high to be aggressive, but not too low to be considered merely friendly. It was another club no-no. The client initiated, not the girl. Part of me no longer cared about the rules.

It was because part of me wanted him. This strange spark between us was intoxicating and disarming. If I'd run into him at a bar on one of my recruiting crawls, I would have snatched him up in a hot second.

His warm hand crushed mine as he leaned in again, his mouth hovering dangerously close to mine. "How do you suggest I distract you?"

It was a bullshit question and he knew it. Lips descended on me, but this time into the side of my neck, and I gasped. I jolted under his kiss and tilted my chin up and away, giving him better access. The cushion shifted under me as he stood. One hand cupped my jaw while the other ventured inside the jacket, working its way around to my back. He yanked me tight against his hard body, my legs falling to part around him and his wide hips. My cheek rested against the tough skin of his palm while he sucked on my neck, licking and teasing me with teeth.

I goddamn shuddered under his power. *Me.* I struggled to find air through my slack mouth. Jesus, what he was doing felt good.

"What's your name?" he mumbled into my skin.

". . . Paige." For the first time ever, I felt bad about lying, but it was too dangerous to use my real name.

"Fake or real?" He worked a path of kisses down to my collarbone.

I wasn't supposed to touch unless given permission, but I found his head in my hands, my fingers weaving through his soft, thick hair. The long suit sleeves were bunched up at my elbows and constricting, but I liked having the jacket on. I liked wearing part of him.

"Fake," I whispered. "You understand why–"

"Yeah." His rough voice rumbled at the base of my throat. He was coming back up. "I'm going to kiss you again. It won't be an accident."

My heart pounded in my chest and I sucked in a breath. "Dom–"

Too late. His hot mouth crushed against mine and this kiss wasn't gentle. It wasn't sweet or curious. It was demanding. Urgent. Passionate. The kind of kiss a man waited a year to give a lucky woman, and I was that fucking lucky woman. My moan was loud and my hands clenched fistfuls of his hair, trapping him where I wanted him. I was drugged by these strange feelings, and thirsty for more.

He tore his lips away from mine and stared down at me with a discerning and sharp look. "Was that reaction fake or real?"

I couldn't breathe, but I managed to speak on a shaky voice. "Real."

The side of his mouth lifted in a pleased smile. "Then fucking kiss me."

chapter THREE

Sitting on the table with Dom towering over me, his hands inching their way toward my breasts, was exciting. The tingling anticipation built with each painfully slow move, creeping leisurely toward the nipples that were hard and sensitive beneath the silky lining of the jacket.

His tongue was deep in my mouth, each wicked stroke over mine better than the last, urging me to come play. I was more focused on my hands and had several buttons of his shirt undone before I paused.

"Is this okay?" I asked.

He resumed kissing me, giving me his answer by helping me undo the rest. I flung the shirt and my jacket open and shifted until I was all the way at the edge of the table, leaning into him. My breasts pressed against the hard angles of his defined chest and we both sucked in a breath. Skin on warm, soft skin.

"That feels so fucking good," he said.

He didn't have to tell me, not just because I agreed. The evidence that he liked it was hard on my inner thigh. My legs wrapped around his hips, drawing him closer. I reached for his belt buckle, and as I tugged on it, he straightened. A hand locked on my shoulder and shoved me, sending me backward until I was flat on the cushion and staring up at the chandelier.

"Slow down, Paige." His warning was sort of playful, but sort of not. The rough voice made everything sound like a command, and that also made me insane with lust. "You haven't been talking at all."

"You make that hard when you keep breaking my rule."

As I'd fallen onto my back, the hand on my shoulder shifted and caressed down my body, brushing over my breast. It trailed over my waist, down over my hip . . . and down . . .

"Tease," I blurted out. He'd skimmed his fingers in the hollow of my inner thigh. One goddamn inch from where I wanted it.

"It's only teasing if I don't do it eventually." He traced the hollow on the other side. "I could say the same thing about you. Doesn't this have you distracted enough to talk?"

He had a point. I searched for something to get the awkward conversation going. "What do you do in Japan?"

"I confirm US inventory on container ships so it can pass through customs without incurring a tax when it arrives in California."

Wow, thrilling. "Do you like your job?"

His gaze drifted across the landscape of my exposed skin. The opening edges of the jacket were hung on my breasts, covering them, but everything else was on full display. I mean, total display because I had Brazilians religiously.

"My job's necessary to save the company millions of dollars. After another year, I'll come back to new opportunities that weren't available before."

A smile crept across my lips. "You didn't answer my question."

"My job blows, but the money's fucking amazing." His eyes turned serious. "What about you?"

"Me? I like what I do." It came out kind of indifferent.

"Fake?" The coarse skin of his palm glided back up, urging the jacket open to expose a nipple to him.

"Real," I said. "I used to love it, but . . ."

The hand finished its journey to my breast, closing on the skin. His eyes hooded as he watched me arch my back into his touch.

"Why don't you love it anymore?" His rushed breathing was the same as it had been when he first came in the room.

"It's a stupid reason. I don't want to talk about it." I let a hand wander over the ridges of his six-pack abs, staying above the belt.

He leaned over me, supporting himself on one hand while the other traced circles on my nipple. Then, his head dropped down and something wet replaced his touch, caressed me. I moaned. Finally we were moving past freshman year of high school.

"Come on, tell me." Lips fluttered against the curve of my breast. "I can find better ways to distract you."

Oh, fuck it. "My best friend fell in love and is getting married."

He went wooden.

"All of my other friends," I continued, "are already married, or have kids." I couldn't put it into words, but I felt like I'd spent too much time fucking around and I'd missed my window. I didn't want the white picket fences and mini-van life, but I wanted to mean something to someone. I was selfish and greedy. I wanted someone to belong to me. "I feel like I've been left behind."

"Shit," he said, hushed. "I know exactly what you mean."

And then his head dipped back to my breast and drew my nipple into his mouth, sucking at me. A bolt of white-hot pleasure shot between my legs. *Yes.* It was plenty distracting, but he wasn't done yet. The pads of his fingers inched downward until he buried them between my legs.

I moaned. Just the faintest touch had me breathless.

"Do you like this?" he whispered. "Real?"

"Yes, very real."

He searched and found the nub of flesh, swollen and already aching for him, his fingers rolling a small circle and increasing pressure. This moan was loud and grateful. The whiskers dotting his jaw scraped over the valley of my breasts as he pushed the jacket aside and traveled to the other nipple. Cold air washed over the wet skin he'd left behind, making the knot of flesh harder.

"I'm thirty three years old," he said, "and the last of my friends proposed to his girlfriend a month ago. I know they're all wondering what's wrong with me."

It was getting hard to think with how his hand was pleasing me and the almost nonexistent filter I had burned away to nothing in my need. "Is something wrong with you?"

"Other than the fact I'm willing to pay thirty grand to have a conversation? I don't think so."

Shit, we better do more than just have a conversation. I shifted my hips, trying to get him to slip a finger inside me. His lips moved up and returned to mine. Every time he kissed me, it was like the wires crossed in my brain. I didn't want it—and I was desperate for it.

"I didn't have a problem meeting women here, but I didn't get too serious about anything when I found out I was moving to the other side of the world." The heat spreading from his touch made my stomach tighten. "You must be fighting the guys off. What's your story?"

I got my wish when he eased a finger inside me, all the way in.

"I get bored," I gasped, opening my legs wider, and bit down teasingly on his bottom lip. "Most guys aren't up to the challenge of me."

"Are you too much to handle, Paige?" He thrust his middle finger gently into me, his thumb moving on my clit. The sensation drove me crazy with lust. I clawed at the bare skin of his chest, wanting more.

Was I too much? "Definitely," I answered. "Can I have another?"

The blue eyes flared with desire and he straightened to his full height. I loved how he looked. Hair ruffled from my fingers, his shirt undone and hung open, his piercing gaze locked on me, spread out before him.

"Maybe you're too much for other guys," he said, "but not for me." The second finger joined in, filling me where I was damp and hot. I bucked on the cushion top with a cry of pleasure, my hands clenching fistfuls of his dress shirt. I didn't know if I was trying to bring him closer or if it was a simple reaction from the overwhelming desire flooding my veins.

This is the guy who I'd made blush. Twice. "You're in way over your head with me, Dom."

"Says the woman who doesn't like kissing, or talking, and I've gotten you to do both in less than fifteen minutes."

My eyes widened.

"Yeah," he said as he increased the speed of his thrusts, his fingers pumping in and out of me. "I think I'm doing all right."

He was doing better than all right. "Fuck, you're going

to make me come."

The corners of his mouth lifted in a wicked smile. "What will that taste like?"

What—? He dropped down to his knees, bringing his head level with the table.

"Oh, god, yes. Taste it," I begged. The sight of his head positioned between my thighs nearly brought me to orgasm.

"Scoot back and I will," the rough voice said.

I did immediately. Warm breath hovered over my pussy. My muscles tightened in hungry anticipation for his tongue, and then . . .

Flames licked at me where his tongue did. I jolted up onto my bent elbows, but threw my head back as a startled moan tore from my mouth.

"Oh, god, Dom. Fuck me with that mouth."

It hadn't been like this. Not ever. Sometimes a guy liked eating pussy, but that was always for him. I'd put on a show, pretend he was much better than he was until I faked an orgasm and he got excited thinking he'd gotten me off. The sensation now was different. Dom wanted to please me. Not because he wanted to show off his sexual prowess; I think he simply wanted me to enjoy it.

"Are you going to come for me?"

"Yes, yes . . ."

Fingers filled and stretched me, plunging and retreating. The wicked rhythm grew the intensity in my center, and that tongue— It was magic. Pinpricks needled up my spine and my legs shook. I panted for air. I writhed against the mouth sucking and fucking me, his tongue fluttering at a furious tempo.

"Fuck, *fuck*!"

The orgasm seized me and I screamed. Pleasure exploded outward in all directions, sending warm bliss rushing through every cell of my body, and leaving pleasant numbness in its wake. My hands had jerked his head hard up against me, and I relaxed the grip as the pleasure began to fade.

His voice rang out between my punctuated gasps for breath. "It tastes good."

I shuddered. I loved hearing that, but I wondered . . . "Fake?"

He chuckled. "Real." What reason would he have to lie? He had thirty thousand excuses to be honest. His fingers remained inside me. They'd slowed but were still moving. "Tell me something you've never told anyone else."

I struggled to catch my breath and searched for something to satisfy his request.

"My favorite movie is *Airplane.*"

The hand stopped moving, and I made a noise of disappointment. He'd probably wanted something deeper than my admission that my favorite movie was a '70s slapstick comedy.

"Surely you can't be serious," he rumbled.

I smiled like an idiot, thrilled he knew the joke. "I am serious, and don't call me Shirley." The hand resumed its disciplined pace and he climbed to his feet, his other hand wiping his mouth and latching on to my hip.

He was utterly gorgeous and I couldn't wait to get on him, but reminded myself he wanted to go slow. After that orgasm, the least I could do was give him his money's worth.

"Now you," I said. "Something you've never told anyone else before."

"My favorite movie's *Airplane*."

I curled my eyes down into slits. "Fake?"

"Fake," he admitted. "Paige, I'm so fucking hard right now, I think it might kill me."

He wasn't lying; his pants were tented spectacularly. And the pole pitching the tent looked to be impressive. I wanted to see what I was going to be working with, so I sat up. He withdrew his hand from me, his expression confused.

I tilted my head up so my eyes could meet his. "Let me see what I can do about that."

He let out a nervous breath.

"Take off your shirt," I pointed to the wingback in the corner, "and go sit in that chair."

The confusion continued on his face, but he hesitantly unbuttoned his cuffs as I stood up from the table. I waited until he peeled the shirt down past his toned biceps and dropped it on the table before I opened the top drawer and grabbed a handful of condoms, slipping them into the suit pocket. The jacket was so oversized on me the pockets were below my hips.

The aqua eyes stayed on me as he lowered his shirtless body into the chair. I sauntered toward him, a seductive smile splashed on my face and a sway in my hips. Which he probably couldn't see, I realized dimly, due to the jacket. But I'll be damned if I was going to take it off. I wanted him to do that.

"What are you doing?" There was a high level of concern in his voice when I knelt before him and went for his belt.

"I want to suck your cock."

His chest lifted in an enormous breath. "I don't think that's a good idea."

I slid the leather end free, and my fingers focused on undoing the button beneath it. "Why not?"

"I haven't had any in a year and I feel like a virgin. I'll lose it in, like, five seconds." There was that sexy blush. An embarrassed Dom was so adorable.

"Give me some credit," I whispered. The button snapped free and I inched his zipper down over his erection. "I can get you to last at least ten seconds."

His hand closed on my shoulder, worry lacing his voice. "No, then this will be over. I'm not eighteen. I don't bounce back like I used to."

"You feel like a virgin? Come in my mouth." My hands fell onto his hips so my fingers could curl under the waistband of his pants and boxers. "I can be patient and you'll last longer later when you're fucking my pussy."

He stared at me, his devastating eyes unblinking. Then, he lifted his hips in silent agreement so I could pull the fabric out of my way.

"Wow, nice." And it was. His cock wasn't the longest I'd ever seen, but it was definitely better than average, a gentle curve upward, and impossibly thick.

"Real or fake?"

I wouldn't lie about the compliment. I gave him a sincere look. "Real, I promise."

He sucked in a breath through clenched teeth when I wrapped both hands around him, one at the base and the other at the head, and squeezed.

"Shit, woman, my estimated time might have been high."

I grinned. He was fun. When was the last time someone had given me a genuine smile while in the room? I kept my eyes on his when I leaned forward and swept my tongue across the tip of his cock.

He groaned in satisfaction. Or agony. That noise could have applied to either one. Didn't matter, I was going to have him in my mouth. I was excited to see him unravel. Would he blush afterward? I licked my lips and slid him inside, until I was past the ridge of his head.

"Mmm . . . okay, that feels really fucking good." He said it like a warning.

I was just getting started, too. My tongue did a cartwheel over the velvety slit on the head of his cock. His hands on the armrests of the chair tightened until he was white-knuckled.

I released him from my mouth and stared at him, letting my eyes fill with everything I felt. How badly I wanted this. How much pleasure I could give him. How I wanted to be able to do this to him for a while.

I think he held his breath when I took him in my mouth again, this time going all the way down. Holy shit, he was thick. I drew patterns with the tip of my tongue on his flesh.

"Jesus," he groaned.

When I started to bob my head, one of his hands went to his forehead and he tilted his head back, closed his eyes. It looked very much like he was enduring torture, yet in direct conflict to that, "Don't stop," he ordered.

I tried to keep my hands out of the mix, not wanting to overwhelm the born-again virgin until he was ready. He let me move faster on him, taking him as deep as I could, and he hit the back of my throat on every pass. His throbbing cock was slippery with my saliva.

"Slower," he commanded or pleaded.

Unfortunately, it was too late with my aggressive nature. I liked it too much. My hand latched at the base of his cock and began to move in concert with my mouth. I went faster, too. His quick and labored breathing, occasionally interrupted by a moan, made me crazy wet.

"Okay, so I guess you want me to come now." Like he was talking aloud to himself and annoyed with me. It was hot. I hollowed out my cheeks with sucking as I tormented him, enjoying every inch of his skin inside me.

I pulled off of him again, my lips just against his damp, swollen column of flesh that was as hard as a diamond. I was on fire and his eyes were oceans I wanted to drown in.

"I love the way you taste. Do you like fucking my mouth?"

The oceans turned dark and his tone was frosty. "I told you not to stop."

I grinned. Holy hell! There was a dominant side buried inside Dom that had just revealed itself. Harsh hands seized my head and forced my mouth back down on him, and I moaned in ecstasy. I *loved* to be dominated and disciplined.

With his hands trapping me, he took control. His hips thrust into my mouth, beating his cock against my lips and deeper toward the dangerous threshold of my gag reflex. I tried to relax the muscle. I'd been training to deep throat but it was better if I had control when doing it.

"Suck that cock," he ordered. "I'm gonna fill that mouth. Get ready."

I let loose another moan, this one dripping with approval, humming it.

There was a stream of obscenities from him as the hard muscle inside me flexed. Hands jerked my head up and down in rapid, uneven strokes as thick, hot liquid pooled in my mouth. His whole body shuddered as he came, a low and long, deep moan in his gravel voice. It looked like every muscle in Dom was tense, from the thick cord of his neck all the way down to his flexed feet.

The orgasm that rolled through him finally seemed to pass when he came to a stop, and his breathing evened out.

I swallowed and slowly pulled off of him.

The hands in my hair were gentle, angling my face to him, stroking the glossy strands back out of my eyes.

"I didn't mean to be like that," he whispered. "I don't know where that came from." He looked guilty.

"Really? I though it was hot."

He didn't look like he believed me. I put a hand on his knee and pushed up to stand before him. We made quite a pair. Him naked except for the suit pants bunched at his ankles and me naked beneath the open suit jacket.

The white chair made no noise when he sat forward. He reached down and set his palm against my calf, and began to drag the tough skin of his hand up my leg, up the curve of my body.

"You are stunningly beautiful."

My breath caught in my throat. That wasn't the kind of compliment I was used to. "Uh, thank you."

The hand dragged up on to my upper thigh, lifting the suit jacket as it reached my hip. Fingers pressed me forward and he buried his mouth in my flesh, his tongue dipping into the recess of my belly button. I blew out a breath, clamping down on my control. He was going to need to recover before we got to the really good stuff, even though I wanted it all *now*.

Strong, manly hands were inside the jacket. They roamed over the small of my back, down to my ass, fingers drawing me forward. He wanted me closer. I put a knee on the chair armrest.

"Something you've never told anyone else," I said. "You never answered me."

He said nothing. Had he not heard me? Maybe he was too focused on my bare and wet pussy right in front of his face.

"I've never been in love," he said.

chapter FOUR

Dom's hand on my ass followed the curve around my hip, moving to the front, raking his fingernails over the skin as it went.

"There was a girl," he said, "I was with for more than two years. I told her I loved her, but I don't think I did." His hand hovered right above my slit so the heat soaked into my body where hair would be if it hadn't been waxed away.

"What makes you say that?"

"When I caught her fucking another dude, I didn't really care. I mean, I was beyond angry, but I wasn't . . . hurt. I wasn't all that sad."

His eyes were magnetic. An irresistible force compelled me to look at him.

"I can't explain why I didn't love her. She was nice, and funny, and smart . . . although leaving the pictures on her phone of his dick in her mouth wasn't the brightest idea." His hand slipped down so his thumb could roll over my clit. "It was like, whenever I told her I loved her, it felt—"

"Like a lie," I said. My heart thudded in my chest.

"Yes." His enormous startled eyes snapped to mine and were mesmerizing. *Connection.*

I'd been where he had. I spent a year with Joel pretending. Wanting to be in love with him, but I'd failed. I'd learned my lesson the hard way that you can't choose who you love.

"Have you ever been in love?" Dom asked. The thumb rubbed steady circles on my sensitive skin. It made my knees weak. I wasn't going to be able to stand much longer if he continued. Or attempted anything better. Talking about love while he teased me; could this night get more insane?

"No," I lied. "I don't do love."

"Why's that?"

Damn him. He replaced his thumb with his mouth. I steadied myself with a hand on his shoulder and groaned softly. Mine rang out like his did before, satisfaction and agony.

"I don't have any shame in what I do," his mouth made it a struggle to find air, "but others have a hard time with it."

The tongue lapping at me ceased. "You keep, um, working when you're in a relationship?"

"No, but I don't do relationships either. I get bored, remember?" The wet, soft tongue swiped over my entrance. Again, I fisted a hand in his light brown hair that had a soft curl at the ends. Whatever woman had trained him, I owed her. I could let him fuck me with his mouth all night. *Wait . . .*

"I don't want to come like this," I said. "The next one's on your cock."

The hand on my ass hardened. "I'm going to need another minute, or five, and you're getting awfully bossy." His eyes were warm and playful. "Maybe I should strap you back down on the table."

I pushed his head away. My knee moved from the armrest down to the cushion beside his hip. My other knee followed, so I straddled his lap. Shit, I *was* ordering him around. Somewhere along the way, I'd disregarded every rule, including my own. This night had gotten totally out of control, but I wouldn't change it for anything. I sat back so his dick was in front of me and I clenched it in a hand.

"You're already halfway there," I whispered. He was semi-hard as I stroked him.

"It's been a year. You have no idea how much I want this."

Not as much as I do, I almost said. And that? That was the most shocking thing of all. I loved sex, sure, but wanting it this badly with a client? I wouldn't have believed it in a million years.

"I want this, Dom. Very, fucking real."

My brain disconnected and shut down. I reached a hand out to grasp his chin and pull him to me so I could slant my lips on his, feathering the lightest of kisses there. Not enough. My second kiss was better. Lightning crackled between us.

I had kissed him. I *was* kissing him, and that action was not lost on Dom. Touching me got him started, but my mouth on him and my tongue caressing his was the activation switch to turn him on. He twitched in my hand, hardening in a single stroke.

We both broke the kiss at the same time and looked down, stunned at this reaction. I didn't waste a moment more. I yanked a condom out of the pocket and tore the packet open, rolling it down the length of him as he groaned.

He went rigid as I positioned myself over him. Shit, was I moving too fast again? Did he want me some other way?

"What's wrong?" I asked.

He had one hand on my hip and the other slipped behind my neck. "Nothing's wrong. I'm trying to remember this." He let me lower myself down on him so he was right at my entrance. "Tonight's got to get me through the next sexless year."

I slid down, welcomed him inside my body, one fraction at a time. God, his cock was thick. My eyes fell closed as I descended further. The realization that this was it for him was powerful and struck me like a fist to my chest.

At last he was buried as deep as he could go. "Oh, god," I cried out, my voice wrapped in pleasure. He silenced anything else I would have said when he took my mouth with his.

Now I was the only woman he'd been with in a year; the only woman he'd be with in two years if things continued the way he assumed they would. He'd chosen me for this.

The first hesitant move I made sent us both into panic.

"Stop," he said. His hand was firm in its grasp on the nape of my neck. "It feels too good already."

Something tightened in my chest painfully. It was some emotion I couldn't put a label on, or refused to. A need that was scary and thrilling. This connection with him was too powerful to stop.

"I'll do whatever you want, just please don't make me stop," I said. It sounded like I was begging, because I was. My arms crossed behind his back and I leaned forward, kissing him in the crook of his neck.

"Slow," he ordered.

"I can do slow." It was a lie, but I'd do my best. I moved again, shifting up in his lap and back down. The slow, slick slide of his cock inside me was amazing. Holy shit, I think I could come just from riding him like this. Slow and steady.

I began at a torturous pace, so much slower than I was used to, yet it was unbelievably arousing. In response, strong hands peeled the edge of the jacket down past my shoulders, letting the collar bunch at my elbows. As the silk lining fell away, Dom set his warm mouth on my exposed skin, the spot where my neck met my shoulder. His tongue traced a line and left goosebumps in its trail.

He had me encased in his arms and held me tight when his hips hinted I could increase my tempo. So I did. How the fuck did it feel so good?

"Look at me." That rough voice turned my insides into liquid. His hands splayed over my body but his gaze was unrelenting and filled with passion. What we were doing? It didn't feel like fucking. This was something different, something I hadn't done before. The unfamiliar newness left my head spinning.

"I'm going to be thinking about this," he said, "every night for the next year. Every night it will be you."

I gasped loudly and the muscles of my pussy clenched. "Oh my god."

He could have doused me in gasoline and lit me on fire, and it wouldn't have compared to how hot his words made me burn. My self-control was obliterated and I hungered for his kiss. I wanted to sink into his skin as the fire inside me raged brighter and brighter. The need for release came at me like a tornado. Fast, and unpredictable.

Our mouths melded into one. Beads of sweat flowered over our skin since the cold room felt like a sauna. Beneath me, his thrusts were powerful, hitting exactly where they needed to, scratching the itch that would send me over the edge. I couldn't breathe. I couldn't slow down, or look away from the aqua eyes gazing back at me. His ragged breath was warm on my face when he set his forehead against mine.

I was going to come. Any second now. The climb kept going higher, and higher, and higher . . . My toes curled into points and my eyes slammed shut. The pleasure welled up, ready to erupt –

His arms were locked around my body, and this prison began to close in, stilling me. Denying the pleasure that was about to set me free.

"No, no!" I cried, my eyes fluttering open. "I'm so close. Please don't stop."

The tortured look on his face was heartbreaking, and gone a second later, as was the tension in his arm. Oh shit, oh shit . . .

Hands clench my hips and drove me on him. These fast, hard thrusts were each tiny orgasms, teasing the big finish that loomed. "Please," I begged him on every thrust. "Please . . . please . . ."

I crested and screamed all the way down. When I lose control, I really fucking lose control of everything, including my voice. My heart slammed against my chest as ecstasy erupted from my core, deafening my mind. Only sensation remained. So much pleasure, it reached beyond bliss, and it lasted an eternity.

The sensation morphed into something new as he lost control after me. The pulsing inside my body narrowly avoided crossing over into pain since I was on total overload. He gasped and dug in his fingers, holding me while my body milked his orgasm from him. I moaned with each throb of his cock, clamping down on it with the muscles on my walls surrounding him.

He groaned. It was so sexy. Heat drenched us both and pressed us together as we slowly returned to earth. That was when it hit me.

Oh, holy, fucking shit. I'd been so selfish.

He'd wanted to go slow and make a long memory to hold him through the next year, and in my greediness, that memory was now less than ten minutes. Maybe less than five. I'd lost all track of everything.

He clutched me tightly to his heaving chest. I shrugged out of the jacket so I could touch him with my skin completely unhindered. My naked body wrapped around his and I gripped him fiercely. "Dom." My voice was a ghost. "I'm sorry."

He lifted his head and blinked his disoriented eyes. "Sorry?"

"I didn't go slow."

He'd said it himself. No way was he going to be able to recover for a third round anytime soon. My stomach was in knots. I couldn't do this to him. I'd wanted to feel something, and now I fucking did. Crushing guilt. This night was supposed to be about him, not me. I'd stolen what he wanted.

In the quiet, there was only the sound of our breathing slowing, and I knew what I had to do. I climbed off of him.

"Wait," he said, but I ignored it.

I picked his jacket up off of the floor and went to the table so I could set it beside his shirt.

"Come back," he said.

Unsteady feet carried me to the silk robe hanging on the hook. My hand shook when I pulled it down and slipped it on, and turned to finally face him. He was devastatingly handsome, even when his face was full of confusion.

"Please get dressed." My voice was hollow since I was terrified by what I was about to do. "I have to talk to my manager."

He already had the condom off and knotted it, and dropped it into the trash. My eyes were fixed on him as he stood and pulled up his pants. I watched the muscles in his lean arms flex as he did the zipper and then the button, his gaze pinned on me.

My whole body shook. My stomach was lined with lead.

"Why do you have to talk to your manager?"

"Because the deal's off."

chapter
FIVE

Dom froze mid-buckle of his belt. "What?"

I took a hesitant step toward him, then another as my nervous hands tightened the sash at the waist of my robe. "Stay in the room, don't leave until I get back."

Because if he stepped out into the hall, that was it. The transaction was complete and Marquis would escort Dom to the payment room, where I'd never see him again.

The disorientation was clear on Dom's face. "Why is the deal off?"

"Because I didn't do what I was supposed to."

I watched the confusion grow larger in his magnetic eyes. "Which was what? Give me the best sex I've ever had? Believe me, Paige, you delivered. And then some."

My goddamn knees turned to mush. He stormed at me, a blur of skin stretch over muscle and pulled me roughly into his arms.

"What is this?" he asked.

Maybe he thought this was some sort of ploy. A shakedown for more money. I wasn't anywhere near a good enough actress to pull off the fractured feeling I was sure to be displaying.

"I don't want your money," I gasped. "It will make what just happened . . . not real."

My brain scrambled, desperate to find a way to come out the other side of this. I'd rather have this night as whatever the fuck it was, than my percentage of his thirty grand.

I'd have to drive myself to the ER after I left here, because something was very, very wrong with me.

"I don't understand," he said. "I have the money. I mean, I got a huge bonus last month. I can pay–"

"Don't, just wait. I don't know what I'm doing." I shook in his arms. "All I know is I don't want you to be another client. Don't take what we did away from me."

Oh, god, I wanted these foreign emotions to get the fuck out. It helped that Dom looked at me now like I had two heads.

His voice was barely a whisper. "Real?"

"Terrifyingly real." How was Joseph going to react when I told him what I wanted? How was I going to pull this off?

His arms were tight, crushing me to his sweat-damp chest. Beneath it, his heart was racing as fast as my own. A tight laugh rumbled in him, shuddering his shoulders.

"Well," he said finally, "tonight did not go how I thought it would."

"No fucking kidding. I wasn't even supposed to be here," I muttered, distracted with thoughts of the man upstairs with the bank of monitors behind his desk and an earpiece to alert him to any situations. Did Joseph know how big of a situation was brewing in Room One?

"Me, neither," Dom said. "I was supposed to go out with my friend tonight, the one that got engaged, but apparently he's sick."

Any sound in the room faded from my ears.

It wasn't coincidence. The man who leased Logan and Evie's fabulous apartment, he lived temporarily overseas Evie had told me once. He was a friend of Logan's, she'd said. This explained how Dom, who lived in Tokyo, knew about this exclusive and secret blindfold club. Dom's referral had come from Logan.

Like I needed any more bullshit to think about kicking around in my head.

There was a sharp rap on the door and Nina's husky voice rang out. "Everything all right? Can I get you two something?"

I had to go, time was running out. "Stay," I ordered him.

Dom nodded.

Nina startled when I pulled the door open, stepped out into the hall, and closed the door swiftly behind me.

"Oh. Should I let Marques know?" she asked, eying my robe.

"No. I have to talk to Joseph immediately."

There were three other girls on tonight, and two of them had already finished seeing their clients. Only Chantel was on the flickering bank of monitors behind Joseph. She was getting it in the ass with a ball-gag in her mouth. Joseph's indifferent gaze swung away from the screen to land on me and his eyebrows peaked.

My manager was young and attractive. Thin, broad shouldered, and omni-sexual. He had a warm smile when needed, but otherwise maintained a professional veneer.

"This has been an interesting client for you," he commented.

Tell me about it. "I need to ask a favor." My heart beat so loudly, surely Joseph could hear it. "You have to cancel his contract."

He laughed lightly, then sobered. "Payton, you can't be serious."

"Like a fucking heart attack."

Joseph didn't look angry, he looked completely lost. "On what grounds? Seems to me the guy had a good time. He came twice."

The tightness was back in my chest. It was hard to speak, to think, to breathe.

"Please, I know this is crazy but I can't take his money. I'll make it up to you."

Concern flooded Joseph's face. "Why can't you take his money?"

"I don't know if I can do this anymore. It'll make me feel," I gasped, "like a whore."

That was yet another reason why I didn't want Dom to pay. I'd spent my life dealing with assholes calling me all sorts of things that I let roll off my back. Slut. Bitch. Cunt. I didn't care about those, but for some reason, when someone called a spade a spade, it cut deep inside me. *Take the money, whore.* The phrase repeated, over and over in my mind.

"Honey, no." Joseph rose from his desk with alarm. "That's not what you are." He knew how damaging that word was to me. It was to all of his girls. "Don't ever say that, but you know I can't turn him away. If it got out, I'd have everyone demanding a refund."

He had a point. "All right, I need my payment in full. Tonight."

"Payton, that's not possible. Maybe if I had some warning I could have made arrangements, but not at one thirty in the morning."

"Bullshit. You can do it." The profanity and tone wasn't helpful, but I was coming apart.

I wasn't about to screw Joseph out of his three thousand because I'd made this drastic and reckless decision.

All I could do was give Dom back the rest, and consider the three grand as payment for the use of the room. That thought quieted the *whore* looping in my brain somewhat.

Joseph's deep-set eyes hardened. "Yeah, maybe I could pull it together, but I won't."

"Why?" My voice broke on the word. I think my shattered self was unnerving to Joseph.

"The only reason you want that money right now is so you can return it."

"Yeah, so what? It's my money, I can do what I want with it."

I'd never seen Joseph upset before. We'd had some intense situations, but he was always calm and collected through them. The man in front of me was not calm. His face flushed with anger.

"I can't have the girls giving back money either. Same issue. This only works as a business, not a fucking charity."

The walls closed in on me. "I can't . . . please, Joseph. I need this."

Even as I was falling over a cliff into the unknown, my thoughts were on the man waiting in Room One. I didn't want to be gone too long and have him investigate where I'd run off to.

"What happened in that room?" my manager asked. "Did he threaten you?"

"No, no. He . . . I don't know what happened. I lost control and it, like, meant something. It felt real."

"It wasn't real." There was a shift in the man before me as his spine lengthened him to stand his full height. His voice was dark and shocking. "Get on your knees."

What the fuck was this? Cold dread filled my belly. I

craved command, and occasionally Joseph would satisfy that need when a client failed. Underneath, Joseph was ul-tra-dominant. We had a fucked-up, symbiotic relationship at the "office." But now? *Please, not tonight.*

"What? Why?" I said.

"You shouldn't have to ask why."

"Joseph—"

His face streaked with authority, and in the darkened room, lit only by the monitor and a soft desk lamp, it was terrifying. Any other night, I would have been on my knees in an instant. I would have thought this was the hottest it had ever been with Joseph. Instead, I wanted to run.

"Payton, get on your fucking knees. Now. You're going to suck my cock and forget all about him. You belong here. *That's* what's real."

I wanted to cry, if I was capable, but I wasn't. I didn't cry. I understood why Joseph was doing this. His grip was tightening on me as he felt me slipping away.

Joseph's hand undid his belt. It worked the button.

"No," I whispered. "Please, no. I can't do this."

"I don't want to lose you, but if you can't do this . . . what are you doing here?"

He undid his zipper and shoved a hand inside his pants, stroking himself. My gaze drifted from his fly, working its way up to meet his eyes. This moment showed me that I couldn't do this anymore. Any of it.

"I can't."

He stilled and took a deep breath. "That's such a disap-pointment." Hands did up his pants. "I'm sorry, I'm going to have to ask you to get dressed and Julius will escort you to your car."

"No, the guy's still waiting for me in the room, I need–"

"I'm no longer interested in what you need, Payton. You're fired."

The air drained from my lungs. "I get that, but I'm going back to that goddamn room first."

"There's no point." Joseph tapped the earpiece he was still wearing. "Marquis took him to the payment room already. It's over."

I'd stormed to the door in the back and banged my fists against it when the cashier refused to buzz me in. There weren't windows, so I couldn't tell if Dom was still there. Julius hovered nearby like he was afraid of me. He was an enormous black man and built like a truck, but he was also a giant teddy bear. He had a not-so-secret crush on me, and even though I flirted endlessly with him, he never asked me out. He was loyal to Joseph's no-dating, no-fucking policy between employees, even when Joseph himself was not.

My next plan was to get dressed as quickly as possible and wait for Dom outside the club. I hurried into the over-sized cashmere sweater and leggings, yanked my knee-high boots on and rushed to get the buckles done. I snatched my purse and coat off the hook in the dressing room and thundered down the stairs.

The winter Chicago night air assaulted me, and I pulled my wool pea coat closed when I hit the street. It was empty.

"Where is he, Julius? Still in the payment room?"

He stared at the cracks in the sidewalk like there were naked women in them.

"Look at me," I said.

NIKKI SLOANE

"Where you parked at?" He set his hand in the small of my back, guiding me down the street. I tried to dig my heels in.

"Come on, help me out. I have to talk to him."

Julius sighed. "Girl, he paid and Marquis put him in a cab."

"Shit, no." I dug for my phone in my purse, intent on calling Evie, but Julius' face was haunting. "What? What is it?"

"Joseph . . . he, uh, wasn't real happy with the guy."

No, probably not. Dom had made Joseph lose one of his best girls, and Joseph wasn't the type to let that go easily. *Marquis put him in a cab.* Not "got him a cab." *Oh, no.*

"What did Marquis do?"

"He fucked him up. Only a little."

Anger, coupled with more crushing guilt, turned almost immediately to concern. "Is he okay?"

"Yeah. Not rough enough that the guy would think about bringing charges, just enough for him not to come back." A thick, muscle-bound arm wrapped around my waist in a brotherly gesture of comfort. "Marquis told him you skipped out."

"Marquis's a fucking asshole! I didn't."

"I know you didn't, girl. This shit sucks for you, I'm sorry."

We were suddenly at the door of my Jag. We'd been moving this whole time and I hadn't realized it. I felt like a zombie when I produced my keys and unlocked the door.

"Damn, I'm gonna miss you," Julius said, shivering in the cold.

I turned to face him, and threw my arms around his hulking frame. "God, me too." I drew back so I could see his face. "You should have asked me out, you know."

48

"Joseph don't like his people—"

"Fuck Joseph. We could have had fun together."

He gave me a sad smile. "Shit, girl, you would have destroyed me. Good luck to ya."

Julius was so much smarter than he let on.

I didn't need luck, though. I had Logan Stone. He'd given Dom the details to this club and upended my life, which meant Logan also knew how to put me in touch with Dom. He owed that to both of us.

As the engine warmed in my car, I pulled out my phone and something sharp bit into my fingers. It had been smashed, the screen white with spiderweb cracks, and wouldn't turn on. It wasn't personal why he'd done this. I had passwords to the club website and phone numbers of the staff, but still. Fucking Joseph.

Even if I could find a payphone in this city, it's not like I had Evie's number memorized. I couldn't drive over to their place because they'd never hear the intercom from their bedroom to buzz me up, and it was two in the morning.

I went home. I tried to contact her through email, then Facebook and Twitter, which I knew was pointless. Every hour that passed was making this worse. How had Dom been hurt by Marquis? Had he been hurt by my assumed rejection?

At four thirty I started to get really desperate. I drove to a Walgreen's and bought a prepaid phone, then raced back home to comb through old emails on my laptop. At five thirty I had one terrible option. I had Amy's number in an email chain Evie had copied me on between her and Blake.

Blake was Evie's friend, not mine. For a long time, right up until the point Logan stepped into the picture, Evie had been in love with Blake. I had no idea why; the guy was so beneath her. He'd strung Evie along for months, even while he was living with Amy. Confused, he'd said. Bullshit. His dick wanted two women. The only confusion was why he couldn't have both. He'd also let the W word pass his lips while addressing me. His apology afterward did nothing to help. I didn't even acknowledge it.

It had worked out, I guessed, for Blake. Amy was preggo with Blake's kid and they were getting married in a few months, shotgun-wedding style. It had most definitely worked out for Evie. There was no confusion who Logan wanted.

As I contemplated calling and waking a pregnant woman I didn't really know, I kind of got mad at Logan. Did he realize what he'd done by setting Dom in my path? This was all Logan's fault. My eyes burned with exhaustion as I'd been up almost twenty-four hours, and in my weakness, I was okay with assigning all of the blame squarely on him and not myself.

"Hello?" a female voice said.

"Hey, is this Amy? It's Payton. I'm not sure if you remember me, I'm one of Blake's friends." *Liar.* "Is he around? I need to talk to him and it's urgent."

There was a noise as the phone fumbled in hands. In the background, I heard muffled voices. He asked who it was and she said, "Some girl who says she's your friend."

"Hello?" Blake said on a sleepy voice.

"Blake, it's Payton. My phone's broken and I need Evie's number."

"What the fuck? It's like five thirty in the morning."

I tried to remain calm. "I know, I'm sorry, but it's really

important I talk to her right now."

He sighed, and after a few seconds where I assume he was scrolling through his contacts, he rattled off the number.

"Thank you. I'm sorry I woke you guys."

"Yeah, okay." He hung up a second later. Dick.

chapter SIX

The emotions caught up with me before I dialed her number. My job was gone. In a few short months, I'd be out of money. I wasn't really big on saving and I couldn't exactly file for unemployment, either. What was I going to do? My worry for Dom and my need to explain what happened got tabled as this new fear took hold. My whole life had changed when Dom walked in that room.

I went into full panic mode when I called her.

"Who's dead?" she asked, once she realized who it was.

"I am," I said. "I need to talk to you, I'm kind of freaking out. And I'm coming over."

My ass was dragging as I headed for my car. Caffeine was required. I got two coffees at Starbucks on my way to her place. Oh, shit, not her place. It was Dom's. Would he be there? Why didn't I think of that before?

I flew into the apartment when Evie opened the door. The couch was empty, and she looked at me like she didn't know what had happened, so, no. He wasn't here.

"Are you pregnant?" she demanded. Her deep brown hair had been pulled back into a damp bun from her shower, her blue eyes large on mine.

"What? No." I slung coffee on the counter when I pulled my cup from the cardboard tray and she instantly went to clean it up. How Logan had changed my best friend. When we'd roomed together in Amsterdam, she'd kind of been a slob, but creative types usually were.

Evie was girl-next-door pretty. She had a normal, real body-shape to her. Hips that flared, a slim waist, and large boobs. I loved and envied her curves. She wasn't a gym freak like me, but still stayed in shape. She was effortlessly beautiful. I'd been attracted to her from the get-go. The threesome had sort of been her idea, but just as much mine, too.

Women were sexy. I liked what we'd done. Up until Dom, Evie's was the only kiss I'd felt something in. Yet, the threesome with Logan proved to me that while women were fun, I swung much more toward the males when it came to sex.

Ugh. I actually didn't want to think about sex right now. That had to be a first. I felt unglued. My arms and legs had been pulled out and stuck back in at awkward angles. I was rambling about the money, about how I should have been warned, or some shit like that. I probably sounded like a crazy woman. It drove Evie to abandon me in the living room and go wake her fiancé.

I stared out the enormous glass wall. We were forty-four stories up, facing North Beach. The view was to die for. Dom's view. I crossed my arms over my chest, trying to hold myself together. When were these emotions going to wear off? Maybe I should have tried to sleep.

"Payton." Logan's deep voice made me turn.

He looked like hell. His eyes were bloodshot and his nose red. Logan had on a pair of sleep pants and no shirt, his brown hair askew. Sick as a dog, but still hot. It amused me to no end that Evie had been oblivious to him until her night at the club. Of course, he was her boss and she thought he was off-limits, but seriously? That wouldn't have stopped someone like me. Evie had been such a good girl, but was recovering nicely.

"Do you realize what you did?" I said to him.

"He's still pretty wacked out on NyQuil," Evie warned. "Can you please start making sense and tell us what happened?"

"I don't know what happened. He came in, agreed to thirty thousand and said he wanted to talk–"

"Who?" she asked.

"Dominic," Logan answered, burying the heel of his hand in an eye to scrub the sleep away. "I told him about the club when we bailed last night."

Dominic?

Evie's mouth popped open. Her gaze flitted between Logan and me as she figured part of it out, then settled on Logan. "Why did you tell Dominic about the club?"

"Because he's lonely as hell over there, and when we had to cancel, I knew he wouldn't go out by himself." He turned his attention back to me. "What happened?"

"A lot. Look, I need to talk to him. I need to know he's all right."

Suspicion clouded Logan's face. "Why wouldn't he be all right?"

I had so much guilt already, I couldn't bear to see their faces when I told them about Marquis. "It was a really weird night, and I didn't get a chance to say goodbye."

"You're lying," Logan said.

Well, well, well. Usually I was the human bullshit detector. I was unaware Logan was, too.

"He might have gotten hurt when he left."

"What?" Logan's tone was angry. "How?"

"I told you, I don't know. I was upstairs getting fired

when it happened. I know he didn't leave on good terms."

Logan gave me a dark, demanding look. "Meaning?"

"I was told he got roughed up. Logan, please, can you give me his number, or call him yourself?"

"Well, he didn't say anything about it when I talked to him a minute ago." Logan covered his cough and braced a hand on the doorframe to steady himself.

"You talked to him? What did he say?" *That some whore fucked him and ran, and he got beat on by her pimp's lap dog?*

"That he needed my help with something. I take it you two . . ." he searched for the polite way to say it, even though it was unnecessary.

"Fucked? Yeah. He didn't even negotiate," I sank down on the couch. What would Dom need Logan's help with? Dominic, not Dom, I reminded myself.

The couch shifted when Evie sat down beside me. "How did you get fired?"

How was I going to explain any of it? I went with the easiest reason. "I tried to get him out of the deal, and when Joseph refused, I tried to give the money back." I turned my gaze to Evie's shocked face. Get ready, sister, here comes a bigger surprise. "I kissed him."

"Whoa, what?" She knew all about my rule. I didn't like intimacy. No kissing, snuggling, pet names . . . it wasn't me. Too bad I felt nothing like myself last night. Or today.

I tucked my face in my hands. I was a wreck.

There was a quick knock on the door, but it creaked open without an invitation, probably because it was his place. I heard a sharp gasp from Evie beside me.

"Your face," she said.

"It's okay, Evie, you should see the other guy," the rough voice replied, deadpan.

Instinct took over. People had to earn the right to call her Evie. With everything going on, this was what I chose to latch on to? I fucking hated it when some stranger used her nickname like they knew her. My hands fell from my annoyed, exhausted face and I shot to my feet. "Her name is Evelyn."

Dominic dropped the box of donuts he was holding, and the impact with the floor created a mushroom cloud of powdered sugar. He was still in the same suit, looking like he hadn't slept at all. There was a cut on his bottom lip were Marquis had split it, his left eye puffy.

"Paige." It came out on a shocked breath. He stood motionless, even as the cloud billowed and dispersed, his wide eyes trapping mine. "How?"

"My name's not Paige," my voice was soft, "it's Payton."

That got Dominic to move. His head swung to Logan. "Threesome Payton?"

"Yes," I snapped, annoyed that Logan had opened his big mouth again. What was he, a chick? Did he and Dominic stay up late at night talking about celebrity crushes on the phone? "I'm *threesome* Payton, but most people don't call me that."

I'd had sex with every person in this room. I didn't feel shame about it, but I also didn't like it being pointed out either.

Since Dominic didn't move again, Logan picked up the box of donuts and set it on the counter with a thump, then opened his freezer. He dug out a blue gel pouch and offered it to Dominic.

"Yeah, all right," he said to the offer. He took it and pressed it to his swollen eye, keeping his other on me. No one made a sound, making me aware I was going to have to.

"I tried to get you out of the deal. I'm sorry, I didn't realize what was going to happen. I didn't think they'd take it out on you."

He didn't move, like he was a fucking statue. Evie and Logan remained as well, watching the train wreck. It forced me to continue.

"My manager and I couldn't come to an agreement. I tried to get him to pay out my percentage so I could give the rest back to you. It's all fucked up and I left. Or got fired. I wanted to get back to the room, but you'd already paid–"

"Sort of–"

". . . and they wouldn't let me in. Then Julius said Marquis had messed you up because of how angry Joseph was with me."

The blue gel pouch came down off his eye. "I don't know who any of those people are, but you've got your facts wrong, Payton." He said my name with emphasis, as if trying it out for the first time. "The big guy came in and said it was time to go. I only owed three grand, he said, *At the lady's request.*"

I felt sick with relief, if that was even possible. Oh, Joseph. "I don't understand."

"Yeah, I didn't either. So I kept asking about you, where you were, and what happened. He warned me to let it go, but I wasn't ready to." He gave a lopsided, sad smile. "I'm stubborn like that."

"Marquis hit you because you wouldn't leave?"

"His second punch was more persuasive. I don't remember the first five minutes of the cab ride."

"You need to ice that," Logan reminded him. "It looks like hell."

Dominic put the pack back on his eye. "Thanks, Mom." His attention shifted back to me. "Have you been here the whole time? I went back to the club, looking for you."

I struggled not to let the impact his words had on me show. Instead I stared down at the dusty spot on the floor from the donut explosion. "No, I just got here. My phone got trashed so I came to get your number from Logan."

"You okay?" Evie whispered to me. I nodded. She grabbed Logan's hand and tugged him backward. "Let's get you back in bed, boss, before you pass out."

Logan didn't look like he wanted to leave, but she had total command over him, and I didn't think she had done this for any other reason than to give Dominic and me privacy. The moment the door softly shut behind them, the air between the two of us grew thick and intense.

"Why did you want my number from Logan?" His rough yet gentle voice was fascinating.

"I was worried about what happened to you."

"I'm okay," he said. "Was that all?"

I lifted my eyes back to his, refusing to give. "What did you need Logan's help with?"

A slow smile spread on his lips. At least, on the side of his face that wasn't hidden under an ice pack. "Finding you. Do you have any idea how crazy it is, you being here? This is technically my place. How did you know I knew him?"

"You were referred by another client, you live overseas. Logan and Evie, our newly engaged friends, canceled on me last night, too." Meaning even if Logan hadn't gotten sick, we would have wound up meeting. But, fuck. It would have been so normal. I probably would have fucked him and promptly forgotten him.

Maybe.

I wasn't quite so sure when he approached now.

"You didn't answer my question, *Payton*."

"What question was that, *Dominic*?"

Again the ice pack came down; this time he tossed it on the counter. His expression told me he liked hearing the full name on my lips as much as I liked hearing my name on his. I knew exactly which question he was talking about.

"Was that all you wanted my number for? To check on my well-being?"

Things were different here than they were in the club. I felt less in control on his turf, and now that I knew he was okay, exhaustion threatened to overwhelm me.

"No." I was usually direct, but my sleepy state made me honest. "I wanted to see you again." Holy shit, saying that out loud was scary. What was happening to me?

He reached a cautious hand out and set it on my hip. Everything was changing much too fast. The man touching me, his warmth seeping into my cashmere-covered hip, was not a client.

"Are you okay?" His voice was low and soft. "Getting let go from that place . . ."

"It was time. I couldn't do it anymore." Not sure if that was what he was really asking. He probably assumed my relationship at the club wasn't one that would let me walk away easily, even though that was the case. "Don't know what fuck I'm going to do now, though."

He grasped my other hip, locking me in his hands.

"Sure you do," he said. "Come home with me."

There it was, the question I heard from almost every client. And now, this time I actually considered it. Dominic was so close. I felt him buried under my skin and working his way in deeper.

"Aren't you already home?"

A half-smile curled on his busted lip. "Yeah, but other people currently reside in this domicile. Come back to my hotel room with me. Have you slept since last night?"

"No."

"Me neither. Let's sleep together." He grinned. It looked ridiculous with his developing black eye, and yet sort of sexy, and I found myself giving him a smile.

Fuck, I was in so much trouble.

chapter
SEVEN

Evie answered the bedroom door immediately when I knocked softly. She must have been listening, although it was probably impossible not to.

"You call me later." This was an order from her to me, although her focus was on the man in the living room.

"You bet your ass, I will," I said.

Dominic finished cleaning up the mess from the donuts while I put on my coat. "There's coffee." I gestured to the extra one in the cardboard tray I'd brought in. "Evie won't want it, and I think Logan's already asleep."

He pulled the cup from the tray. "Can I interest you in a floor donut?"

"I'm good." No, that wasn't true. I was tired. "Where's your hotel?" *Please be close by.*

"The Hilton by Millennium Park."

Thank god. "Let's go, I'm in the parking garage."

Dominic climbed into the passenger seat, his eyes roaming over the interior of my new Jaguar. "This is a nice car."

Hell yeah, it was nice. It was $80,000 nice.

"Thanks." Too bad I was going to have to sell it. I'd bought it outright, which was part of the reason I had no savings. I shoved the thought away as I pulled out of the parking space.

He was silent at first. When we were stopped at a red, he clicked up the volume on a Black Keys song from the satellite radio. "*Lonely Boy.*" The irony was not lost on me.

"Does it hurt?" I asked. "Your eye?"

"Not really. I took some Advil at four."

The silence was awkward and annoying, but talking was a scarier prospect.

"Payton what?" he asked abruptly. "What's your last name?"

I let out a breath. "McCreary. Yours?"

"Ward."

Dominic Ward; that sounded nice. I frowned. Why did it matter? I was going to go to his hotel room and give him a morning to remember. A longer, better memory to take back to Japan, then I'd move on and figure out what the hell I was going to do with my life.

"Use the valet," he said when we neared the hotel. "I'll cover it."

Great, he'll validate my parking after the fuck. What was wrong with me? Why was I all snippy and jittery?

"You said you came home for Thanksgiving, but you're staying at a hotel?" I asked on the elevator ride up.

"My parents live in Milwaukee. I spent the week up there, and came down to hang out with Logan during the weekend."

I almost asked why he didn't stay with Logan and Evie, but thought better of it. Dominic would have wanted a place to bring his hookup back to after drinks last night.

"When are you heading back to Japan?"

"Tomorrow."

I followed him down the hall, calming a bit when he ushered me into his room and flipped the light on. I'd get my confidence and emotions back on the rails once the clothes were off.

Wrong. It was seven in the morning and the sun had

begun to rise. I was dressed. And sober. Dominic crossed the short and generic-looking room, and pulled the curtains closed to block out the daylight. I didn't feel sexy, or in the mood. I stared at the perfectly made king sized bed, wanting to use it solely for its intended purpose. Sleep.

I took off my coat and hung it in the open closet, set my purse on the dresser, and sat down on the edge of the bed to wrangle off the boots. Meanwhile, he peeled out of his suit coat. It was tossed on top of the suitcase stacked on an ottoman, and then Dominic turned his attention on me.

My unsure hands went to the hem of my sweater, lifting it–

"What are you doing?" he said softly. "Come here, I get to do that."

I was barely on my feet when he pulled me up against him, slamming his mouth over mine. His possession was unreal. Exhaustion dried up. Lust stormed onto the scene and demanded control, which I surrendered gladly to her.

His kiss teased me. He used his teeth and his tongue like he really fucking knew what he was doing. It drove my hands around his shoulders, and I sighed into him, my body molding to his.

His fingertips crept under the hem of my sweater and guided it up. He broke the kiss as he freed the garment from my body, revealing the plain black camisole beneath. The sweater made no noise as it dropped to the floor. I was faster with the buttons of his shirt the second time around. My eager hands sought the heated flesh beneath the fabric. God, his body was amazing.

I thought my camisole would be his next victim, but it was my leggings. They were peeled down my legs to my ankles where I stepped out and kicked them away. He'd left my simple black thong on . . . maybe he wanted to take that off last, or leave it on.

This was better. I felt more comfortable now. I undid his belt, released his pants, and they flowed to the floor. He caught my wrists in his hands when I slid fingers inside the top of his boxers.

His mouth was by the shell of my ear and he whispered it there. "No."

"Am I going too fast again?" Luckily, it came out concerned and not frustrated, although I was feeling both of those equally.

"I said I wanted to sleep with you, and I meant it."

He kissed my forehead and abandoned me by the foot of the bed. It was so he could go to the far side and tug the covers down. I stood in disbelief as he sat and slid one foot after the other into bed, glancing at the empty spot beside him. "Coming?"

"No. I don't do *that*."

He stared at me. "You don't sleep? Are you a vampire?"

Tension balled my hands into fists and I set them on my waist. "I'm serious."

The blue eyes . . . well, the good one, gave me a sharp, calculating look. "Another one of your rules?" When I nodded, he added, "Great. I had so much difficulty with your other ones. Now come to bed."

I bent down and snatched my leggings up off the floor, intending to get dressed.

"Payton." The unease in his voice got me to halt. "I haven't acclimated to the time change. My head is killing me, and I'm exhausted. You were eye-fucking this bed when we got in here, don't think I didn't notice." He combed a hand through his hair and let it fall on the empty pillow that he wanted to be mine. "Let's get some rest before round two. I'm sure we'll both need it." He gave me a wicked smile that was all sin and sex. "I know you will."

His persuasive speech got me to stay in the room, but he needed to be knocked down a peg for being so smug.

"Fine." I came over to the bed. "But I sleep in the nude."

He was ready for this. "Not today, you don't. I'm not sleeping with a hard-on."

"Then control yourself and don't look." I pulled the camisole off in a swift move, immediately followed by the bra. "And don't touch, either." The panties were gone a heartbeat later.

He rolled away from me at the sight of my naked body. "Fuck, woman, you're the devil."

"I warned you," I said, taking the sheets in my hand. "Too much to handle." I slipped into the bed, turned away, and stayed right by the edge, giving him a wide berth.

The mattress rocked as he moved. A hand snaked over my belly and yanked my back against his chest so he was spooning me.

"Not for me," he whispered.

I was aware he left the bed. There was rustling as he dressed and left the room, and returned a few minutes later with the ice bucket full. His eye was bothering him, I assumed, making it hard for him to sleep. He undressed and got back in bed, a towel filled with ice pressed to his face.

It seemed better to sleep than to lie awake and contemplate what the hell I was doing here, so I fell back asleep moments later.

With the curtains closed, it was impossible to tell how long we slept, and the alarm clock was on his side of the bed. I knew he was awake, though. Fingers traced a line down the bare skin of my back, easing the covers down with it until he reached the hollow at the base of my spine.

Then, kisses. His hot mouth moved over my shoulder blades, his stubble scraping my skin like fine sandpaper, working his way toward my neck. Goosebumps pebbled on my legs and I shivered.

"Want me to warm you up?" his rough voice asked.

He didn't wait for an answer. His hand skimmed over my hip, gliding up my belly and through my cleavage so he could use his fingertips to turn my face toward him. Dominic's kiss was slow and sultry; his tongue's wicked stroke was slower still. I was determined to do better this time. To not take over and let him go slow, but this kiss was like flooring his foot on my accelerator.

"No." A hand was firm on my hip, stopping me from turning on the bed to face him.

"No?" I let my voice go teasing. His chest was up against my back, and I shifted, rubbing my ass against him where only cotton stood between us. He was already raring to go. Good, me too.

The hand went tighter still, fingers pressing into my flesh. "We're doing this my way." He pushed his hard cock back against me. "Slow. Long. Neither one of us is going to come unless I want it."

I shivered again, excited by his aggressive words, but my controlling personality instinctively kicked in. "Good luck with that."

The hand yanked me flat on my back and he was up on an elbow, peering down at me with a stern look. "I don't need luck." His eye wasn't too bad, but it was swollen and bluish, and the added day's worth of stubble covering his strong jawline and the dark look made this handsome man appear dangerous. Hotter than the leather seats of my Jaguar in August.

He harmlessly slapped my hand away when it tried to grip him through his boxers, and he raised an eyebrow, challenging me to try again. My next attempt was just as unsuccessful and a wicked smile warmed on my face. I pretended to lead with my right, and while he was occupied with that, my left closed around him.

"Fuck," he groaned, his hands wrapping around my wrists and slamming them up above my head, pinning them to the mattress. It forced him over me, bringing us chest to hard chest. My nipples tightened. Legs settled around his hips, drawing him up against me. Could he feel how wet he'd made me with those thin boxers on?

His head dropped down, bringing his lips beside my ear. "Slow, Payton."

I blew out a frustrated breath when his mouth brushed over my sensitive skin. I'd never had this before. Outside of the club, I was always the one in charge. Guys were too turned on, too lazy, or lacked the balls to take control away from me.

Not this one. His tongue slid down my neck, his hot breath cool in its trail. Dominic had given me the smallest peek at his dominant side at the club, and I could tell the more comfortable he became with me, the more likely it was to come out and play.

"I lied before, when I said I can go slow," I said.

He sort of laughed, his face in the valley between my tits. "Yeah, I learned that lesson the hard way." He rolled his tongue on my nipple, then scraped his teeth over it. Right on the knife's edge of painful and pleasurable. My legs clamped tighter on his hips, urging him to grind on me.

Instead, he pulled away and back on his knees so he was kneeling between my spread legs, his gaze wandering down my bare body as if assessing me. The hands on my wrists were gone, and he grabbed the ice bucket, setting it beside me, then stuck his hand in.

Was he getting some ice to tease me with?

"Touch yourself," he said. It came out almost as an order. "I want to watch you play with that pretty little pussy."

His hand never moved from the ice bucket. My right hand did as requested and my eyes stayed on his. Watching his face flood with heat when I circled my clit was almost as enjoyable as the sensation of my fingers rolling on the wet button of flesh.

He watched, his gaze intent on my hand moving back and forth, until I let out a soft moan. Only the gleam in his eyes a fraction before he moved let me know something was up. He yanked my right hand away, once again pinning it beneath his hold.

"Use your other hand," he said. "That should slow you down."

My mouth went slack. I wasn't left handed. It was awkward as hell using my non-dominant hand, and frustrating, too. It felt good, but not as good as I knew it could. "Aren't you an evil fucking genius?" I accused.

The ice in the bucket sloshed when he pulled his hand out, his skin pink from the cold water. It stole all the breath from my lungs when one of those icy fingers plunged deep inside me. My back bowed up off the mattress and I threw my head back, too startled to make a noise.

"You like that?" His rough voice. I wanted to hear more. I wanted to come from his words, but right now it was probably going to be from the shockingly cold finger fucking me.

"Shit, it feels so good," I said when I finally found my voice.

He moved at a leisurely pace while my fingers fumbled over my flesh, desperate to get my release. My right hand tried to escape his grip. It'd be so much faster that way . . .

"Dominic." My hips moved in time with his slow thrusts, begging him without words, but then my words began too. "Please."

"Please what? You want another, or you want your hand back?"

The fucked up thing was I didn't even know. "Yes."

He made a noise of amusement. He thought this was funny? I was writhing under his touch, half-restrained, out of my mind with lust and desire. So close to coming all over that hand.

"Sorry, you little liar. I think you need to be taught a lesson." The finger retreated.

"No," I said, but it died on my tongue when the finger that had been inside me slid into my mouth.

I licked it clean and watched the muscles along his jaw flex as his nostrils flared with desire. I was aching painfully, but at least his little lesson had side effects for him as well.

The moment the finger was gone from my mouth, I blurted it out. "Fuck me, please. I want your cock inside me."

His expression was playfully smug. "Do you not understand the concept of going slow? Did no one explain to you how that works?"

"Less talking, more fucking." I was so turned on, I was dripping between my legs. I abandoned my goal of getting myself off with my left hand. It wasn't going to happen, and he wasn't watching anyway. He let my fingers dip under the waist of elastic and close around the soft yet firm column of flesh beneath.

I stroked him. Over and over. And even though his breathing became rapid and uneven, he didn't move. He sat back on his heels and let me give him a sloppy handjob with my unskilled left hand.

"I'm going to let go of you now," he said. "I'm hoping you've learned your lesson." He leaned over me, his lips crushing against mine as his hand relaxed, releasing me. "It's taking everything I've got not to bury my dick inside you and lose it immediately. Don't make it any harder on me."

Did he realize what he was asking me to do? I craved to dominate and be dominated. Joseph demanded my submission and I thought that was undeniably hot. But this? To willingly give my submission to Dominic? That concept was a scorching five hundred degrees. So much hotter than anything else.

It came out less confident than I'd ever sounded in bed. "I can try."

We tangled our bodies then. Hands held the sides of my face and I crossed my arms behind his back, gripping my forearms to keep my hands from drifting. I clenched my teeth together as he explored every curve of my body. Hands, then mouth. Submitting to him like this, knowing

I was pleasing him instead of myself . . . oh, god. I couldn't think about it. Tomorrow he'd be gone and take this fascinating new experience with him.

My eyes were shut tight when the bed rocked and he went to the suit jacket, yanking out a foil packet. He lost his boxers on the way back to me, unleashing that huge cock I was desperate for. The torturous agony stifled me when he dropped the unopened condom wrapper on my stomach. The waiting was killing me.

Slow. Oh so slow. He knelt between my bent knees and dipped down, his tongue swiped over my pussy. One long, agonizingly teasing lick at a time, just the tip of his tongue.

Again.

And again. I fisted a hand in his hair, but kept myself from pressing him against me and demanding more.

"So," he mumbled from in between my legs, "what are you going to do now that you're unemployed?"

My head spun. He wanted to talk about that with a face full of my pussy? "I don't know, and right now, I don't give a fuck. All I care about is what you're doing."

A chuckle rumbled from below. "Yeah?" He pushed two fingers inside and I gasped, moaning in satisfaction. They pulsed inside me, working together with that tongue. What he was doing felt amazing, but I was starting to get light-headed from how hard he had me breathing.

"Are you going to . . . let me come?" I asked between gasps. Heat and pleasure rolled in waves through my body. I couldn't do slow much longer. I was beside myself with need, feeling more fractured every second, and each wicked thrust and swirl of his tongue widened that fracture.

"How do you want it? Like this?" His voice was hushed.

"Or on my —"

"Oh god, on your cock. I'll do anything for it."

The desperate tone in my voice was pathetic. I couldn't believe it. Less than twenty-four hours after meeting him, and he had me begging for it. *Me.* The one who men shelled out thousands of dollars for the chance to stick it in me.

His head snapped up, his expression startled. "Anything?"

I closed my eyes, enjoying the heightened sensation and focus when the visual wasn't allowed.

"Name it." He'd seen my willing list. He knew what I was up for.

He only hesitated for a single breath. "Come to Japan."

chapter
EIGHT

I scrambled backward off of his hand, the condom on my stomach falling to the sheets. "What?"

He grabbed the wrapper and tore it open. "Come back with me. You can stay a week or two, hang at my place. I'm in corporate housing that's meant for families, so I've got a spare bedroom. I'll cover your airfare."

"Are you serious right now?"

He gave me a half-smile. "Real." His chest was moving rapidly, but no idea if it was from the foreplay or the shocking offer he'd just made. "You said you wanted to go. You've got free time, and I've got my bonus."

"We don't even know each other."

He rolled the condom on slowly and methodically, my gaze fixated on his hands. "That's not true. I know lots about you, and your silly rules you let me break. I know what you taste like here," he touched my lips with the soft pad of his index finger and drew it down my body, all the way to between my thighs, "and here. What you sound like when you come."

"Dominic."

"I know you're best friends with Evie—"

"Evelyn."

"—the girl who agreed to marry my best friend, and he likes you."

"Yeah, of course he likes *Threesome* Payton," I snapped.

His face skewed. "That's not how I meant." He trapped

my waist in his hands, hauling me toward him so I was flat on my back, beneath him. His expression shifted to serious. "Can I be honest?"

I stared up at him. Wasn't he always? My hand pressed against the center of his chest, although I didn't remember putting it there. Beneath my palm, I could feel his heart racing. I nodded quickly.

"I don't want to go back to Tokyo, worried I might have walked away from something here."

Now it was my heart's turn to race, although from what I wasn't sure. Fear? Excitement? Did he feel this strange and scary connection as strongly as I did?

"Come on," he whispered, nudging me with the tip right at my entrance. "Don't you want this?"

"Your cock, or a free trip to Japan?"

He smirked. "Yes."

There wasn't much discussion going on in my head. Two weeks in Japan, for free, with this fuck-stick of a man? No way was I going to live with regret the rest of my life about turning the offer down. And as a signing bonus, I got the hard cock I wanted. Right, fucking, now.

"All right, sure."

Obviously, he didn't think it was going to be so easy, because he froze. "Really?"

"Yeah, now seal the deal," I groaned, rubbing against him. I shifted my hips, trying to line up with him and –

Yes. He pushed inside me, my body gasping with pleasure.

"Shit, your cock is huge. It feels so good—"

He put his hand over my mouth, silencing me. "Not. Another. Word." It came out through clenched teeth. "I know how good it feels, and I'm trying not to think about it."

Adorable, embarrassed Dom. *Welcome back.*

The hand shifted away, only to be replaced by his mouth, and his hips drew back, tentative. Then, they surged forward. Our kiss broke as we moaned collectively, and then hard lips returned to mine, demanding.

That indecent, deliberate rhythm as he pounded into me was just as exciting as it had been last time, only now there was a new layer to it. No added pressure. Because what we were doing? We'd be doing this again at least once more over the next two weeks. Probably a lot more, if he could keep up.

My hands slipped around his back so I could dig my perfectly manicured nails in. His tempo increased, as did the intensity of Dominic's kiss. A hand tangled in my hair, gently tugging my head back, and his kiss descended to the base of my throat.

"Two weeks," he rumbled, like he was murmuring to himself.

"I'm going to wear your ass out."

His hands seized my breasts and teeth nipped at my neck. "We'll see about that."

The slap of our bodies grew loud, punctuating the air, but the bed remained quiet as he drove into me. Harder. Faster. Not that I was complaining, but where the fuck did slow go? Whatever we'd done at the club before, this was something else. This was most definitely fucking. He claimed me with his cock, over and over again. Aggressive and dominating, owning me. I cried out, about to be overwhelmed.

"This ass is mine for the next two weeks," he said. It was like he'd just thrown me into a pool, submerging me in ecstasy. I shuddered in his arms, my scream quieted by his hand as I came violently, arching my back and sucking down air through my nose. I continued to gasp even when the hand fell away, but he didn't slow his pace.

Instead, Dominic rolled his hips against me, grinding my clit.

"Fuck," I said breathless, my eyes slamming shut. "You're going to make me come again."

"Sounds like a plan."

He dropped into fourth gear. It wasn't gentle, and holy shit, I loved it. A deep sound of approval ripped from my chest. He rose up on balled fists so he could slam into me, driving me into the mattress with force.

Maybe the environment at the club had thrown him off, coupled with his unwanted dry spell. But not here with a bed and a woman beneath him, one who'd begged him for this. Now Dominic was in his element.

A bead of sweat rolled down his temple, another between the chiseled sculpture of his chest. I wanted to lick it off. So I rose up onto my elbows, and somehow, despite everything else we'd done, this was the motion that upended the ice bucket on the bed, sending a tidal wave of freezing water rolling my way.

I screamed when it hit my heated skin, jerked away, and scrambled off to stand by the bed.

"You all right?" His arms were around me in an instant.

"I'm fine, but that was really fucking cold." I used a hand to wipe at the damp skin, and as the shock of it began to fade, amusement took its place. "You don't have to literally dump cold water on me to make me slow down."

The aqua eyes blinked once and his lips twitched. "Who

said anything about slowing down?" His frame leaned toward me, urging me backward like a dance partner, leading me to the desk. He lifted and seated me there, his hands pushing my knees apart so he could shove himself inside in one quick move.

"Holy shit," I said. I had no choice but to cross my heels behind his waist, put my hands on his shoulders, and hang on for the ride. "I knew it."

"What?" It came from him between two mind-erasing thrusts, his thighs banging into the wood below us.

"You're a man who knows how to fuck."

He grinned. Maybe he blushed, but we were both flushed from what we were doing so I couldn't tell. "The stuff you say," he flexed inside me, "makes me so goddamn hard."

He didn't let me speak again. Either he kept my mouth busy with his or he had me too focused on the tension he'd filled me with. It grew enormous in less than a minute when his hand settled over my clit, stirring there while he rammed me.

We made the desk rock. Its steady thump against the wall left no doubt what was happening in this room. Oh, and I was screaming, too, probably something about his cock. I lost control on that desktop, my legs quaking as he made me come harder than I thought I ever had. It melted my brain when he came, right after me, one hand squeezing my hip so hard I was going to have a bruise there.

Totally worth it.

Pleasure detonated inside as he jerked and seized, the muscles beneath my hands straining. His head fell forward, dropping onto my heaving chest while we struggled to find air.

Sex with Dominic was like . . . it wasn't like anything I could compare it to. Maybe spending your whole life driving a Volvo and suddenly finding yourself behind the wheel of a Lamborghini. I couldn't wait to take him for another drive.

The heavy, sweaty head on me rose away and he trapped my face in his hands. "You're unbelievable, you know that?"

The kiss he gave me was tender and disorienting. My melted brain couldn't render a response, so I sat on the desk, the edge digging into my thighs, and let him have complete control.

He made a noise of dissatisfaction as he withdrew from me and helped me off the desktop, my bare skin squealing on the veneer. "We've got a lot of shit to do before we can do that again."

What? Holy crap, he'd actually fucked my brains out. "Hmm?"

"Japan? Packing. Airplane tickets."

"Oh, yeah."

He stared at me, confused. A slow smile widened on his face. "You okay?"

"It's been a helluva day."

I let him guide me into the bathroom where he started the shower. "No kidding." He righted himself and turned his full attention on me. I could feel the subtle caress of his gaze as it wandered over me. "Not going to lie, I really like how it turned out."

We stunned the future Mrs. Logan Stone into silence when Dominic floated our plans past Evie and Logan at dinner. We were seated at a booth in a cozy Italian restaurant, and it was a noisy Saturday night. Had she not heard over the dull roar coming from the bar area nearby? Or did she think this was the craziest idea she'd ever heard?

If honest, yeah, this was crazy. After the shower, reality began to set in, and then it really took hold as Dominic rode in my Jag back to my place. He sat in my living room and spent the next two hours on his iPad upgrading his ticket to business class so we could sit beside each other on the flight.

I'd been fired. And I was going to Tokyo.

I kept repeating the words to myself as I packed. I was excited. And terrified.

"I need your passport." His gritty voice came through my bedroom doorway.

I delivered it to him. "No comments about the photo."

A smile teased his lips as he flipped it open and took in my ridiculous hair from five years ago. Then, his smile froze.

"You're only twenty five?" He scrubbed a hand over his face.

"Yeah, you dirty old man. Don't worry, I'll be careful with you. Don't want you to break a hip or anything."

He gave me a playfully annoyed look and went back to entering in the info.

I spent the remainder of the short afternoon handling administrative issues, like paying my rent, arranging for my Jag to stay in the parking garage, and then I purchased a replacement iPhone. Thank god all my contacts were backed up. I texted Evie, and that brought us to the cozy Italian restaurant.

"Wow," was all Logan could get out, his gaze drifting from Dominic to me. The longer he considered it, though, the more he seemed to like the idea. A pleasant smile filled his face. "That's going to be interesting."

"Yeah," Dominic said.

"It's just two weeks." I tore off a piece of garlic bread and set it on my plate, ignoring Evie's wide stare from across the table.

"Is he paying for it?" she asked quietly.

I smirked. "Just the trip."

On the car ride to my place, Dominic gave me his go-to 'Can I be honest?' line.

"I'm not offering this trip," he said, "because I have plans of . . . keeping your services on retainer."

While we were stopped at a light, I faked shock. "You won't be paying for this pussy again?" He struggled to find words, but I laughed lightly. "Keep in mind, free pussy usually costs more."

Turned out it cost just a little less. My last minute business class ticket came in at nine grand. He'd pulled out his credit card and typed those numbers in like it was nothing.

Evie pulled me aside as we finished in the bathroom.

"What is happening?" Her expression was nervous. "You want this?"

"Go to a kick-ass city, all expenses paid, with a guy who's sexy as fuck? Yeah, I want this."

"Have you thought about it seriously?" Her face skewed into an unreadable look. "I don't really know him all that well, but Logan says he's a good guy. But he's not . . . like you."

I gave her a plain look, silently asking her to get to the point.

"He's going to get attached. Logan said he's lonely. You're going to hurt him – not on purpose, but it's going to happen."

She didn't say it mean. We'd known each other for a while now. She, like Joseph, knew I didn't do attachments. But I knew something about Dominic both she and Logan didn't. He'd never been in love. It stood to reason he could survive two weeks with me. He was going to be at work a large percentage of the time I was there anyway.

"I've made it clear that's not allowed to happen." Not technically true yet, but I had a thirteen-hour flight to explain it.

Her look was skeptical, but I was confident. I was good looking, but really. My personality was an acquired taste, and few found it all that appealing. The chances of that happening were slim.

chapter
NINE

After dinner we hit the clubs with more of Logan and Dominic's friends. He'd spent most of the evening discussing inside jokes with them and catching up, and Evie and I talked wedding.

At one point I went to the bar to get another cosmo, and a hand touched my shoulder.

"Can I buy you a drink?"

The guy looked like a younger version of Paul Rudd. Kind of goofy, but friendly cute. I'm always interested when a guy like this hits on me. I like the confidence and ambition. He knows, solely based on looks, I'm probably out of his league. But maybe he also knows most guys are too intimidated to hit on me. So I should have liked this guy right away because he's not a pussy.

But something foreign sprung up in me instead of my usual flirting smile. A shocking response, "Oh, thanks, but I'm here with someone."

Again, something was definitely wrong with me. Why did I turn down a free drink? I wasn't taken.

The guy nodded and he tried not to appear disappointed, but a look flashed in his eyes. Rejection. I latched a hand on his arm.

"I'm not blowing you off," I said. He had the balls to try, and I didn't want him to be discouraged in the future. I let my gaze linger over him with a bit of exaggerated hunger. "Yesterday I would have definitely said yes."

He blinked, stunned. A faint, teasing smile rose on his face. "Well, where were you yesterday then?" When he left and a new cosmo appeared on the bar, I returned to the table. Dominic's questioning gaze was locked on me.

"Friend of yours?"

Oh, shit. That wasn't a questioning look in his eyes. That was possessiveness. Which should have made me angry, but instead, it sort of turned me on. He'd spent serious bank on me. I was okay with him demanding a little loyalty.

"No, just a guy who thought I looked thirsty."

"Yeah, he looked real *concerned* about you."

Conversation at the table ceased at Dominic's dark tone and every head swiveled toward me. Evie's eyes went so wide they were almost completely white. She expected me to raise hell at this.

Instead I calmly took a sip of my drink, enjoying the bite of the vodka. "You're going to have to do something about that tone, Mr. Ward, or you won't be enjoying my company for very long."

He pushed back from the table and stood, looming over me. "Can I talk to you for a moment?" He gestured to the back.

I slammed my drink and followed him toward the bathrooms, weaving my way through the throng of people until we were past them and in a quiet, dark corner of the deserted game room, wedged between two pinball machines that had seen less action than Dominic had in the last year.

He pressed me up against the wood paneled wall and brought his face in close so I could hear his rough voice over the loud, jovial bar atmosphere in the next room over.

"This ass is mine for the next two weeks. I thought I

made that clear."

There was a rush of heat between my legs. I looped a hand behind his neck and yanked him in to my kiss. Yeah. My kiss. The more dominating he got, the more I responded to it.

"You made it crystal clear. But let me make something clear, Dominic. Don't get attached to me." I took one of his hands and shoved it between my legs. "Or this. Two weeks, and I'm moving on."

The hand massaged me through the skinny jeans I was wearing. He took one of my hands and put it on his crotch, where he was already half-hard.

"Better not get attached to this, then."

Normally over-the-clothes bullshit wouldn't do a thing for me, but I fucking loved being an exhibitionist. The idea of someone catching us groping each other back here was arousing. I used both hands to undo his belt buckle and drop his zipper so I could wrap my hands around his cock, which was now at full attention.

To my delight, he didn't protest this new level of naughtiness. I was against the wall, between the two pinball machines, and his large back was to the door, blocking the view of anyone who might come in.

"Yeah," he said, his gaze watching my hands stroke him. "Harder."

He blew out a breath through his teeth when I did as told, and his hand went to undo my pants, but I shifted away. "Uh, uh. This ass isn't officially yours until we're over international water. Right now," I tightened my grip further, "you're mine."

Heat flashed in his eyes, and he allowed it. He set his

hands on the glass tops of the machines at our sides and submitted to me. Oh, god. It was so hot.

Switch, I believe is the term. Even though I worked at a BDSM club for about a year, I still felt new to the lifestyle. I'd never gotten into a real relationship or role with a partner, other than the occasional scene with Joseph. But I knew enough to know what I was. Sometimes I wanted the control, and sometimes I want to surrender it. Tonight, I was the top.

I pumped faster on the pulsing cock in my hands, spreading the drops of wetness around when he started to get close. In the dimly lit game room, his strikingly blue eyes looked less like the deep ocean and more like shallow, sandy waters.

"Are you going to come for me?" I demanded.

Alarm filled his face. "In your hands?"

"Worried you'll make a mess?" I knelt before him and tugged the sides of his open fly out of my way.

"You're going to blow me right here?" He glanced around.

Yeah, I was. I licked the crown of his cock and held it steady as he twitched in reaction. I closed my mouth around him and sank down, taking him as deep as I could. The power this gave me, the command over him, I got drunk off of it in an instant. I slipped him between my tight lips. My tongue did somersaults. I sucked as hard as I could and steadied one hand on his hip, controlling the pace.

"You dirty, little slut. You like the way that cock tastes?"

I froze, the filthy talk from him was so unexpected I momentarily forgot what I was doing. I looked up.

His face was red. "I've watched way too much porn in the last year. I'll be quiet."

I pulled back off of him, keeping my grip firm around the base. "No, don't fucking do that." My breathing was rapid and I could feel my soaked panties clinging to me. "You're making me so wet. I love the way you taste." I leaned back and swirled my tongue over his saliva-drenched flesh. "I've been wanting to suck you off all damn day."

I attacked him and he groaned with pleasure. Hands threaded into my hair and held my head still as he battled me for control to build a tempo, sawing his cock in and out of my mouth. Rough and unapologetic, just the way I like it. But I pushed his hands away and paused.

"Put them back on the glass. No touching."

He must have done as instructed because I heard skin slap down on the glass.

I pumped him twice more and scraped him with my teeth on the last pass. "Are you going to come for me, Dominic? I don't like waiting."

"Stop teasing me and I fucking will." The gravel voice was almost threatening and nuclear hot.

I used my hands. One formed a tight circle that followed my lips as they slid up and down, and the other hand cupped him. He was panting for air above me. He was so close. I held him there on the brink for a moment, slowing my rapid tempo down and the noise he made was like anguish.

Then I surged forward and pushed him through to the other side of his pleasure.

"Fuck," he whispered. "Here it comes. Take it."

I did, gladly. The thick, hot liquid leaped into my mouth as he shuddered and groaned, and the thick slab of flesh pulsed on my tongue, flexing with every spurt until there was nothing left.

I swallowed him down and gave him a moment to rest without movement. Truthfully, I needed a moment to catch my breath. I don't think I'd ever been this turned on from giving head in my life. I was a mess. He fell out of my mouth and I helped him zip, and then stood back up on my heels. With them on, I wasn't much shorter than him, which I liked.

"Are you still thirsty, or did I take care of that for you?"

My mouth hung open at his crude statement but slowly I twisted it into a smile. "You say the most shocking things sometimes. It'd help if you weren't blushing like a schoolgirl when you did it."

A hand settled in the small of my back and he leaned in, tipping his forehead against mine. "You have some weird effect over me."

My pulse raced at this confession, and faster still when he closed the last inch of distance between our lips and brought them together. Sparks. Tingles. All the mushy stuff I thought I was supposed to have felt the first time I'd kissed a boy growing up, but didn't. Why now? Why with him? As the kiss deepened, his effect over me did too. My legs went weak.

"I kind of like the Payton effect," he whispered.

Two weeks of this could be dangerous, and I was no longer sure for which one of us.

The downside to the Jag was that I usually wound up the DD. It was close to two in the morning when Dominic, Logan, and Evie got in and I drove them to Dominic's apartment that he leased to Logan. After we said our goodbyes, I drove my sexy travel companion to his hotel and pulled in front of the door.

"I don't think the valet's on this late," he said.

"I'm not staying tonight."

The aqua eyes focus on me with confusion. "Why not?"

Because I needed to get my head on about this. But I told him the other reason. "Because if I go upstairs with you, you're going to want to go slow and I want to get some sleep tonight."

"We don't have to fool around, we could just sleep."

My grip tightened on the steering wheel. "I don't do that, remember?"

His triumphant look was annoying. He thought he could get me to disregard that rule again easily, but he was mistaken. I was deadly serious. I wanted to sleep in my own bed tonight. I was exhausted. His gaze left mine and drifted to the clock in the dash and disappointment washed over him.

"Okay." Fingertips touched my cheek, slid under my chin, and turned it into his kiss. "I'll meet you at the United counter at the international terminal at ten." He pushed open the door and threw me a final look. "Don't be late. It'll freak me out."

I laughed lightly. "Don't worry, I'll be there."

I left a message on my mother's voicemail in the morning, letting her know I was headed out on a business trip to Japan for two weeks. She was probably at church. We only communicated through voicemail messages these days, which was fine by me. It was mostly lies anyway. I'd make up stories about my high-powered job that allowed me to live on the Gold Coast and drive a new Jag, and she'd lie about missing me and hoping we could get together. Just as soon as that busy schedule of hers settled down.

I took the CTA out to O'Hare, dragging my enormous suitcase onto the cramped train car that smelled like urine. Passport? Check. iPad? Check. Anxiety? Check and check. I was nervous about the trip, but more about the flight. I fucking hated flying. We'd have to hit the bar as soon as we were through security.

I stood just inside the sliding doors of Terminal Five by the United counter, one hand on my bag and the other worrying the hem of the pale yellow infinity scarf looped around my neck.

10:02 a.m., the clock over the departure schedule said. Where the hell was he? I shed my winter coat and proceeded to shove it inside the already stuffed suitcase.

"Payton."

My hands froze at his deep voice. I swear, it was like it shot straight between my legs when he said my name. I slowly righted myself and gave him a once-over. Faded jeans and a striped T-shirt that was cut lean and hinted at all the wonderful things going on beneath it. Instead of going dry at the sight of him, my mouth grew damp. Like I was drooling.

What the fuck? Get a grip.

"Hi." Yeah, my breathy voice wasn't helping either.

He'd stopped a few feet short of me, and the strap of his laptop bag cut a diagonal between his pecs. The terminal was busy like it usually was, but I barely noticed. The only thing stealing my focus was the urge to kiss him hello. But I couldn't decide if it was a good idea or not. I wasn't his girlfriend, and I worried it would send the wrong message. I wanted him to think of this as a friends with benefits type of deal.

He seemed to be evaluating me as much as I was him. Unsure of what was allowed and what wasn't. I gave up fighting sense and logic. I liked living in the now and dealing with consequences later, so it spilled from my lips.

"You gonna fucking kiss me, or what?"

He didn't move toward me. The blue eyes heated over a playful smile. "Oh, you're into that now? What about your rule?"

"You have some weird effect over me." It was meant to sound off-handed and indifferent, but I think he heard right through it to the meaning that lay beneath the surface.

"Yeah?" The bag he was toting rolled closer to me, until he was only a breath away. "Good."

He kissed me. Soft and slow, but building with fire at the end, and when he drew back, he lingered so close I wanted him to come back and do it again. That was when I had an inkling I might actually be in over my head.

chapter TEN

Dominic thought I was kidding when I mentioned I was a nervous flier. At the lounge he watched two screwdrivers disappear into me and then canceled my attempt to score a third.

"Are you trying to get hammered?"

"That's the plan."

The soothing words about safety and odds that fell from him while we waited to board did nothing for me. Yeah, I knew I was safe, but that was the rational side of my brain. The irrational side was the one in control right now. It was the one that poured panic into my stomach when I followed Dominic down the jetway.

Shaky hands buckled my seatbelt. "Stop it," I muttered to myself, willing the tremors to go away.

"Hey." He took my hand and laced our fingers together. It temporarily disrupted my oncoming panic attack. It forced me to recall our first night together and all the sexy hand-holding. "Can I be honest?"

"Why do you ask that? You always seem to be." I liked that about him. "What is it?"

"You're still beautiful when you're scared out of your mind. Why'd you agree to come with me if you hate this? I mean, you knew we weren't taking a boat."

"I'm not scared out of my mind," I snapped at his backhanded compliment. "I just don't like this part. I'll be fine once we're up and leveled off, and I'm not going to let it stop me from getting what I want."

He shoved his laptop bag under the seat in front of him with his foot, not releasing my hand. I sat in the window seat and Dominic in the aisle, and I scanned the seats around us. Business class was considerably nicer than economy. Spacious chairs with their own screens. Yes, this was a much better place to die than the cattle-car section behind us.

"Can I do anything to help? Distract you or something?"

I could barely focus on the words. "Um, I guess. With what?"

"I thought maybe we could get to know some more about each other. A crash course–"

"Don't say that word."

He nodded, understanding but also kind of amused. Jerk.

"Tell me about yourself." His hand squeezed mine.

I was buzzing from the screwdrivers and my stomach twisted in knots. I didn't like talking about myself and I felt too vulnerable right now. "Not much to tell."

"Come on. If there's one thing you're not, it's boring." His shifted in his seat, adjusting so his shoulders were angled more my direction. "What's your family like?"

"My family?" I scowled. Ugh, no. I didn't want to talk about them.

He looked concerned. "You don't have family?"

"No, I do." I straightened my scarf and tried not to listen to the sounds from outside the cabin. It was probably just luggage being loaded, but every mechanical noise or thump from below set me more on edge. "My parents live in Orland Park. Kyle, my older brother, he moved out to New York City a few years ago."

"What do they do?"

In my altered state, I didn't edit. "They're all profes-sional liars."

"What?"

"Lawyers. I don't want to talk about them." I shook off his grip and crossed my arms over my chest. I had to deflect. "Milwaukee, huh?"

Given my defensive body language, he looked okay with switching gears. "Yeah. I'm a middle child. Two sisters, both married and have kids."

"Are you guys close?"

He shrugged. "Sure."

There was a heavy thud and my seat vibrated. The lug-gage compartment closing, or maybe the jetway retracting, or the engine falling off the wing. I combed a hand through my hair and bit down on my bottom lip. He was well aware of my nerves. And it seemed like he decided to use it to his advantage.

"How'd you start working at the club?" His voice was low and curious. "You've got a degree, and not from some shit school, either."

I accused him with my eyes and my words. "How the hell do you know that?"

"Logan mentioned it, after the night you guys . . ."

My fear mixed with annoyance. "What exactly did his big mouth tell you?"

"Basics. That you and Evie—"

"You don't get to call her that. It's Evelyn."

"You and Logan both call her Evie. I don't know her as anything else, so get over it." I sighed in frustration. An-other one of my rules he wanted to disregard. "Anyway," he continued, "he said you two girls were fooling around when he came home. Do you . . . do that a lot?"

"No. It was a first time for me, for us." Actually, the only time. "What else did he tell you?"

That subtle color developed over his cheekbones. "You asked if you could join them and she agreed."

I waited for more, but nothing else came. "That's it?"

"I don't really want the details on Logan's sex life. He said the threeway was insane, like in a good way, but he spent the whole time worried she was going to freak out and he was going to fuck things up with her."

That wasn't surprising, but it was the first time I'd heard this. Evie and I didn't talk about it. Not in a "that never happened" way, more in a "we don't need to" way. A one-time, relationship-risking experience for all of us, that we luckily made it out of unscathed.

"Did you like it?" He asked it casually, but there was a tiny edge. Oh, he was curious. Such a male.

"Yeah. I don't have any regrets." The cabin attendant was shutting the overhead compartments, and every click felt like I was ticking closer to my doom. "This is weird, talking about it. Logan and I . . . he's your friend."

Dominic's face twisted into a grimace. "Yeah, I try not to think about that part. Mostly the stuff before he got involved."

The buzz and fear made my brain sluggish. "You think about me and Evie together?" Despite everything, I kind of laughed. "She's going to be your best friend's wife."

"Sorry, the idea of you with another woman? Way too hot not to think about."

"It was hot." Desire pooled in his eyes. Oh my god, maybe I could run with this distraction. I leaned into him, my lips close to his neck. "I don't know which I liked better, fucking her with my fingers, or with my tongue."

He exhaled loudly and shifted uncomfortably in his seat.

"She was dripping wet for me. Her pussy was so warm and soft, and she made these little whimpers when I was going down on her. She screams when she comes."

He clasped his hands in his lap, so obviously hiding his response. "Fuck, don't tell me any more right now."

Right now. Because he wouldn't mind hearing more later. "You said you wanted to help me."

"And you find tormenting me helpful?" His dark, annoyed tone was sexy.

"I do. I like watching you like this."

"Like what?"

I searched for the word, and found it. "Frustrated."

The aqua shifted into a stormy blue and his jaw set. "I'm going to teach you a lesson when we get to my place."

I scoffed. "A lesson?"

"Yeah, a lesson in frustration. I'll teach you all about it, Payton."

This time it was me who exhaled loudly. He'd gone a year without sex. I might be about to endure a lesson from a master.

Dominic let me dig into his backstory while we rocketed down the runway and sailed into the air. He went to the University of Wisconsin and was Logan's roommate freshman year. The girl Dominic had dated and who cheated on him, her name was Brook, and they'd met at work his second year at Chase Sports, the massive sports apparel company he still worked for.

He painted a picture of a person sort of like me. Even though he'd done everything to follow a normal life plan—college, a nine-to-five, a steady relationship—he drifted and was restless. Unlike him, I'd embraced my wild side, believing that would solve my restlessness, but I realized working at the club was just a distraction. A temporary fix. Something else was the problem, or missing.

Soon after the *fasten seatbelt* light went off, the Asian man across the aisle from Dominic was clearly having difficulty getting his monitor to work – I didn't think he realized it was a touch-screen because he kept hitting the buttons on the armrest.

"*Osoreirimasu,*" Dominic said. Then showed the man by leaning over and tapping his screen. I wasn't sure which one of us was more surprised, the man or me, to hear Japanese come from Dominic's mouth. The man nodded a thank you.

"What?" Dominic seemed puzzled by my reaction.

Obviously he spoke Japanese. I just hadn't thought about it. "It caught me off guard, that's all." And the language was a weird fit on him. "How much Japanese do you know?"

"I'm not too bad. It's hard to learn, but I've been studying it for a few years now. You speak any other languages?"

"Nope. I only learned a few phrases in Dutch while I was in Amsterdam. Everyone speaks English there."

We lapsed into silence, and now that I was calm, I guessed Dominic wanted to try to scratch the surface of Payton McCreary again.

"You never answered my question about how you started working at the club."

"I hit on Joseph one night when I was out with friends. He recruited me."

"Joseph. Your . . . manager."

I nodded and picked at my nails. I knew what he wanted. An explanation about why I was the way I was, but how could I give him one when deep down I had no fucking clue myself? "I like sex. Surely that's not a surprise."

"No, it's not," he gave an amused smile, "and don't call me Shirley." The *Airplane* callback.

"Before, I worked as a customer service rep for a media company. I goddamn hated it. At the club, I got paid to do something I like."

"How long did you work for Joseph?"

"A little less than a year."

He fidgeted in his seat, snapping and unsnapping the cover of his iPad.

"Ask it, Dominic."

He still hesitated. Not wanting to know and yet desperate to. "How many guys have you been with?"

"I don't keep count. You want the ballpark?" He broke off eye contact. I didn't know why I cared what he thought. It never bothered me before. I'd dealt with slut-shaming since high school. "I saw one client a night, every Friday and Saturday. I didn't work every weekend, but most, but sometimes I couldn't reach a deal with a client. I had some regulars too."

Dominic's shoulders tightened. "Less than a hundred."

"At the club? Yeah. There were some before, you know, my time in high school and college." I clenched my teeth when I saw the disappointment in his eyes. Like he was embarrassed for me. Acid rose in my stomach. "And what's your number?"

"Less."

Obviously less. He hadn't had any in the last year, during which I'd been a professional. "Don't put that fucking double-standard on me. Do you know how many guys go trolling the bars for a new girl every weekend? Why is it okay for you guys to rack up numbers, but I'm not allowed to do the same?"

His eyebrows pulled together and he looked like there was a struggle raging inside him. Maybe he knew what I was saying was true, but he still didn't like it. Oh, well.

"I'm not going to be embarrassed about it. At least *I've* never paid for sex."

There was that sparkling Payton personality. His back snapped straight and he scowled. I'd hurt him, but he didn't get to have it both ways.

"I'm sorry," I said, "but you don't get to judge me for working at the club when you're the one who walked through the door."

He blinked oh-so-slowly, and the hurt from his eyes faded. It came out unsteady and hushed. "You're right."

That wasn't what I expected. Most people got angry and defensive when they were called out. All he did was consider my statement, and then accept it. Perhaps with a bit of reluctance, but he accepted it anyway.

"Like you, I didn't keep count, but I'd guess my number is somewhere around fifty. And not to sound like a cocky piece of shit, but it would be higher if I wasn't in Tokyo."

I couldn't help it. My eyes raked over his magnificent body. Oh, yeah.

"Someone mentioned to me once," he said, his eyes

warming a shade, "that I could walk into a bar and women would be willing to drop their panties for me. I'm not sure if I believe her, though. She may or may not be a vampire."

How did he do that? How did he readjust his emotions so easily? I was worked up, expecting an argument, and he just dissipated everything. Another sign I was in trouble with this one.

Shit, Dominic was dangerous.

chapter ELEVEN

It was four in the afternoon Tokyo time when we landed, but it felt like two in the morning to me. My eyes were heavy and burning for more sleep, but otherwise I was charged and excited. We'd each gotten a decent nap in during the flight.

Japan. I knew nothing of it other than the glamorized version from movies and TV. It was supposed to be the mecca of the cutting edge, fashion and technology. But Dominic said that wasn't quite true. Parts of Japan had less technology than rural, small-town America did. Cash was still king, not plastic. ATMs were inside the banks, which closed at six. Fax machines were preferred over email.

The airport was beautiful, modern, and bustling with travelers, and after we got through customs and immigration and claimed our luggage, Dominic led me to the counter and bought us train passes.

The station was mostly empty. Beneath our feet, glossy white tiles looked clean enough to eat off of. We waited behind a glass wall for the train. Chicago and Amsterdam's public transit was nothing like this. The seats on the equally clean rail car were a deep red, stain-free, and plush.

"You tired?" Dominic asked as we rode through a tunnel. The darkness made me yawn.

"A little, but I'm all right. How far is your place?"

"Fifteen minutes on the rail, then a ten minute walk."

He didn't seem too tired, either. I wondered if he'd asked because he was working out his 'lesson plan' in his head. Halfway through the flight I'd made a mile-high club joke, and he responded by telling me to keep it in my pants until we landed.

The train approached the station, and I got my first look of Tokyo from the ground. The sun had set not long ago, but the lights were on. Gleaming steel buildings stretched to the sky. To be honest, it wasn't so different from Chicago. Busy and corporate, with taxis and cars pushed up together while trying to navigate the streets, and pedestrians with heads down, buried in their cell phones.

But the signage. Everywhere, and the characters were unrecognizable to my American eyes. Once we stepped off the train and made our way from the impressive station, I began to feel like an alien. We looked like no one else, and the conversations that passed by were shocking. The European languages have some sort of familiarity to English, but not this.

As Dominic approached a set of double glass doors, a doorman nodded and pulled it open.

"*Konnichiwa*," Dominic said, and the doorman echoed it back, a pleasant expression on his face. The lobby of the apartment building was elegant but generic. We paused at the desk for Dominic to pick up his mail, and then rode an elevator up.

"I'm in Japan," I said out loud.

Dominic smirked. "I'm aware." He shifted his weight so he was close, his body leaning into mine and his voice dropping low. "Every part of me is aware." I tried not to shiver from that delicious voice.

Like the lobby, his corporate apartment was elegant and generic, but western style. No sliding paper doors or tan mat floors. It was small by Chicago standards, probably even New York standards. When we stepped over the threshold, Dominic's shoes came off in Japanese tradition. I followed suit.

To the left was a tiny kitchen space, not much more than a sink and the stove top, separated by a foot of counter. Cabinets overhead and below, a pantry, and a small refrigerator beside that. The square, black dining table divided the kitchen from the living area, also known as the couch. This room was smaller than Evie's old apartment, but more effective at maximizing space.

"The master room's to the right," he said, sorting through the mail and dropping it on the table. "The guest room's there." He gestured to the doorway beside the fridge. "You want something to drink?"

"Sure."

It was abruptly awkward for me as he pulled two clear, odd-shaped bottles from the fridge. I was at his place, completely dependent on him. At his mercy. Oh god, I hadn't thought this through.

"What happens tomorrow?" I asked while he opened the bottles and something rattled.

"What do you mean?" He extended it to me and I took it. Soda of some sort, but there was a weird clear orb in the neck of the bottle.

"You have to work, right?" I took a swig of the drink, but the ball floated in the neck and clogged it so I only got half a sip. Lemon-lime, and not too bad.

"I do. There are lots of different tours you can go on. I've got some brochures left over from when my parents were here."

I tried again to take a sip, but the stupid thing rolled right back into the neck. "This drink is defective."

"You don't like the marble soda?" There was a gleam in his eyes. Arrogance. Hot, but annoying.

No dice on my third attempt. "I can't get it to work."

"That must be *frustrating* for you."

The air grew thick between us in an instant. His lesson had begun. There was a thunk as he set his bottle down on the table and stalked toward me. My pulse jumped. I sure as shit wasn't tired now. A wicked expression twisted on his face. Lust. He pulled the bottle from my hand. Another thump of glass on wood as it was set down.

"I just realized I didn't give you a proper tour."

His arms banded around my waist and squeezed, lifting me up until my feet no longer were on the floor. He was carrying me to his bedroom, and I figured I'd make it easier on him. That way we could get there faster. My legs wrapped around his hips.

He took a hand off me to quickly flip the switch on the wall when we were through the door, and I got a brief look at the room before I sailed down onto my back on the bed. Purples and golds, with boring artwork on the walls. He lived here, but it seemed like he'd made no effort to make it his home. The room barely fit the bed, which was thankfully a queen-sized one. I was going to fuck him all over this apartment, but I was happy to start here.

He stood at the edge of the bed and peeled off my socks while I rose up on my elbows and yanked the scarf over my head. It made no sound when I flung it away. His fingers slipped under the hem of my lightweight sweater and forced it upward. It was cast off. It was a mad dash to get naked after that. Or so I thought. I jerked at the back of his shirt and pulled it over his head as his hands fumbled at the button of my jeans.

We were both down to our underwear when I began to scoot back up on the bed to put my head on a pillow.

"Wrong," he said. His hands grabbed fistfuls of the comforter I was lying on and dragged it toward him, carrying me along with it. His hands closed on my knees and slid upward. Over my thighs, over the baby blue lace band covering my hips, and up. The coarse skin of his palms brushed over my ribs and his hands splayed as he continued. Thumbs trailed over my bra-clad breasts, to my shoulders, and slowed at my neck.

They reached their final destination at my jaw. His fingers skimmed over my cheekbones in a soft caress. He leaned over me, lowering to deliver that mesmerizing kiss. I tipped my head into it, my eyes falling shut as the warmth of his skin closed in.

My eyes fluttered open.

He'd stopped, just a breath away. I lifted my head to meet him—

Nope. Those hands cupping my face had a purpose, and it was to prevent me from doing that. He'd locked my head in place, teasing the kiss I originally claimed I didn't want, and he already knew I was desperate for.

I shifted. I struggled against his hold, but he was prepared. When I decided to employ distraction, he was ready for that, too. The moment my hand touched his thick cock through his boxers, he stepped back from the bed.

"Give me your hands," he demanded. There was something yellow in his. My scarf. Oh, he was feeling comfortable with me now. Here in his bed where he was going to own my ass for the next two weeks.

"If I don't?" My voice was filled with excitement and sex.

"Your lesson will last longer."

I pretended to be reluctant about surrendering my control, but surely he could tell this was a lie. He took the scarf, which was nothing more than a giant loop of fabric, and knotted it, cinching my wrists together.

"Too tight?"

"It's fine." I was a little surprised he hadn't pussed out and gone easy. The knot was kind of tight. He pushed my arms over my head and took a knee beside my hip. He left one hand on my bound wrists, just resting there. Like it was guarding them.

Soft lips skimmed over my chest. The whiskers on his chin tickled me as he worked lower. His mouth opened and his tongue traced the edge of my bra, and the plan was kind of transparent.

"How slow are we going to go tonight?"

He didn't laugh. Instead, his head lifted and locked eyes with me. His gaze dripped with seduction. "Until you think you might die."

This wasn't playful Dominic. This was some other kind of creature. Fire poured into my center and pooled in my body.

His hot mouth clamped down on my breast, moisture soaking through the fine lace as he sucked at me. His tongue kneaded my flesh. I clamped my legs together, unbearably turned on. He roved over to the other breast and repeated it until my nipples were hard and sensitive, my breasts full and swollen.

"Can you come like this?" he asked. "Just from my mouth sucking on your tits?"

A tight noise escaped my throat. Normally the answer would be a *no*, it certainly always had been. Still, he knew what the hell he was doing. He'd timed it perfectly. As he nipped at me, I arched my back and his hand sank beneath my body. It searched for the clasp of my bra. It took him a few seconds, maybe more than one try, and tension sprang free from the band.

"One handed." I gave him an impressed look.

"I've very talented."

The bra slipped up over my elbows and he abandoned it there by my bound wrist.

"Fuck," I moaned. His mouth was hotter without the lace in the way. I watched the tip of his tongue roll a lazy circle around my erect nipple, his hand holding the breast in place.

"Better?" he rumbled. "Do you want to come like this?"

Like he was sure he could get me there with just his mouth. *Could he?* Another circle and a soft bite made it seem possible.

"I . . ."

Fingernails slipped down over my stomach as his hand journeyed lower. Yes, lower. That would definitely get me there. They inched under the lace and I opened my legs to welcome them. Two fingers stirred me. I moaned loudly.

"Jesus, Payton, you've made a mess down here."

I smirked. "You did that."

The fingers were suddenly gone, and wetness smeared over my nipple, followed by his tongue. "Your pussy tastes so good."

Holy shit, if he did that again, I was going to come. My

lower body protested that his touch was gone, but my skin above was hyper-aware. Every caress and lash of his mouth brought me closer to the brink.

A soft whimper fell from my lips. It was like a signal to him.

"Keep your hands here," he ordered. His voice was an even mixture of playful and threatening.

Dominic slid back off the bed and knelt between my parted legs, and my breathing became shallow. Like with the bra, his tongue teased the edge where lace gave way to skin, this time on the inside of my legs. Only here, it wasn't as pleasant.

"I want your mouth on me so bad, it hurts," I said.

He stayed silent. Not ignoring me, though. A soft kiss was planted on the lace. Then, another. This one lingered, and that sinful tongue got involved. My stomach clenched.

"Take my panties off."

"I will when I'm good and ready." He sucked at the damp fabric and licked me through it. "I don't need to take them off to do this." Fingertips curled around the inside seam and pulled them to the side.

I unleashed a startled moan when he fucked me with his tongue. Slow. Sensual. Like he had all the time in the world, and wasn't aware he had brought me almost to the edge. One fast swirl, or a finger running over my clit and I'd be done for.

"I'm right there. Oh, god . . ."

His mouth shifted away and he released the panties, letting them snap back into place. I took a deep breath in through my nose and blew it out of my mouth. I knew what this was. My body was aching for release, but he wasn't going to allow it yet.

"I understand the lesson," I said. "Please, can we—"

He laughed. "You think we're done? Payton, shit, we're just getting started."

He backed me down from orgasming at least a half-dozen times. With his fingers and with his mouth again. He'd taken off my panties the second time he went down on me. Tremors shook my legs and my arms began to go numb from the lack of movement, but I did my best to keep them in place. Dominic showed no signs of letting up anytime soon.

"Are you brinking me?" I asked, struggling for breath.

"What's that?"

"Where you take me to the brink of orgasm and back off."

The smile I got was evil. "Oh, then, yeah. That's exactly what I'm doing."

Each time I got close, he either stopped or changed techniques. The second option was worse because it was new, different pleasure right on the heels of the sensation that was supposed to send me over the edge.

"Oh, shit, please." My voice was shaky. He was back to kneeling between my legs. This time he used both his mouth and his fingers. *Please let this be the time he allows it.*

"Do you want to come?"

"Yes." I was out of my mind. I couldn't focus on anything else.

He paused his mouth, but that pair of fingers continued their slow press in and out, and I shifted my hips in time with them.

"Do you *need* to come?"

With every cell in my body. "Oh, god, yes."

"How badly do you want to? Tell me."

My skin was on fire, yet covered with goosebumps. My eyes closed under his power, which I was drowning in. "I'm going to lose my fucking mind. Please, Dominic. *Please.*"

He carved a path with that mouth, from entrance to clit and I sucked in a breath. Yes, yes, yes . . .

No. He ceased everything and shot to his feet. No longer touching or tasting me.

"Then, come," he ordered. His dark gaze focused on me, watching. I clamped my legs together, squeezing every muscle in my lower body, trying to send myself over the edge when he'd abandoned me teetering there.

And . . . and . . . it wasn't going to happen. A deep sound of frustration broke free from my chest.

"This lesson is the fucking worst. I'm over it." I brought my arms down. I could get this knot undone with some maneuvering, and I'd finish what he refused to.

But his mouth crashed into mine, stunning me motionless. Hands slid beneath me and forced me back up the bed, his naked body along with it. The boxers must have come off when he was going down on me the millionth time, and his hard length pressed against me.

My head hit the pillow at the same instant he yanked open a drawer in the nightstand. A box tore open. A wrapper crinkled as he rolled onto his back beside me and his hands moved, covering himself.

My teeth chattered. Not with cold, or fear, but some side effect of the insane need gnawing at me. Need. For him. When he was ready, he threaded his head through the circle of my tied arms and positioned himself over me.

"You want this cock inside you? Say it." He slid it in my

wet folds, priming himself, or just being more of a tease.

"Fuck, I want your big, hard cock inside me."

He flashed a victorious smile, and claimed my mouth the same moment he claimed my body. My groan of enjoyment sounded suspiciously like suffering. The tight fit of him inside me . . . it felt so impossibly good.

Then he moved.

Hips rolled, touching me inside and out. He was on top of me, inside me, all over me . . . fucking everywhere. His subtle movements increased the tension in my core.

Something like a sob swelled in my chest. The ache for release. So strong I could taste it. Everything else faded out. Just the need remained. I moaned and cried out, thrashed beneath him. I couldn't breathe. I wasn't sure I could go on living if he didn't get me there.

His lips were by my ear but it sounded like his voice was in my head. In my fucking thoughts. "Are you going to come for me?"

I hissed out the word. "Yes."

"How badly do you want to come for me?" His thrust was deep. Wicked, and possessive. "I want to hear the desperation in your voice."

Desperation was right. I began to panic. My whole body shook and I clutched him as best I could with my hands tied. "I want to, so bad. So. Fucking. Bad."

"I think you're ready." His head ducked out from the loop of my arms and—

Terror descended into my voice. "Dominic!"

He pulled out of me and sat back on his heels, his eyes incredibly intense. "Come for me. Now. Right fucking now. Don't make me wait another second."

This command in that rough voice lit a fuse that spiraled into me, burning deeper and deeper, until it set off the explosion. My mind drained of thought. Eyes rolled back in my head. Holy fuck. I arched my back and screamed. "Shit, I'm coming! *I'm coming!*"

He wasn't even touching me. Dominic sat shock-still, watching the pleasure seize and tense my body; hot, consuming, and leaving nothing in its wake. I couldn't find air and didn't give a fuck. I wanted this to last forever. Wanted him to make it go on forever. The sharp edge of the orgasm flooded through me and washed away slowly, one layer at a time.

"Did you like that?" His voice was audio sin.

I nodded, unable to speak. Still couldn't really breathe. The orgasm had been so intense, I needed more time to recover. As I did that, I was only faintly aware he was undoing the scarf from my wrists. Everything was tingling.

His warm body pressed against mine when it was done and I had my hands free. They settled on his broad shoulders, drifting downward when he shifted between my legs and his cock began to sink into me again.

Dominic had made me come without touching me. Sure, he'd prepped me, but in the end it was his rough, dirty voice that got me there. Had he done it because he worried my orgasm would set off his, or had he done it simply because he could? Didn't matter once he resumed fucking me. Nothing did but that connection to him, and those deep, furious thrusts that put me back on the climb toward ecstasy.

And that kiss. That fucking kiss. I moaned into his soft mouth, not wanting my lips to leave his. His skin felt like it was on fire beneath my palms, which slid further down so

I could dig my nails into his ass. My legs wrapped tighter around his waist and I rose up off the mattress, trying to meet him like I couldn't get enough of his cock. Because I couldn't. His joke about not getting attached to it drifted through my head.

It was a million degrees trapped underneath him and we were both sweating. His hair was damp around the temples and I could feel the hair sticking to the back of my neck, but no way was I going to let him slow down, and the determined look on his face said that wasn't going to happen anyway.

"Fuck," he groaned, burying his face in the side of my neck, his ragged breathing loud in my ear. "You feel so good. I'm not going to let you leave this bed for the next two weeks."

But I had plans. Sex on the dining table. The couch. Maybe the shower if it was big enough. He dipped a hand beneath my back, slipping down to grab a handful of my ass and squeeze, hard.

The tension wound tighter inside, making it difficult to focus on anything else. Fuck. Too good. I was going to explode.

"You're going to . . . make me come . . . again." Could barely breathe.

He gave me a teasing look. "That's the plan, genius."

The hand not holding my ass latched on to my breast so he could tilt it up into his mouth, skimming over the sensitive skin with the sharp edge of his teeth. I cried out, squeezing my legs harder around him and bringing my knees up so they were almost beside his head. My back arched up as pleasure mounted and took hold, gripping me in another orgasm. Weaker than the first spectacular one, but still fucking awesome.

"Sssh," he whispered while grinning.

"You don't like . . . that I'm vocal?" I panted out.

"Are you kidding me? I do, but my neighbors probably don't."

"Fuck your neighbors."

His grin turned down into a playful scowl. "Why the hell would I do that? I'd rather fuck you, and we know you like it. Evident from all the screaming."

Oh, those damn aqua eyes flashed cocky and arrogant.

"Maybe it's your turn to learn a lesson," I said. I seized his large biceps with my hands and shoved him off of me, hard.

"What are you–"

I had him flat on his back and I scrambled up on my knees. Reverse cowgirl is so motherfucking sexy, but getting there isn't, especially when you're moving fast. But by the time he figured it out, it was too late. I straddled his hips, reached down to grab a handful of his hard cock, and slid down, taking him inside me.

Dominic's groan was loud and long. His hands tightened on my waist like he had some hope of controlling me. Forget it. I was on top in every sense of the word now. I sat up straight on him, rocking him deep inside.

"Payton." It came from behind me, alarmed. "Shit, wait a minute."

"Why?" My lips peeled back in a smile. "You don't like it?" I increased the tempo, rotating my hips and flexing my interior muscles. "Don't you like it when I fuck you?"

"Jesus, wait!" He sounded borderline panicked.

Nope. I leaned back toward him, dragging his hands away from my hips, depositing them on my breasts, and rode. Hard. Fast. Teaching him the lesson that I could fuck just as good as he could. Maybe I could make him scream.

The angle was just right between us so he hit my G-spot. I left one hand on top of his that clung to me, and the other ventured lower. It took a detour at my clit for a moment, then I let it wander lower, touching his balls.

"Goddamnit!"

Beneath me, his body writhed. The hands on my skin pulled and pushed, urging me to move faster. Yeah, he'd given up on trying not to come. Now his body took over and it showed me how he wanted it.

"Fuck, fuck . . ." It played an endless loop from him, mindless while the man under me went rigid. *"Fuck!"* He sucked in an enormous breath, and pushed it out in a loud moan. Not a scream, but louder than I'd heard him before. Then, the pulse deep inside, signaling his drawn-out release. Every twitch and flex I could feel, and I could feel it everywhere.

I slowed my breathing, taking a minute to blink back to reality, although I was still buzzing. The hands around me gently lifted me off of him and rolled me onto my side so I was against the cool sheets, and then his arm folded over me.

Spooning me. Again. I told myself I was allowing it because I was exhausted and blissed-out. Not because I kind of didn't mind it. Because that would be crazy. My eyes closed when lips brushed over my neck, and an involuntary shiver crept over me, followed by goosebumps.

"You're cold?" he asked, whisper-quiet.

"No. You're causing that," I admitted.

He let out a soft noise that sounded suspiciously like satisfaction.

Not sure how long we lay there. Minutes, hours, days . . . whatever. Eventually he got up, disposed of the condom in the bathroom, then went to the kitchen, returning with glass of water for me, and that annoying soda for him.

I drank and set my glass on the nightstand, then rolled over to face him.

"I've been meaning to ask you," I said, "about the thirty grand. Did you not know you were supposed to negotiate?"

He was on his back, one hand propped up behind his head, and gave me a lazy smile. "I knew."

"Okay, so you're stupid about money."

The lazy smile stretched wider. "Maybe. Or maybe I wasn't interested in wasting time discussing it, plus the whole thing . . ." His eyebrows pulled together into a more serious expression. "Haggling about money and saying, 'No, she's only worth this much–'" Those blue eyes blinked slowly. "I was already extremely uncomfortable with what I was doing. I didn't want to assign a dollar value to you like you were livestock. I just wanted that part over as fast as possible."

"Aw, that's nice. But all I hear is that you're incredibly stupid about money."

"Maybe what you should hear is that I know a good value when I see it."

chapter
THIRTEEN

I must have dozed off. When I woke, it was dark in the room and Dominic's heavy, deep breathing beside me announced he was asleep. Thankfully he was on his side of the bed so I was able to slip out without him knowing. I shut his bedroom door quietly behind me then pulled my luggage to the second bedroom.

This one was done in greens and was smaller than his. No window. The bed wasn't much bigger than my college dorm bed, but as it was unoccupied and I was still exhausted, it looked great. I pulled on a pair of shorts and a shirt, because I'd lied to Dominic the other day. I didn't sleep in the nude unless I had to.

I curled up under the covers and passed out.

Only to wake with his arm around me, making me the little spoon once again. What the fuck? My bleary eyes surveyed the room. Purple, not green. Big bed, not little. His room. "How the hell did I get here?"

"Plane," he rumbled, half-asleep.

"No, asshole. How'd I get in this bed?"

There was a hand attached to the arm thrown over me, and that hand was beneath my shirt, his palm warm against my belly. "I got lonely and dragged your ass back here. Now stop talking so I can sleep. I have to work tomorrow."

I tried to get up, but the hand went firm.

"Don't even think about it."

Fire flooded into me. "I told you. I. Don't. Do. This."

NIKKI SLOANE

The bed rocked subtly as he rose up on an arm and loomed over me. Only the faint blue light from his alarm clock lit the room, but I could see his face clearly enough. It was set and determined.

"I. Don't. Care." Annoyance coated his voice. "My bed's been empty for a year and you think I'm going to let the most beautiful woman I've seen sleep in the other room?"

I stared up at him and tried to assemble my words, but apparently he wasn't finished.

"I brought you ten thousand miles to be here with me. Not on the other side of my apartment. What's the big deal? You get night-terrors or something?"

"No," I scoffed. "But it's . . ." God, I didn't want to have this conversation, now or ever.

"But it's what?"

I sighed. "It's too intimate."

Of course he began to laugh. If I wasn't pissed that he was laughing at me, I might have thought his laugh sound-ed nice. Deep, yet warm and infectious. Instead, I flung his hand off of me.

He scrambled to regain control. "Hey, stop that. Come on, this is stupid. We've had sex how many times already? We're way past intimate."

That's not how I viewed it at all. Seeing him naked, sleeping with him . . . that wasn't intimacy. The day-to-day, real life was what I didn't want. I wouldn't mind a peek be-hind the curtain of Dominic, but he sure as shit wasn't going to get one behind mine.

I flopped down, turning over in a huff, and heard him settle back down.

I knew this was stupid, and if I ever wanted to belong to

someone else, I was going to have to let them in. Yet I'd only done that once in my life and been burned so spectacularly, I couldn't stomach the thought of trying again. I'd held Joel at a safe distance and hidden behind the sex, but my strategy had only worked for so long.

The bedroom was silent other than Dominic's breathing which deepened as he fell asleep. Now I was wide-awake, staring at the ceiling of his Japanese apartment. How much longer should I stay here? I had to be firm about this sleeping arrangement. I'd let him have the kissing, but no more blowing past my rules.

I waited.

Gently extracted myself from his embrace.

And waited again. Then, I escaped from his bed the second time, channeling my inner ninja. I was relieved to stand my ground as I crossed the living area for the guest bedroom, but worried what action he was going to take when he figured out he was alone again. Would he storm into the bedroom, flip the lights on, and demand I get back into bed with him?

No, it was worse.

His heavy arm was around me again, crushing me against his body that was like a fucking furnace.

"Morning," he murmured when I stirred.

"Seriously?" I was disoriented with sleep, wanting to fall back into it. Too tired to argue right at that moment. "Can you at least get on your side?"

"I am on my side. This bed is tiny."

What? My eyes fluttered open to see the green wall. He'd crawled into bed with me, rather than attempt the move again.

"You're obnoxious."

He chuckled. "You didn't leave me any other choice." Beneath the sheets, his large hand curled around me tighter. "You hungry?"

The thought of food woke me some. "What time is it?"

"Five-thirty."

Turning over to face him almost sent me off the bed because there was no room to maneuver. The bedroom door was open and early morning light came in from the living area. His eye was almost back to normal with just a faint purple shadow clung below it.

"What are you making me for breakfast?"

His hand settled in the small of my back with ease. "What makes you think I'm making you breakfast?"

"I'm your guest. It's polite, and I didn't exactly get a good night's sleep."

"That's your fault, not mine. You chose this bed." Before I could protest, he covered my mouth with his. His soft lips pressed to mine and encouraged my participation. The spark between us flared, burning brighter and hotter as his tongue gently slipped into my mouth. The thought slammed into me. Dominic . . . was he even better at kissing than he was at fucking?

I didn't get a chance to test the theory. He drew back abruptly and sat up, taking his warmth away. He ran a hand over the scruff covering his jaw, and turned his gaze toward the kitchen.

"What do you want for breakfast?" he asked.

"I want what we were just doing." I reached a hand out and set it on his arm, tugging him back toward me, but he wouldn't budge.

He blew out a short breath. "Yeah, me, too, but I don't have time."

"You can be late."

There was that deep laugh. "Late? That word doesn't exist in Japanese culture."

I sat up and tossed the covers back, wanting the desire to drain from my body. It was alarming how quickly he'd turned me on. "Fine. What do you have to eat?"

"Frosted Flakes." He stood. "I don't have any milk, though."

"Delicious." My eyes were fixed on his body.

A smile broke on his face. He must have put his boxers back on before coming into my room, but they were the only thing covering his insane body. I enjoyed every defined curve of his chest and the notched washboard abs below it, leading my eyes like an arrow downward.

I swung one foot then the other and stood, stretching my arms up over my head. He took the lead from me. His gaze caressed down over my tight and thin white tank top and lingered there for a moment at the swell of my breasts before working lower to the shorts and my bare legs. The muscles along his jawline flexed, and I'd swear I saw him swallow hard.

"I have to leave this room now, devil woman." And he fled to the kitchen.

I crunched a bowl of dry cereal and stared at the Japanese version of Tony the Tiger while Dominic showered and dressed. Seeing him packaged in a suit was a close second to the boxers, and he smelled earthy and manly as he came close, pouring himself a cup of coffee.

"Not to sound all domestic," I said with a mouthful of

cereal, "but when will you be home?"

He hesitated. "I stay until the ship's secured. They stick as close to the schedule as they can, but there's a lot of uncontrolled variables that usually derail it."

I understood what he hadn't exactly said. "You don't know."

"If inventory is balanced, the wind doesn't interfere with the crane, and the ship doesn't have any maintenance issues, they pull out of the port at five. I'll text you if that changes." He went to the narrow bookshelf beside the couch and pulled out glossy brochures, splashing them on the dining table. A pen appeared from his suit pocket and he scribbled a note on it.

"WiFi password." A yellow map was pulled from the pile of papers. "This is the map of the train. Take this if you go out. Some of the trains don't have any English and you'll get lost." He shifted his weight from one foot to the other as if uncomfortable.

"What's with you?"

"This is weird, just leaving you here to, like, fend for yourself. I didn't prepare you at all."

His guilty expression reinforced this, as if he felt he were abandoning me. Which was totally unnecessary, but kind of sweet.

"Oh my god, I'll be fine."

His face said he was far from convinced. "There's a *konbini* right by the station, you remember how to get there?" He dug out his wallet and pulled out a handful of yen.

"I do, but I don't know what that is."

"It's a convenience mart. They've got groceries."

When he held out the wad of money toward me I stared

at it, unmoving. "You want me to buy your groceries?"

"No. I mean, I don't know. There's not a lot to eat here. I wasn't expecting to have company."

He was flustered, and every moment longer I stood without taking his money seemed to make it worse. Uncomfortable Dominic wasn't far off from embarrassed Dominic. Cute. I enjoyed it for a second and then closed my hand on the cash.

"Any requests?"

"I'm not picky, but don't buy anything unless you're sure what's inside." A look crossed his face, a shudder of a memory.

"Learned that one the hard way, huh?"

He nodded and finished his coffee. His eyes fell like he was going to check his watch, but discovered his wrist was bare. Instead, he checked the time on the microwave clock. "I have to head out. You sure you're okay? You can text me if you need help."

His concern was starting to annoy me. I'd traveled all over Europe, and lived on my own in downtown Chicago. "Seriously, I'll manage."

He set a key on the counter. "Okay. Here's the spare key when you go out."

And with that settled, it dropped us squarely in the middle of 'how the hell do we say goodbye?' Did I throw out a 'have a good day at work?' Give him a hug? His blue eyes studied me, gauging my body language or waiting for me to initiate the farewell.

"Well," he said, "have fun."

It was like his feet were glued to the floor, though, and his expression looked pained. Like he was displeased with himself for saying those words. His head tilted slightly, bent toward me. "You gonna fucking kiss me, or what?"

It sounded amazing in his rough voice, and even though I knew it was a bad idea, I did it anyway.

It was close to lunchtime when I realized I needed a game plan on seeing the sights. I'd showered and dressed, then fired up my laptop at his dining table and read up on Japanese tourism. And while researching the different places I wanted to go, I fell down into the spiral of the Internet and wound up reading history of Japan articles on Wikipedia. I'd always been a sucker for learning new things.

The rumble in my stomach reminded me it was time to venture outside.

It was overwhelming, and exotic, and I loved every freaking minute of shopping in the *konbini,* from the strange produce on display to the brightly colored boxes lining the shelves. Some of which I had absolutely no idea of what they contained. Thankfully, most had English in small print somewhere. The clerk flashed me a vacant look when I was finished and rang me up.

Something as routine as grocery shopping was exciting. I loved the foreignness of it. On my way back to the apartment, amazing smells came from a restaurant and I considered going in, but then thought better of it. The chances of me understanding the menu or ordering weren't great.

I texted Evie to let her know things were good. It was noon Tokyo time, which was a whopping fifteen hours ahead of Chicago, meaning it was nine at night there, yesterday. I could hardly wrap my head around it.

The sun had faded from the window when I finished composing my list of the places I was going to tour over the coming days, and my phone buzzed with a text from Dominic.

> Should be back around 5:30. Want to go out for dinner?

Like a date? I pushed the question away. I did want to go out, and my opportunities with Dominic as my guide were limited, so I said yes.

I was seated at the kitchen table and peered at him over the top of my computer when he came through the front door and toed off his shoes. My hands gripped the sharp edge of the wood. Hopefully he didn't notice. Goddamn, he was good looking. I was going to put that suit on the floor in ten seconds flat.

"Hi." He shot me a sexy smirk. "Give me a minute to change." He hurried across the living area and disappeared into his bedroom. I don't know what I expected, but that was surprising. I blinked, trying to sort out this weird feeling.

Oh, fucking hell. I wanted his kiss and was annoyed he'd bypassed it. I pushed back from the table and my eyes narrowed on his open door. Hangers shifted around in there and gave the telltale sound as a shirt was yanked off with haste.

I'd just made it to the doorway when he reappeared, dressed in dark jeans and a casual, patterned button down shirt. "Ready?"

He didn't wait for me to answer. Instead he guided me to the door, barely giving me a chance to put on my shoes and grab my jacket and purse. How the hell did he get changed so fast?

"Where's the fire?" I demanded when he all but shoved me into the hall.

The question was ignored. He locked the door and let out a tremendous sigh. Like relief. "That was close."

"What is your deal?"

A hand was warm on my hip, pressing me toward the elevator. "We had to get out of there before we had sex."

"What?" He had me spinning. "You don't want that?"

The blue eyes glared at me like I was the idiot in this situation. "Are you kidding? Of course I want that. I've been thinking about it all damn day, but I can at least buy you dinner first."

I've been thinking about it all damn day. This was bad. The warning alarms sounding in my head quieted to nothing when he tugged me into the awaiting elevator and crushed his lips to mine.

"Where are we going?" I asked when we boarded the train. He'd hurried me through the streets back to the station we'd come from yesterday.

"There's a restaurant near the Shibuya crossing."

We had to stand since the car was already full. Dominic reached up and grabbed one of the hanging straps from the ceiling, and put a firm arm around my waist. My breath caught in my throat. Once again, I shouldn't, but I liked this. He'd done it for safety so I wouldn't lose my balance if the train jerked, but I couldn't help but like the display. As if I were his. I softened and my arms naturally encircled him.

Shibuya. The name was familiar. "I think that's on my list."

"What list?" His voice was hushed and uneven. Maybe

in reaction to what I'd done.

"All the stuff I'm going to see. I brought it along because I wanted to get your opinion."

We looked like a couple. The other people gave us absolutely zero percent of their attention. Like in Chicago, the train was a cross-section of the different subcultures of the city. A white-collar salaryman in a finely tailored suit rode beside a younger man in a brightly patterned hoodie whose hair was spiked and slanted to the side in a wild style. And behind them, two teenage girls in school uniforms. We were the only Westerners on the train. The only *Gaijin*.

I watched the urban landscape whiz past the window at a crazy velocity.

"It's so quiet," I whispered. Not just the car, but the train itself. I was used to the rumble and clank of the L and its screeching brakes. Not this train. Only a faint hum was noticeable.

A smile warmed his eyes. "They know how to do public transit here. One morning I'll make you ride the train during rush hour. That's an experience."

My first traditional meal in Tokyo was amazing. Like shopping in the *konbini*, I enjoyed every minute. Taking off my shoes at the door and walking across the tan, woven tatami mats. Sitting on the floor at the low table surrounded by paper sliding doors. The green tea. The food.

And of course, the man across from me who ate with chopsticks like he'd used them his whole damn life. He didn't judge me for not having the faintest clue how to use them. He helped. Maybe it was nice for him to not feel like the biggest foreigner in the room for once, but I think he got a kick out of watching my pleasant reaction to everything. I kind of loved all of this.

For the first time since my sophomore year of college, conversation with the opposite sex wasn't so hard. I don't know if it was Dominic, or the sake, or a combination of both. We chatted about our day after he'd ordered for us. Japanese coming out of his mouth was still bizarre, but interesting.

We went over my list, and he made comments about a few, like "crowded, but worth it," or "tourist trap." There were some he hadn't done yet, and seemed thrilled when I asked if he wanted to go together. I decided I was done worrying about him getting attached. I'd deal with it later if it happened.

"I expected you to balk," he announced, a grin teasing his lips. "That was pretty far out of the comfort range of American cuisine."

I gave a soft laugh as I surveyed the mostly empty bowls before me. It had been fish with the head on, rice, and something that looked like seaweed, and it had all been delicious. I gave a sly and seductive smile. "You haven't figured out yet that I'm the adventurous type?"

His eyes hazed with lust. "No, your list the night we met made that clear." He downed the last of his sake like it would give him courage. "About that, I was wondering . . ."

My pulse ticked up a notch. "Was there something on there that interests you?"

Just below his cheekbones, the skin flushed a subtle pink. "Yeah. First column, uh, third one down."

"Sorry, I don't remember which one that was." Total lie. I knew *exactly* what it was, but he was way too cute when he was like this.

"Let's just say it rhymes with schmay-nal."

I choked on my sake. "God, Dominic," I laughed, "if you can't say it, you don't get to do it."

He just blinked and looked like he didn't know what to do. His broad shoulders lifted in a hesitant breath. "I haven't before."

chapter
FOURTEEN

Holy shit, after fifty-some women he'd never had anal sex. "Really?"

His blush deepened another shade as he nodded and his voice dropped low. "Do you like it?"

"Oh, yeah." I grinned.

"Real?"

"Real. I'm definitely up for it." I was excited to give him a lesson in that kind of pleasure. But then reality crashed down on me and I skewed my face.

"What is it?" He looked alarmed.

"I'm going to need some help because you're so big."

I think he stopped breathing. He was so tense, the compliment barely registered. "What kind of help?"

"Like, help you can buy at an adult store," I said, softly. "Surely there's one around here—"

He rubbed a hand behind his neck, working out the tension. "Trust me, there are plenty. And don't call me Shirley." He bit down on his lip, and his eyes glinted with desire. "In fact, I think there are several in Shibuya. Let's go." He threw down a wad of yen, and started to get up from the table.

His eagerness made me chuckle.

Shibuya Center Town was a massive intersection in the heart of a shopping district, and every square inch of flat surface was either covered in signage or jumbotron dis-

130

plays of moving images. The advertisement was in your face, soaking into every pore, seeping in until I was overwhelmed. It made Times Square seem like it was nothing.

Dominic and I stood at the window of the Starbucks on the second floor of a nearby building and watched as the light changed, and an enormous wave of people took off, power walking across the dotted white bands on the pavement, signifying the crosswalk. It was a sight to behold.

I lived in downtown Chicago and crossed busy streets every day, but somehow this was new and different and exciting. "I want to do it."

"Cross?" he asked, amused. "We will."

We watched the crowds for at least twenty minutes as they moved through the intersections, the overhead neon lights of billboards flashing different images and splashing rainbows of color on them. That seemed to be as long as Dominic could stand it. Clearly he had other things on his mind.

Such a male.

We queued up with the other people at the edge of the road, and when the light changed, off we went. The throng of people moved at a fast clip, and Dominic's hand curled around mine, urging me to keep up, stay with him, and stop gawking. The city . . . it felt alive.

The sex shop wasn't hard to find, given the enormous cartoon penis in the window with an English speech bubble that said "Best Fucking Shop in All of Japan!" We wound down a spiral staircase into a basement. Once inside, it wasn't any different than the sex shops in Amsterdam. Dildos and vibrators and costumes, and all the other stuff you expect to find.

His warm hand squeezed mine.

"Can I be honest?" he asked. When I nodded, he continued, "Pretty much whatever you want in here, I'll buy it. Seriously. I'll buy you two of everything." His eyes darted to the costume of a sexy school girl.

"Okay, I want that." I pointed to the three foot long dildo behind a glass case. The one that had something that looked suspiciously like teeth at the end. I did my best to look serious, but he laughed.

"Okay, freak, but it'll make me feel inadequate, and if you want me to bite you, all you have to do is ask."

A vision of Dominic's head between my legs, teasing me with his teeth, flashed through my mind and filled me with desire.

We giggled like teenagers at some of the more ridiculous stuff like the plastic vaginas or blatant copyright infringement.

"Christmas is coming up," Dominic said, holding up a vibrator that looked like Mickey Mouse. "You could get this for Evie and let it take her to the happiest place on earth."

"Evelyn," I corrected, even though I knew it was a lost cause. He just smirked.

I grabbed a bottle of lube and a toy and made my way to the counter, but he ensnared my waist with his hands, pulling me so my back was against his firm chest and his lips by my ear. "What else? That's not all you want, is it?"

"You know, you have me at a disadvantage. You've seen my willing list, but I haven't seen yours."

The rough voice was soft, yet rumbled like thunder. "I'm up for whatever. Whatever makes you come apart. Whatever makes you scream with pleasure. It doesn't *always* have to be my mouth or my cock that gets you there."

A delicious shudder swept through my body, which he had to feel since he had me flattened against him. My brain went blank with lust. Shaky but determined hands snatched more things up, most of it not registering. Vibrator. Blindfold. Handcuffs, I think.

The trip back to his apartment was a hazy fog of lust and anticipation. The train was less crowded now and we sat on the red seats, my hand between his legs, although he kept pushing it down.

"C'mon," I whispered into the side of his neck. The sex shop had turned me on like a mad woman. "Don't you want to reenact that scene from *Risky Business*? This train's way cleaner than the L."

"Yeah, no shit, risky business. I'll have my train privileges revoked and fuck up my job if we get caught." He gave me a look of pure desire. "We'll be home in ten minutes, you exhibitionist."

"And then you're going to fuck this ass?"

He exhaled sharply. "C'mon, don't make me walk back to my place with a raging hard-on."

Dominic fumbled with his apartment lock, and then the door burst open. He hurled off his shoes, keeping one hand on the generic brown sack from our shopping excursion.

"Take off your shoes," he ordered.

I stepped out of them and was whisked into his room. He'd made the bed this morning, but his suit was thrown on it. He ignored it. The bag thudded to the mattress as he used both hands to pull at my clothes, stretching my sweater over my head, and worked to undo my jeans. I undid the top few buttons of his shirt and reached behind his back to tug it off.

"Okay," he said, pushing the jeans down over my hips and I stepped out of them one bunched leg at a time. "Do I need to do anything differently when—?"

I put a finger on his lips, silencing him. "This is going to seem ironic coming from me, but slow down. You're definitely going to enjoy it, but I need to be in charge to make sure I do, too. Okay?"

He gently pulled my finger away from his lips and nodded. "It's the Payton effect. I lose my shit around you." He leaned in painstakingly slow, and kissed me. Was he aware I lost my shit whenever he did that? My fingertips curled in the hair at the base of his skull, fisting a handful. I gasped against this kiss. Every layer of it and I fell deeper and deeper under the spell of him.

I tugged his belt open and shoved his pants down, anxious to have him in my hands. A low, guttural moan dragged from his lips.

"First," I said, stroking the smooth, hard length of him, "you're going to go down on me. And when I get close, you're going to take out that starter toy and fuck me with it until it's wet, and then push it in my ass. Slowly. All the way to the ring at the base."

"Oh, Jesus, I think I just came a little."

He was impossibly hard in my hands. I marveled at the velvet-like feel of his flesh against my fingertips.

"Second, you're going to fuck me with this cock until I'm begging you to take it out and fuck me in the ass." His hot, wet lips latched onto my earlobe, biting softly and creating an electric shock that surged straight through me. "Then, you can decide when to give me what I want."

His breath washed over my shoulder as he sighed and

lifted his head to stare down at me. The color of his irises was a deep blue tonight, almost a shade of cobalt. Hands closed on my shoulders and pushed me backward onto the bed.

"So I'm supposed to start here?"

Dominic didn't waste any time. He ran a hand through my legs and over my panties, moments before fingers curled around the waistband and yanked them down. My legs were pushed apart as his knees thudded to the carpet and his mouth descended on me.

"Fuck," I cried.

It wasn't going to take me long at this rate. I threaded both hands through his hair, gripping him to me. Shudders built inside my core, vibrating out with every caress of his tongue.

"Dominic."

My brain threatened to go offline, but I heard rustling of the bag, followed by plastic, and thankfully before I had to say anything, he disappeared into the bathroom. The faucet ran for a minute, and he returned, a towel drying the French pink jelly toy that was long and egg shaped, tapered at one end and had a large base at the other.

He cast the towel aside. Eyes swept over my naked flesh and I did the same to him. That tan, ridged skin with a dusting of chest hair, and below . . . the helmet of his thick cock standing out, reaching for me. *Soon.* He knelt back down beside the bed and followed the plan I'd laid out for him.

I sighed when his lips sucked on my clit, and gasped when the toy intruded into my pussy. I was dripping wet and it went in easily.

"Oh god," I moaned. "I want that to be your cock."

"Do you want to come like this?"

My eyes fell closed and I bit down on my bottom lip. *Yes,* the sinful voice whispered back, but I knew it would be so much better if I waited. I shook my head. It took an enormous amount of self-restraint to back up on the bed, away from his tongue. I already felt like I was going to rattle apart and we'd barely started.

I turned over and pushed up on my hands and knees, silently telling him what he should do now. Breath came and went rapidly for both of us.

"You ready?" His voice was soft and unsure.

"Oh my god, yes."

Fingertips grazed my left ass cheek, gently pulling it to the side, and then it was there, right at that forbidden entrance. It started to advance.

"Yes," I encouraged and it went deeper, stretching me.

"You like that?" He didn't ask it like he was curious, because lord knows I was giving him plenty of evidence that I did. He wanted to hear how much I liked it.

"Mmm, hmm. It feels so dirty, but good. More."

He complied and it encroached further. The stretching was uncomfortable but I knew it would pass and pleasure lurked on the other side. I placed a hand between my legs and touched myself, distracting from the initial discomfort, and heat spiraled through me.

"Oh, fuck," he whispered when the base was up against me. "I'm hard as a rock right now. That's so hot, getting you ready for my cock like this. Your ass in the air, waiting for me to fuck you."

I moaned and leaned forward, pressing my cheek flat against his bed and closed my eyes. Pleasure rippled through me. "Touch me."

"You want me to play with this pussy?"

"Yes." It fell from my lips broken and whisper-quiet when he did. Thick fingers explored and plunged inside, then drew back and teased. I rocked my hips against his hand, teetering dangerously close to orgasm.

"Take over for a second," he commanded. "I'll be right back."

So he could go to the nightstand and get a coin-shaped packet. My fingers hunted over my slit, searching for bliss. Tension welled inside. Begged for release. *Shit.* I needed him now. Ached for him. I whimpered when he was sheathed and knelt behind me on the bed. The rough skin of his palms was set on my hips, steadying himself.

"I've been thinking about this moment all day," he rumbled, although it was quiet, "when I first push inside you." The tip of his cock was against my entrance, gently pressing in. "All I could think about was this. How good you feel." He slipped inside, just the head. Oh, god. Behind closed eyelids, my eyes rolled backward. I couldn't breathe. "How good you make me feel."

Further and further he descended into me, one inch at a time. My hands balled the sheet beneath them into fists. It was like he was closing the circuit between us, and electricity poured now through my body when the connection was complete.

"Did you think about me today?" It was meant to sound casual, but he'd failed. There was too much curiosity and hope in his words to hide.

"Yes." I'd thought about him way more than I wanted to admit.

"You did, huh?" The voice behind me was pleased, and

it earned me that first thrust, injecting me with a wave of pleasure, making me moan. "What did you think about?"

How could I answer? I was much too focused on what he was doing and the toy in my ass, which was starting to feel really fucking good.

"C'mon," he goaded. "Don't I have you distracted enough to talk?"

"I thought about how I'm going to suck you off in the shower tomorrow morning before you leave for work." Maybe telling him ruined the spontaneity of it, but he'd asked. "You know, only if it won't make you late."

"It won't make me late. I last all of a minute when I'm inside that filthy mouth of yours." It rang out like he was annoyed with himself.

His cock pulled back and surged forward.

This was my favorite position. Him behind me and in control, easily able to dominate with a hand in my hair or the sharp crack of his hand on my ass. And that angle . . . it made him feel even larger and long, and it rubbed right at that perfect spot to make me come both inside and out.

Dominic established his pace, and fingertips trailed up along my spine, sliding over my skin and giving me shivers. Those fingers paused at the bra clasp and undid it, then continued their journey up to the nape of my neck, where they settled, cupping at the place my neck joined my shoulders.

I exhaled loudly. There was no pressure or tension in his grasp, it just rested there like that was its home, but the gesture was incredibly dominating. I pushed back with my hips, trying to match his rhythm.

"I like it rough," I blurted out. My approaching orgasm was all I could think about.

"How rough?" He drove into me. Every crash of his body against mine pulled double-duty, pleasing me with his cock and that toy in my ass. "*Safe word* rough?"

"Yes."

The hand tightened a degree. The tiniest shade of pressure as if only trying to make me aware of its presence. "That's a conversation I'd like to have, but not right now." The hand twined in my hair, taking a fistful and pulling my head back. Not hard or painful in the slightest, but still aggressive and controlling. "Right now, I want you thinking about my cock filling your pussy. Thinking about how it's going to feel in your ass."

And . . . that's all it took. The hand released my hair. I tore apart with my orgasm, smashing my face into the mattress so I could scream. Ecstasy rippled and flooded upward, burning across nerve endings and leaving cold bliss in its aftermath.

"Shit, you're so fucking sexy when you come." He continued his relentless rhythm, pounding away at me, one hand tight on my waist.

"Fuck me in the ass. Make me come again."

He made a noise that came from the back of his throat. Disapproval. "That sounded like an order. I thought you were supposed to beg."

"Please."

"Better," he growled. "But not good enough."

Had I created a monster? "Please, Dominic. You said you were going to own my ass. Don't you want to? Don't you want to fuck this dirty little slut where she needs you to?"

He made a sharp sound of satisfaction, and my words sent him into a flurry of action. He pulled out. The toy in my ass retreated and dropped to the towel on the bed. The paper bag rustled again and there was a snap as the bottle of lube popped open.

Silky fingertips spread it everywhere, massaging me for a moment. I moaned at the touch, and murmured words of encouragement as he did the same to himself. I pushed back up on my arms, glanced over my shoulder, and locked my eyes with his gorgeous ones.

"Go slow at first," I whispered.

His face was ultra-serious. "I will."

I turned back to bury my face against the sheets, my hands splayed out in front. The bed shifted as he positioned himself. His cock nudged at the taboo spot. Deep breath.

I exhaled through clenched teeth as the head of his cock pushed its way in. Not the best feeling in the world. I gripped the sheets tightly.

"Okay?" he asked. The hands on my waist tensed.

"Keep going."

He did. The stretch got worse and I bit down on my bottom lip, but it lessened when he began to move back and forth.

"Holy fuck," he groaned, his voice heavy with pleasure.

It was getting difficult to breathe again. "You . . . like it?"

"It feels different," he said on a low voice. "It feels good. Really, fucking, good."

He went further with every slow pass, and I crossed the threshold from discomfort back to comfort. "Faster," I urged.

His quiet moan was erotic. Hearing his pleasure helped me find my own so much faster. Dominic's rapid, loud breathing was punctuated by the gentle slap of our skin as he began to fuck me.

"Yes," I whimpered. Oh, it was starting to feel good now. I shoved a hand between my legs, teasing my clit as his dick sawed in and out of me.

"Oh, Jesus, Payton."

Once again, a hand slid up the length of my spine, only this time I arched my back into it, rising up on my free hand. He lowered down onto a hand, so his damp chest was pressed to my back, and his other hand curved around my body, cupping my breast. His lips trembled by my ear, occasionally planting kisses when he wasn't struggling to find air.

"Do you like being in my ass?"

"Fuck, yes." He rolled my nipple between two fingers and pinched it. "Does it feel good for you?"

"I fucking *love* it."

He was thrusting hard at an urgent pace. His desperate breaths said he wasn't going to last long. Thank god because I was right there with him. My fingers on my clit were frantic. I was on fire. Crazy with lust. Out of my mind with need.

The room closed in and the air thickened with desire and sex. Something intense grew closer with each gasp we sought. I was trembling. Going to come any minute now and I wanted him with me. I slipped two fingers inside my pussy, grinding on the heel of my palm as my fingers massaged him through the wall of my channel.

"Shit, what are you . . . fuck. *Fuck!*" His heated hand on my breast squeezed, gripping me as his body hardened and shuddered. I could feel the moan of his release resonate through his chest in the seconds before my climax started.

"Oh my god, Dominic," I cried. I don't know how long my orgasm lasted. Just that it was sharp. Intense.

Out of this world.

I collapsed forward off of him onto my belly, and he dropped down just to the side, his arm and leg over me. My spent muscles were shaking and twitching, which he could probably feel.

I slowed my breathing with my face turned away from him. His arm began to move. Lazy, gentle strokes over my back. Caressing me.

"Look at me," he asked softly. His face was creased with worry. "Are you all right?"

I gave him a huge smile. "All right? I'm way better than all right. What about you?"

"Yeah. Way better than all right, too." The kiss he gave me was tender and dangerous. "That was . . . You're amazing."

I held my breath. Not sure what I should say. He didn't seem to mind my silence. He kissed me again, then slipped away to the bathroom. While he was gone, I tried to keep my mind empty. I didn't like that he was gone, especially when he was only ten feet away and just behind a goddamn door. I didn't want to think about it, or the realization I was one day closer to leaving. I'd just gotten here.

When he came back, I went into the bathroom and cleaned up, and when I came out, it was dark in the bedroom.

"Dominic?" My shin located the side of the bed and I groaned.

"Sorry." A strong arm closed around me, and the other one swept under my knees, lifting me up into his arms.

"What are you doing?" I gasped.

"Getting a head start on our discussion of sleeping arrangements."

"No—"

The sneaky bastard only had to carry me a single step,

then knelt on the bed, laying me down with his arm locked around me. "Come on. Don't make us sleep in that other bed."

"I'm *not*. You're supposed to stay here."

"Forget it. If you get up, I'm gonna follow you."

I struggled against the arm. Sort of. Not my best effort. Part of me didn't care anymore. Time with Dominic was limited, and he obviously wanted this badly . . . I could allow this.

I blew out an exasperated sigh. "Let me up so I can put on my sleeping stuff."

"Yeah, I was surprised to discover clothes on you last night after you told me you sleep in the nude."

"I lied."

My eyes had adjusted to the darkness so I could see the white of his teeth as he grinned. "So, I'm supposed to believe if I let you go, you're going to put on some clothes and come back to me?"

My heart raced at the implication and my voice tightened its pitch. "Only one way to find out."

His hold eased to release me. There was a click and his lamp sprung to life, bathing us in warm light.

The walk across his apartment was ten miles there and twenty miles back. Uphill. I didn't like this awkward feeling. Didn't like being so unsure of what I was doing. I'd tugged on my tank top and shorts while my stomach did somersaults. I stepped into the doorway.

Dominic sat up in the bed, the covers around his waist. I noted the rapid rise and fall of his bare chest, and let my gaze drift up. His eyes were captivating, and stunned me motionless. His serious expression spoke volumes. Like he sensed how crossing this physical threshold was really crossing a greater one for me. Letting him not just get his way, but letting him get . . . close.

I found my breath when the corner of his perfect mouth turned up into a smile. "I almost sent out a search party."

"It's easy to get lost because your place is so huge."

I planted one foot in the room. Then, the other as I approached the bed. Could he see how anxious I was about this? It meant no backtracking. I'd be sharing a bed with him the rest of my time here.

His embrace was comforting and soothing to my jagged nerves. Live in the now, I repeated to myself. Worry about the consequences later.

chapter
FIFTEEN

I knelt before him in the tub while he stood under the stream of water with his cock buried halfway down my throat. I liked the echo of his moans across the tiled walls, and liked him snapping to attention under my command even better.

His hand brushed over my cheek, pushing back a damp clump of my hair. "Jesus, were you hungry for this cock?"

It was true. His alarm had gone off this morning and we'd stumbled sleepy-eyed to the shower, and I'd dropped my knees to the porcelain in one half of a heartbeat.

I moaned when his hand curled around the back of my head and guided me to go faster. To slide that thick, hard cock between my tight lips. It was difficult to keep my eyes open with the water misting in my face, but no fucking way was I not going to look at his body. Water poured over his hardened frame, cascaded down over the contours of the muscles beneath his smooth skin.

This moan was deep and long, and the hand clenched in my wet hair. "You like that cock in your mouth, you dirty girl? Because I fucking do."

My eyes turned up to his, blinking rapidly in the falling water. Oh, he liked that connection of our gazes while my mouth sucked on him, and his face twisted with pleasure. His expression was primal.

Aggressive hands locked on the sides of my face. His hips moved rapidly, pumping in and out . . . fucking my mouth. A growl ripped from his chest as he approached his orgasm, and I flicked my tongue over him with each stroke.

"Oh, god," he said, "here it comes."

I moaned my approval, accepting it as he shot into the back of my throat. Pulse after pulse, mirrored with moans from above. There just wasn't anything hotter than listening to him come. Between my legs I was slick and hot with desire.

His rapid breathing began to ebb. I put a hand on the wet tile of the wall to pull myself up, but abruptly he had me up and my back flat against it. The wall was cold, but the contrast between it and the hot man over me was nice.

"Safe word," he said in a low voice, just louder than the shower. "I have questions about that." His hand followed the rivulets of water coursing down between my breasts, over my belly, but he stopped at the apex of my thighs. One calculated stroke between my folds and I was trembling. How the hell did he do that?

"Mostly," he continued, his gaze on the hand stroking me, "what do you want me to do to you that you're worried might go too far?"

I bit down on my lip, closed my eyes, and my head thudded back against the tile. What he was doing to me downstairs was unreal. His touch was like nothing else.

"The safe word," I said on hurried breath, "I doubt I'll need to use it, but . . . oh, shit, I want your fingers inside me."

"Not yet. I guess what I'm trying to say is I don't know if I can do rough. Like the schmay-nal, it's not something I've done before." The pads of his fingers kneaded my clit, alternating pressure and speeds. "What did you have in mind?"

"It's kind of hard to think when you're doing that."

"What, this?" He slipped a finger inside me and I groaned in satisfaction. "What do you like? Besides being tied up, you've made that clear. You want me to pull harder on your hair?"

"Yes," I purred.

"You want me to spank you?"

It came out dripping with lust from me. "Yes."

"You want . . . all of it? Like, whips and paddles and . . .?" His voice was decidedly less confident. "Because I don't, like, have any experience."

The truth was I hadn't gotten into any of the heavier BDSM with props. That was all about trust and building a relationship with your partner, which was something I refused to do. But I was curious about it. And for the first time, there was an option in front of me. If he was willing, why couldn't Dominic and I learn something new together? Teach each other a lesson?

"I'm interested in it," I admitted, "but that's a new area for me, too."

His hand withdrew from me and caressed down my thigh to behind my knee. It was so he could raise my leg and set my foot on the shower ledge, opening me wide to him. The porcelain squeaked when he lumbered down onto his knees in front of me.

"Any thoughts on the word?" He braced a hand on the inside of my thigh and pressed me open, using the thumb of his other hand to pull back the hood on my clit. There was only a hint of that tongue, but on my exposed, sensitized skin it was a shock and I jerked.

"Jaguar."

He chuckled and the rumble wafted up through the steam. It faded away, and the tongue danced over me once again.

I gasped and my knees went weak. "Your safe word?"

"Do I need a safe word? I'm a lot bigger than you."

Sure, it'd be easy for him to stop me with those thick, powerful arms, but . . . "It's not about that. It's a kill order. Everything's supposed to stop. And, what if I want to tie you up?"

"Good luck there. I like being able to use my hands." To prove his point, he buried two fingers deep inside my pussy, all the way to the knuckles. "But, it's fine. I'll use the same word."

Of course he would. I might have been annoyed, except that hand . . . And that mouth . . . *Fuck.*

The visual of him kneeling before me, the water beating down on his back, running off of him through the deep valley of his spine only intensified the desire and ache in me. I was ready to succumb to the flutter of his warm tongue over my swollen flesh in a crescendo that was going to be very, very loud.

"Do you want to come for me?" he asked.

"Yes."

"Do you *need* to come? Are you so fucking desperate for it?"

My breath hung in my throat as I recognized the pattern from before. "Yes."

His mouth resumed fucking me for another amazing thirty seconds, and he pulled back completely as I clung at the edge of climax. Anticipation crawled over my skin. Everything was hyperaware of what he was about to say next. His hooded eyes pinned mine. The expression darkening his face was beyond authority.

"Then come for me. Right now."

Thankfully I slapped a hand over my mouth as I tipped over the edge and the tremble seized every muscle, locking me up. I screamed against my palm, my back arching from the wet tile. Hot ecstasy sped through my veins like liquid fire. It felt so, *so* good.

As I floated back down into reality, Dominic had an enormous grin on his face. Thrilled with himself. And why not? He'd gotten me to come on command with much less workup this time around. I wouldn't have believed it was possible, and now he'd done it twice.

"You," he said, rising to his feet and towering over me, "have no idea how insane it makes me listening to that. I'm going to be hearing that scream in my head the rest of the day."

I set a hand in the center of his chest, although I didn't know why. I liked touching him. Then his lips collided with mine. Touching was nice and all, but I liked kissing him better.

It became a morning ritual. The alarm clock would sound, and strong but gentle arms pulled me to the shower. I was more than willing.

I was fucking addicted.

By the time the weekend hit, I was in big trouble. I'd been so worried about him getting attached that I was too blind to see what was really going on. *I'd* been the one to do it. Me.

We'd fallen into a comfortable schedule. He'd go to work and I'd go out and explore the city, armed with my English train map. First, I did temples, gazing at the tiered towers and taking tours to learn about the fascinating history. Then, it was lush gardens full of delicate trees and meticulously groomed landscaping. Dominic brought dinner home late after work some nights, and other times we'd go out.

There was a gym in the basement of the apartment building, and on Friday evening we worked out together. Well, it consisted of me running on a treadmill and him lifting weights, but I sure enjoyed the show. I didn't need the treadmill to get my heartrate up. And once we were done downstairs, he gave me a thorough workout upstairs, too.

Couch sex, check.

Saturday morning I rolled out of bed and padded out into the living room, wearing my tank top and boxer shorts, my hair disheveled from the sexcapades the night before, but it wasn't a big deal. I was hoping to Skype with Evie, and she'd certainly seen me in a greater state of undress.

I glared at Dominic's laptop on the bookshelf.

He'd tripped over my power cord two days ago and bent the jack so my laptop wouldn't charge. The replacement cord he'd bought was supposed to arrive on Tuesday, and he insisted I use his laptop in the meantime.

"Don't judge me for the enormous amount of porn on there," he'd said, his face coloring red. "That how I survived here."

I wanted to remind him who he was talking to, but didn't. God, he was so adorable when he was embarrassed.

I opened the silver MacBook and launched Skype, not paying any attention to it as I checked my email. So when it rang with an incoming call, I didn't realize I'd clicked 'Accept' until I'd already done it.

The box expanded to fill the screen and a brunette,

seated on a couch with a glass of wine in one hand, came into view. She was pretty but kind of wholesome looking, like she had that cute librarian thing going on. Probably ten years older than me.

I felt my eyes grow large as she peered at the screen, stunned to see me seated on the other side of the camera and not her younger brother Dominic.

"Hello," she said, sounding curious. "Who are you?"

Shit! It was too late to slam the computer shut, she'd already seen me.

"Uh, hi. I'm . . . a friend of Dominic's. Sorry, I didn't mean to—"

She leaned forward to her screen like she was taking a closer look at me. A faint smile curled on her lips. "You're American? And pretty. Where the heck did he find you?"

"Naked in a blindfold club" wasn't going to work, so I skewed the truth. "I'm on a long vacation in Tokyo." I had to find something to distract. "You're Meredith?"

Oh, that was the wrong thing to say. Her faint smile got wider. Yes, I knew his sisters' names. And the smile she gave me now was identical to the one I often got from the man in the room next door.

"How long have you two been together?"

Together? Like a couple? "We're not dating."

She blinked her skeptical eyes at me, probably staring at my bedhead and my braless tits beneath my tank top. "It's, what, eight-thirty in the morning there?"

She had a point, but I didn't care for her passive-aggressive statement. "And? Just because I fuck him doesn't automatically make him my boyfriend."

Shit. Why couldn't I keep my stupid mouth shut?

She gasped and frowned. "I can think of one thing it makes *you*."

My annoyance with the bitch went from zero to sixty in much less than four seconds. "Yup, you're right, that's what I am." I reached forward to slam the computer closed—

"Wait, wait! Crap, sorry." Her scowl intensified, but I could tell it was at herself. "It's none of my business. Please, I'm sorry."

I drew back my hand and shot her a dark look.

"I'm glad he's . . . made a friend," Meredith said. This was free from judgment and my heart rate ticked down a notch. "You know my name. What's yours?"

I wanted off this call as soon as possible. I didn't want her to ask whatever her next question was going to be. "Payton."

"Where are you from?"

Ugh. "Chicago."

Meredith's pretty eyes widened in surprise. "Oh, wow, small world. Dom's got a place in Chicago."

I swallowed hard. *Dom.* The flashback to our first night together was unavoidable. "Yeah, I think he mentioned that. Hey, he's still asleep, so I'm—"

"What do you do?" She took a sip of her wine and set it down on the desk. When I didn't answer immediately, she blinked and tilted her head to the side. "Oh, no. Don't tell me you're like a model or something."

"Or something." At least I didn't have to lie to her.

"Damn it. His ego is already huge, and now he's going to brag about dating a model."

The laugh I gave was involuntary. "Not a model, and again, we're not dating."

I'd swear I could feel that penetrating gaze of hers all the way from across the Pacific. She was protective of her younger brother. We sat in silence, evaluating each other, for a long moment.

"Where the fuck's my morning blowjob?" Dominic teased from the doorway, one hand buried beneath his boxers. He couldn't see the computer screen, but he heard the sharp gasp come from the speaker.

"*Oh my god*, Dominic!" Horror splashed on his sister's face.

"Meredith?" He snatched up a blanket off the couch and banded it around his waist, then thundered over to the laptop to confirm. He gave me a 'WTF?' look.

"She was trying to call you," I said. "I didn't mean to answer it."

That look faded and was replaced with amusement. The couch jostled as he dropped down beside me, throwing an arm casually over the back. Around me.

"Seriously, I'd smack Mike if he talked to me like that," Meredith said. It looked like she hadn't quite recovered from the comment.

He brushed it off. "I see you've met Payton. What's up?"

"Not much. Mom's been guilting us all in to calling you more often, and I saw you were online."

I climbed off the couch, pretending to want to give them privacy, but all I really wanted was to get the fuck away. Because I liked Dominic. I was exclusive to him. Living with him. Now I'd met some of his family. If that wasn't the definition of an acting girlfriend, I didn't know what was.

My shower was almost over when he came into the bathroom and stepped into the tub beside me.

"That was informative." There was a sharp edge to his words. I turned to face him and was greeted with a scowl. "Not dating, huh? What the fuck are we doing then?"

I wished I hadn't answered that call for the millionth time, and put my hands on my hips. "I told you, from the *very* beginning, I don't do relationships."

"Just like you don't do conversation." The aqua eyes flared with accusation. "Like you don't do kissing." His voice rose steadily as he closed the distance between us. "Like you don't sleep beside me."

"That's all you. You ignored my rules!"

"Yeah, I did. And get ready, because I'm gonna ignore this one, too." His jaw tightened and his eyes were pure and determined. "Go and put up your walls, Payton. They don't stop me."

They didn't even slow him down.

His kiss was wild and ferocious. An assault that I couldn't defend against, even as the panicked voice in my head urged me to. His touch lit me on fire. Made me come alive.

"This is more than just fucking," he said, his kiss traveling lower. "I know you feel it. C'mon, tell me I'm wrong." His challenge was issued at the base of my throat, his hands cradling my head.

I was unraveling like a pulled string on a sweater. If Dominic kept tugging, I was going to come apart completely. His kiss carved a path toward my lips but he pulled back at the last second. His expression was intense and inescapable. "Is this just fucking?"

There was no point in lying. My voice was breathy. "No. It's more."

He squeezed me to him so tightly I could barely breathe,

and dragged me back under the stream of water while his kiss obliterated all thought except for one. I'd told him that night at the club I didn't do relationships, but I'd also told him I didn't do love.

Was he going to disregard that rule, too?

chapter
SIXTEEN

My flight home was Friday afternoon, which meant I had three days left with him. Neither one of us mentioned it. We didn't talk about if this *relationship* was going to continue with ten thousand miles between us, or how it was going to work if it did. Maybe he was like me, pushing away the things he didn't want to deal with until he was out of time.

The weekend had gone faster than the elevator that took us to the top of the Skytree tower on Saturday, which gave us unbelievable views of the city. It had gone faster than the bullet train that took us the two hours to the base of Mount Fuji on Sunday. We'd done a tour and a gondola ride to the summit of the gorgeous, snowcapped volcano that was the icon of Japan.

Last night, it had been Kabukicho – Tokyo's famous red light district. Nothing in common with Amsterdam's red light district except for the lewd signage in a mixture of languages.

Neon. Neon *everything*. So many signs you didn't know where to look, and you felt like you were on some futuristic porn movie set. This was where the love hotels were and the hostess bars Dominic had talked about. We gawked and grinned together at the perversion, and shrugged away from the barkers who tried to get us to come inside their bars. Shit, it was fun.

But tonight, we both wanted a break from all the Japanese.

"An American dinner," I'd told him as he got ready for work. "That's what you're getting tonight, because I don't know how to make anything else."

There was a smug look on his face. "Cooking dinner for me? Such a good little housewife."

"I'm going to rip your balls off if you ever say that again."

His smile continued when he leaned down and kissed me goodbye.

My first thought was spaghetti. No. No noodles. Something fried and greasy. After I ran three miles on the treadmill in the basement, I went to the market and got everything I'd need to make fried chicken.

At six o'clock I'd successfully decimated his clean, tiny kitchen. But the test batch I cooked was awesome, and, holy shit, I was excited to get to do this. A normal, low-key dinner with Dominic, whom I sort of belonged to now.

My phone rang. Dominic. Why didn't he just text me? Calls were outrageously expensive.

"Payton." His voice was weird. "I'm on the train heading home, but I've got to turn around. The ship's coming back to port with some instrument malfunction."

My gaze dropped down to the mess of dishes and the sack of flour on the counter.

"I have to stay with the inventory," he continued, "until the ship pulls back out again or I make the call to receive the inventory back into production."

I didn't want him to hear the disappointment in my voice. "How long are you going to be?"

"Hours. I'm sorry."

I sat down at the dining table, feeling like I weighed five hundred pounds. "It's not your fault."

"I know, but . . . still."

Three days left with him, and now one of them had been taken away.

"I understand," I said, my voice tight. "I'll see you when you get home."

There was a soft sigh. "Please don't wait up for me. I'll feel even worse if you do."

I held my tongue from asking if I had anything better to do. "Okay. Hope they get it figured out soon."

"Me, too." He paused. "I'll see you in the morning."

After the call was over, I fried up the chicken, ate a little, and put it in the comically small refrigerator. I drank one of the beers I'd bought, surfed mindlessly on the Internet for a while, and avoided thinking about him or what next week was going to be like. Probably a lot like this. No, it'd be fucking worse. I hadn't even thought about the time difference.

One week ago I'd thrown a fit about sleeping arrangements. Now I was alone in his bed, pissed off, wishing he was here. Not just for the sex either, although I had no complaints there. Every day since our safe word discussion he'd edged a little closer to the line I'd asked him to cross.

Sometime later, the bed jostled and woke me.

"You're awake?" he whispered.

"Yeah." I rolled over and tossed my arm around him without thought, but the action wasn't lost on either of us. I didn't snuggle, I merely allowed him to. Something as simple as this was huge for me. I kept my voice even, but my arm where it was. "What time is it?"

"A little after two." Dominic drew me in closer so I was tucked beside him. I had a hand on his chest, and beneath my fingertips, his heart raced.

"Are you okay?" I asked.

"I'm fine."

I didn't need to see his face, which I couldn't in the darkened bedroom anyway, to know he was lying. "What is it?"

"Come to work with me tomorrow. You can ride the train during rush hour and get the full experience."

"Is it bring your girlfriend to work day?" I asked, skeptical.

His heart beat faster. "My what?"

Jesus, what was with me tonight? Who was I turning into? "Shut up, you obviously heard me. All I meant was, is that all right?"

His hand skimmed over my forearm, past my elbow, traveling up to my shoulder. "It's okay. I'll give you a quick tour and we'll stay out of the way. I probably don't need to be in the office until later anyway."

The warm hand settled on my jaw, his thumb brushing over my cheek. I was curious to see where he worked. "Okay, sure."

For the first night since we'd arrived here, there was no sex. Instead he gave me a kiss that was slow and hypnotic. He kissed me like a man with all the time in the world, though we had only two days left. I didn't just allow this kiss, I liked it. I craved more. I craved being in his strong embrace. His effect over me . . . I was fucking defenseless.

"No," Dominic said in the shower. "We don't have time for that."

Of course I took it as a challenge.

Harsh hands yanked me upright as I tried to kneel. "I'm

serious. My cock's off limits right now."

"I don't know," I gazed down, "sure doesn't look like he's closed for business."

The vibrant blue eyes glinted with lust. "You've trained him. Just getting near this shower gets him hard as a rock."

"You don't want me to help with that?" I purred through the steamy air. "Don't you want my lips wrapped around you, sucking you until you're dry?"

His gaze turned cloudy as he rinsed the last of his shampoo from his hair and I followed the bubbles cascading down his slippery skin.

"Are you already done with your shower?" he asked.

I nodded. We had plenty of time–

He yanked back the shower curtain and forced me from the tub.

"What are you doing?" I yelled. I stood on the rug, drenched and dripping, glaring at him as he yanked the curtain closed, separating us.

"I don't trust myself with you, devil woman. Go put some clothes on. I'll be done in a minute."

My blood boiled while I shivered in the cold.

"Wear a skirt," came from behind the curtain.

I made a loud noise of frustration and stormed away.

"Are you really that mad because I didn't let you go down on me?" he asked when we were pulling on shoes at the front door. I'd sipped my coffee in total silence. Hadn't said a word to him since the shower.

Yeah, I was mad. I only had a few mornings left with him. Why had he denied it? "Maybe I'm worried something's wrong with you. What guy turns that down?"

He gave me a weird smile. "Maybe the one trying to

keep you from falling into a routine. You know, so you don't get *bored*."

That just made me more annoyed. I marched beside him toward the station, pulling my jacket tight around me. It was cold and overcast this morning, matching my mood.

"Are you claustrophobic?" Dominic stood beside me as we queued up to board the train. All around us, business people waited, polite and orderly. It was mostly men with briefcases and newspapers tucked under an arm.

"No," I answered. "Why?"

"They're going to pack us into the train car. Like, literally. Stay close to me or we'll end up on opposite sides."

The train's light leaped into view and focused as it barreled at us. It slowed to a stop, the doors peeled open, and there was a surge from behind, propelling us forward. I gasped as we compressed with the line of people in front of us, mobbing onto the car where it was already standing room only.

I pivoted in my spot, only to shuffle backward as the wall of people continued to push and thicken. I was pressed up against Dominic, but also the Japanese salarymen around me. Jesus, when were the people going to stop trying to get on? I was crushed against the people around me. At the doors, a pair of conductors pushed at the body parts sticking through the doorway until the doors could finally close.

I could feel the man behind me breathing, I was that tight against him. I looked at the other human sardines around me. No one cared. They stood in total silence. No one on cell phones. No one moved, not that they could, I assumed out of respect. Dominic was right. This was wild. We stood chest to chest and I lifted my gaze to connect with his.

I smiled, wanting him to know I was enjoying this.

He was tired. He'd only gotten three hours of sleep last night. But when he returned the smile, the exhaustion faded from his eyes.

It was a fifteen minute train ride and it delivered us close to the harbor. The salty smell and seabirds announced which way to go, but I put my hand in his anyway. Fuck my rules about getting intimate. It was futile. I was attached, and going to stay attached as long as possible.

There was a small building no larger than a trailer sandwiched between a seemingly endless maze of different colored containers, some towers stacked six high. I ascended the metal stairs behind Dominic while he unlocked the door and pulled the clipboard from the box attached to it.

His office was organized, but also like stepping back into the 1990s. A massive desktop computer. Fax machine. Filing cabinets. Stacks and stacks of paper. The window on one side of the narrow office faced the cranes that loomed over the water's edge.

I stared at the sad looking office, and I got angry.

"You spend all day here?"

"When I'm not counting inventory." He scanned the clipboard and set it on the desk.

"This place sucks."

He laughed. "Yeah, it's not great. Come on, I'll show you around."

We walked through the rows of containers as he described his system for receiving the inventory through customs . . . basically it was a lot of paperwork. It wasn't the most boring job in the world, but close.

I followed him as we wound deeper and deeper into the

container maze. "Where are we going?"

He pulled me to a stop, his eyes shifting left, then right. Hands closed on my hips and urged me around the corner until metal was hard against my back. We were in the shadow of a tall tower, stacked very close to another. Secluded and hidden, but not out of the realm of possibility that someone could wander by. As we'd worked our way to this spot, we'd passed a dock worker, and I could hear forklifts running in the distance.

My pulse quickened when he tugged loose the belt on my wool jacket as if desperate to get inside. His hot mouth claimed mine as he continued to undo the buttons and flung the jacket open. His fingers were under my shirt instantly, gliding over my belly and sliding upward.

"Your hands are freezing!"

He chuckled. "It's warm in here."

The cup of my bra was tugged out of his way, and his icy hand closed over my breast, pressing me back into the metal wall.

"Is someone going to catch us?"

"You'd like that, wouldn't you?" His mouth roved over mine. "If someone came around the corner and saw me fucking you?"

My body burst into flames with desire. "You're going to fuck me here?"

The heat of his body left as he pulled back and the expression on his face was immoral. "Only if you're good. And *quiet.*" His hands balled fistfuls of the maxi skirt I was wearing. "Can you be quiet, Payton?"

I nodded.

"I don't know if I believe you. Let's find out."

He tugged off his outer coat and dropped it to the ground, leaving him in his suit and tie that was like the male equivalent of lingerie. Then, hands pushed up my skirt as he sank to his knees, kneeling on his coat. Cold air hit my knees and thighs where my boots stopped, and I held the skirt for him. He liked having use of his hands, after all.

His fingers hooked under one side of my thong. Dominic used both hands on it, gripping and pulling hard until the elastic stretched beyond capacity and the destroyed underwear fell to my ankles. I stepped out of it eagerly, lust making my knees weak.

I moaned softly as his fingers parted me. I bit my bottom lip when he leaned forward and licked me.

"God, you taste good," he whispered.

I shivered from his words, not the cold. My hands clenched the skirt tighter, straining against the fabric. Staying quiet was going to be the most difficult thing I'd ever done in my life.

"Is this why you wouldn't let me go down on you this morning?"

"Ssh."

I swallowed a breath. His tongue stroked and massaged my clit. Heat swelled and expanded in my chest, strangling my breath. *Quiet,* I whispered to myself. *Prove you can do this or he might not give you what you really want, that connection.*

He slipped a finger inside me and it felt so fucking good but I made barely a sound.

"Do you want to come?"

He'd programmed me with his words, night after night of it. The starting sequence triggered waves of pleasure deep inside, and anticipation left me breathless. "Yes."

"Do you *need* to come? Would you do anything for it?"

I was already too frantic to notice the subtle difference. "Yes." The next thing he said would be the order I was desperate to obey.

His gaze turned up to me, his eyes shockingly blue. "Then, stay with me."

chapter
SEVENTEEN

My stomach twisted into knots, and this unexpected command threw my brain into chaos. "What?"

Dominic continued to work his finger in and out of me, keeping me right on the edge of the orgasm. There was a crease in his forehead and his expression was uncertain.

"I need another week." He took a deep breath and his voice plummeted to a hush. "I'm not ready to let you go."

All this had been calculated. Last night his heart had hammered out of his chest because he was setting this plan into motion. The plan to manipulate me into staying. I should have been upset, but this was a stay of execution.

"Please." He kissed me softly where the ache for him was unbearable.

I sighed when a second finger speared into me. It filled me with more need until there was room for nothing else. My hand tangled in his hair. Not stopping, just desperate to touch him.

"You don't need to hurry back, right?" he said. "Another week." His soft tongue teased and begged, and was more convincing when it wasn't using words. "Stay."

This was crossing into dangerous ground, but there was no other answer. "Yes."

He exhaled loudly as his shoulders relaxed. "Holy fuck, come for me. Right now."

My eyes slammed shut. The vise of the orgasm gripped me. His hands braced my hips against the wall while my body rocked and writhed with pulsing pleasure. My strangled cry was crushed under his lips, wet with my own taste. Another week with him. *Yes.*

I was tingling and still in the floating, weightless place he took me to, when one hand abandoned my hip. It tugged his belt open. A zipper rang out. His pants slid down to his ankles when the condom wrapper was in his hands.

"Dominic," I moaned. My hands dove under his boxers and lowered the waistband down over his cock, helping him get ready to take me. You'd think we'd gone a year without sex and not a single day from the desperation in me. I hooked one of my legs around him. "Fuck me. Fuck me now."

He held his dick in his hand, positioning it against me, and when the angle was right, he slipped his hands under my ass and lifted so I could slide down on his thick, impossibly hard cock. I took all of him in deep, and he blew out a sharp breath right by my ear.

"You needed this, didn't you?" he asked.

The rough voice . . . it pumped desire in my veins. "Yes. Oh my god, yes."

"Is it all you can think about, like me?"

My arms crossed behind his neck and I held on as he began to fuck me against the side of the container. It escaped my lips. "Yes."

His teeth skimmed the pulse pounding in my neck. The climb toward another orgasm began, tugging me upward, and this one threatened to be epic. I panted and moaned. My hands clutched at his suit jacket while Dominic drove into me.

What would we look like if one of his coworkers stumbled upon us? Dominic's ass was only half covered by those boxers and my boots were locked at the ankles around his back. Would the man run off? Would he stay and watch? Fuck, the idea turned me on.

"Are you close?" Dominic asked.

I nodded. "I'm gonna come all over you."

Abruptly his rhythm slowed and his voice was harsh. "No, you're not."

My eyes popped open in alarm. What just happened?

"You'll come," he said, "when I tell you to, and *only* when I tell you to."

Holy. Fucking. Shit. I don't know if I'd ever heard anything hotter in my whole life. My ass was cold in the briny ocean air as he thrust deep and hard, and I held my pleasure at bay for him. The quiet, repetitive thud of my backside thumping against the hollow metal container sounded vaguely like industrial work and not Dominic pounding into me and making me quiver at the edge.

His hands dug into my ass, tightening. Oh, he was getting close.

"Do you want to come?"

I sobbed my reply with a noise of twisted need. Then, panic. "It'll be loud."

He slammed into me, pinning me against the wall and my legs clamped around him to hold on. His rough hand slid across my mouth and covered it to silence my impending scream.

"Come for me," he ordered. "Right now."

I groaned against his palm while my whole body shuddered, my pussy clenching at his cock. The orgasm burned up from my legs until I was completely engulfed in flames.

"You," he said on a broken breath, "are mine."

Everything focused in on him and forced the orgasm to last a lifetime. I would have screamed, but he held his hand firm on me. Kept me quiet, all the way through his own orgasm. Inside me, he jerked again and again. Dominic was going to ruin me. No man would ever take me like this. Possess me as he did. And in this moment, I didn't give a fuck.

His lips slipped over mine, pressing gently in a sultry kiss. My head spun. His effect over me strengthened every time we did this.

"I thought you were going to say no," he whispered.

He helped me down off of him, but I had to take a moment to recover, leaning against the wall as my skirt fell back into place. Dominic hurried to do up his pants, dusted off his coat, and slipped an arm in the sleeve.

I felt out of control, but, happy. "Well, I haven't been to the Imperial Palace yet."

A smile broke out on his face. "Oh, of course."

There was a rumble from beyond the wall of containers and Dominic's face turned serious. He again glanced at his bare wrist, then dug his phone out of his pocket and checked the time.

"Hey . . ." His arms circled my waist.

I understood. "Let me guess, take your girlfriend to work day is over."

His eyebrow notched up, like he was amused. "Unfortunately, it is. Do you remember which stop you need to get off at when you take the train back?"

"Yeah."

His forehead was warm against mine. "Thank you."

"For the fuck?" I teased. "No, thank you." I didn't want to talk about what he was really thanking me for. It was scary how quickly I'd agreed to stay.

The corner of his mouth lifted into a knowing smile. "I'll walk you back, and then I'm going straight to my office to reschedule your ticket."

I rode the train past the stop to his place, taking it all the way to Harajuku. I needed to walk to clear my head and get a fucking grip, and what better place to do it than Tokyo's fashion district?

One more week, that's it. We were both attached, obviously, and time was only going to make it harder to leave. I'd agreed to stay because I was a junkie and Dominic was my drug.

Harajuku was wall-to-wall shops and restaurants, and I strolled the streets along with other *Gaijins* and tourists, my eyes vacantly scanning the shop windows. I wasn't paying any attention to what I was doing. I ended up standing in line outside of a storefront. Standing in line was so normal here, I didn't notice for a long moment.

In front of and behind me was a seemingly endless line of young women. All beautiful, although I'd always thought Asian women were gorgeous. Their fair skin, glossy dark hair, and delicate frames. I totally got why a lot of men were crazy for Asian women.

I watched the line feed into the building and the women who came out were sometimes carrying a pink paper bag and folder. Free samples? I thought about getting out of the line and moving ahead to see what was going on, but I'd lose my place and eventually I'd get there. I could always step out when I got to the front.

At the door, the woman did a double-take. She said something that was probably a question, but I shook my head. "I'm sorry, I don't speak Japanese."

The woman waved that off and gestured for me to go inside. Okay. If she was cool with it, I guessed I was too. I was curious what was inside that had women lined up around the block.

The room was mostly empty. There was a long table with a group of people seated behind it, and a video camera on a tripod to one side. The talking at the table stopped when I stepped inside.

One of the women at the table stood and bowed, and said something that had to be directed at me. I returned the bow, trying to imitate hers and repeated that I didn't speak Japanese.

There was discussion between them. It didn't seem like anyone spoke English. The woman standing came to me and motioned for me to turn around. Like she wanted me to leave –

No. She wanted me to turn in place. That was when I noticed the pictures on the table before them. Headshots.

I turned in place so they could evaluate me. Then, the woman walked forward, pivoted and walked back to me. She wanted me to do a runway walk? God, I felt like an idiot. What the heck was I doing here? I put one foot in front of the other and strolled across the room, and turned back to return to my spot. This was going to make for a hilarious story tonight.

More discussion among the group of people. They asked me something, but I could only shrug.

"Thank you," I said, backing up toward the exit. "I'm

sorry for taking up your time."

"*Tomaru,*" one of the men said. He reached behind him and plucked up one of the pink bags from the floor. And then he pulled out a pair of . . .

Underwear. Sexy, too. Baby pink with ruffles.

The man pointed from the underwear to me. I giggled, which was probably highly unprofessional, but this was so insane I couldn't help it. Then, I finally got the bright idea on how to solve the language issue.

"Is everything okay?" That's how Dominic answered the phone.

"Yeah, but I need your help," I said, putting it on speaker. "Do you have a minute? Can you translate for me?"

"Translate what?"

The people behind the table stared, their mouths open. They probably couldn't believe this rude American girl had the audacity to get on the phone right in the middle of a model casting call. But what the hell did I have to lose?

"Say, 'Would you like me to try that on?'"

There was a pause, and then Japanese came from the phone I outstretched toward the table. The man holding the pink underwear dropped it back in the bag and said a long phrase.

"Where are you?" Dominic asked.

"You tell me. I think I'm auditioning to be an underwear model?"

"Uh . . . they need a Japanese model for today. But they have a swimsuit shoot on Friday where they're looking for international girls. And, they like you."

I smiled, kind of thrilled. "Okay, so how do we make that happen?"

Japanese came once again from the phone. We worked it out so I would strip and walk in my underwear and if they continued to like what they saw, they'd give me the address and time of the photo shoot on Friday.

"Payton," Dominic's voice was urgent. "You can't do this."

My neck began to get hot. Was he really so possessive of me that he didn't want these casting people to see me in my underwear? Wasn't he fucking aware of what I had done for a living?

"Oh my god, just because I'm yours doesn't mean you get to tell me what to do."

It sounded like he fumbled with the phone. "I don't have a problem with that, but you don't have any underwear on. Remember?"

I blinked, and then chuckled. He was probably bright red on the other end of the line. "Don't worry, they've got some stuff here for me to try on."

"Oh." He let out a sigh of relief. "Okay."

"Thanks for your help."

"No problem. I can't wait to hear about this tonight."

On Friday evening, he came home with carryout dinner and was eager to hear the story about the shoot.

"It was way less glamorous than it sounds," I said with a mouthful of sushi. "They sell swimsuits in catalogs, at least, that's what the photographer told me."

"But the fact remains, I'm now dating a swimsuit model."

"You're such a guy." Meredith was right, he was going to rub it in. "The whole thing took, like, two hours." It didn't pay much, but it had been fun. "Oh, I got to keep the suits."

"Bikinis?"

"A few, yeah."

His bottle of beer clunked on the table. "You'll have to model them for me."

"You want to see them?" I gave a small laugh. "Of course, because you like checking inventory."

"I like looking at your sexy-ass body, is what I like doing."

It was silly to attempt a fashion show. I only modeled one before he pulled the strings loose and we sank to the living room floor. I'd become an expert at getting him out of his suit.

Saturday morning I Skyped with Evie while Dominic slept. She stared at me like I had two heads.

"Boyfriend," she repeated.

"Yeah."

She blinked and looked like she was evaluating me to see if I were an imposter. "Okay. So, what happens whenever you get back here? I mean, you're coming back, right?"

Was she crazy? "Yeah, I'm coming back." I couldn't live in Japan. It was a nice place to visit and all, but Dominic was right. People all around and yet it was isolating. I didn't think I'd ever feel like I belonged here. I'd mentioned that to Dominic yesterday and he shot me a strange look, maybe an 'I told you so.' "I don't know what happens. We don't, like, talk about it."

"You're going to have to, eventually."

"I know," I said, annoyed.

"Hey." Her body straightened in her chair. "I got a weird call yesterday from Joseph."

Ugh. I'd deleted the few voicemails he'd left me, without listening to them. He'd always call when I was asleep, probably unaware I was on the other side of the earth.

"What'd he want?"

"He asked if I knew where you were. He said he really needs to talk to you."

Forget it. That part of my life was in the rearview. "What did you tell him?"

"That you were out of town. Is that okay?"

"Yeah, it's fine. I'm sure he wants to see if I'll come back to the club."

She shot me a sly smile. "Don't think the *boyfriend* would like that."

I snorted. "No, he wouldn't."

If last weekend went fast, this weekend went at warp speed. I blinked and it was Monday. I blinked again, and it was Tuesday. Every morning was one day closer to leaving, and I started to panic. I was in bad shape as he got ready Wednesday morning to go to work. I sat in his bed and stared blankly at the generic art on the wall. What was I going home to on Friday? What was I leaving here?

"Are you okay?" he asked, cinching the tie at his neck. It probably freaked him out that I was sitting like a statue.

"I'm thinking about how it's going to work."

"What?"

We needed to have the conversation. It'd been put off long enough. "After I leave on Friday."

His hands froze. He turned slowly, his expression unreadable. "How do you want it to work?"

Hearing his voice unstable gave me a sinking, sick feeling. "I don't know. How do you want it to work?" It was immature to throw the ball right back in his court when I was the one who initiated it, but fuck it. I was suddenly terrified.

His chest expanded as he sucked in a large breath. "How do I want it? You stay through New Years. That's how I want it."

My eyes went so large, my eyeballs almost fell out of my head. "Are you crazy? That's another two weeks."

"Yeah." He ran a hand through his hair and approached the bed, hesitant. "I looked at pushing your ticket back another week and the flights between Christmas and New Year's are like double the price."

I swallowed, even though my mouth was dry. Two more weeks. A total of five weeks with him. Holy shit.

"If you only want to stay another week, I'll pay it. It's worth it for another week with you. But, can I be honest?" He sank down on the bed to sit beside me, his face only inches away. "I already know I'll ask for another week by the end of it."

"Dominic, I can't."

"Why? Because you want to spend the holidays with your family that you don't even like talking about?" He said it softly, not accusing. "Wouldn't you rather spend it with me?"

Hell yeah, but . . . "My apartment. My car."

"You can't pay your rent online? Logan could put your car in my parking space, my place has two spots."

Logan driving my Jag? I scowled. I'd let him fuck me, but wasn't sure if I trusted him to drive my baby. How messed up was that? Dominic's hands cupped my face, not allowing me to look anywhere but into those piercing eyes.

"I know I wasn't supposed to," he said on a low voice, "but I got attached. I think I was already, when you told me it wasn't allowed."

"Just another one of my rules you ignored." I don't know

who I was annoyed at. I was just as attached as he was.

"When are you going to learn that lesson?" There was a hint of humor in his voice, maybe an attempt to mask the anxiety beneath.

"What lesson?"

"I don't like boundaries. And definitely not ten thousand boundaries between us."

There was a stab of pain in my chest. "I don't want to leave," I admitted, "but I can't stay here."

"I know. Just through the holidays. It's my first Christmas away from home and I know it's going to be rough." His expression changed to one like he was in pain. "But it'll be impossible without you."

The hands on the sides of my face were firm when I tried to look away. His face was haunting. Agreeing to this was most definitely going to blow up, but I ignored the nagging voice. I wanted this.

"Fine. Two more weeks." Even though I hadn't moved, I was out of breath. It came out shaky when it was supposed to be stern. "Because I still haven't seen the Imperial Palace."

His laugh was deep and shook the bed. Then, his kiss leveled me.

Dominic took two steps into the apartment and paused.

"I got a Christmas tree," I said.

"I can see that."

His gaze was fixed on the cheap bonsai tree I'd bought at one of tourist shops nearby, and had decorated with white Christmas lights. It was sort of a joke, but sort of not. I could deal with Dominic needing to work on Christmas day since it wasn't a holiday here, but I couldn't pretend Christmas didn't exist at all.

"I like it." His lips curled back in a smile. "If I stick your presents under there, are you going to peek?"

"Presents? Plural?" I'd only gotten him one thing. "Maybe you should give me some ideas of what you want so you can have plural gifts, too."

"Payton," he laughed. "You already gave me what I wanted, you don't need to get me anything."

"Bullshit. Ideas, now."

He smirked. "Another week?"

"No. What else?"

He pulled off his suit jacket and slipped it on the back of one of the dining chairs, leaning forward with his hands on it, as if deep in thought. "Sorry, I got nothing." He snapped upright abruptly. "And I can prove it." A hand disappeared into his interior pocket and pulled out an envelope, extending it to me.

"What's this?" The letter inside was all in Japanese, except for the handwritten word in the bottom corner. "Negative." There was a signature beneath it.

Warm color rose in Dominic's cheeks. "I had a physical the other day. I know you can't read that, so I had the doctor write my test results in English."

"Clean bill of health?" I played dumb. "Good for you."

"Don't pretend like you have no idea where I'm going with this."

I grinned. One night after he'd fucked my brains out, the condom had broken and I'd calmed him by telling him I got the birth control shot once every three months, so we were safe. And he knew I was clean because the club posted the date of our last monthly STD test on the bottom of our willing list.

I set the letter down and my hands worked the knot of his tie loose. "You want to be inside this pussy with nothing between us?"

He exhaled loudly. "God, yes. Are you cool with that?"

A shiver flashed down my spine. "Oh, yeah."

Lips traced over my neck while one of his hands cupped my ass. "And the green light on that is when?"

I'd gotten my period a few days ago, and wasn't into that kind of messy sex. It'd been blow jobs and above the waist stuff for us since. "We should be fine tomorrow. Christmas Eve."

"That reminds me. You want to do presents before I go to work on Christmas day or are you okay to wait until after?"

"I think we'll be rushed in the morning. Let's just do it after."

His hands held me to his hard, firm body, where I was beginning to feel like I fit perfectly.

"Works for me. Do you have a job that day?"

I'd gotten called up for another photo shoot. The second time it had been bras. The third was thigh-high stockings. I had been paid in cash each time, which was nice since I didn't have a work visa, and I'd used the money to buy Dominic's Christmas present.

The nicest, most elegant watch I could afford. I'd found his watch with a broken link soon after I arrived and offered to drop it off for repair, but he said it was too cheap to fix. So I'd spent every last bit of yen I'd made. If honest, I was excited about this. Every time he looked at this watch, hopefully he'd think of me and our time together.

We sat on the floor of his living room with the overhead light off, so only the twinkling bonsai tree lit the room. Our opened presents were spread around us, along with the ripped Japanese newspaper we'd both used to wrap each other's gifts.

My first gift I opened had been *Airplane* on DVD. The second gift was a 1:16 replica toy car. My Jaguar F-Type.

"I know you've been missing it," he said.

"I like that you're cool with my unhealthy obsession with it."

"I think *I* have an unhealthy obsession with it."

The next gift came in a small box, and my trepidation grew when I realized there was definitely going to be jewelry inside. It was a thin silver chain necklace, the tiny pendant was a silver origami crane.

"Is that cheesy?" he asked.

"No," I said. "It's beautiful."

Around Dominic was the necktie I'd bought him— a sapphire blue striped one to match his gorgeous eyes. Then, the school-girl uniform he'd been eying in that sex shop so many weeks ago. He was definitely excited about that. And he was already wearing the watch I'd given him. Which, holy shit, was sexy.

"I've got one more for you," he said, pushing the box toward me.

I peeled back the paper and opened the shoebox. Only there weren't shoes inside. It was that black blindfold I'd bought.

"That," he said, his breathing rushed, "comes with more."

I pulled the blindfold out and looked at him, still puzzled. "More?"

"Yeah. Like, the safe word kind of more."

chapter
EIGHTEEN

Dominic led me to the bedroom and yanked the covers off the bed, then turned his attention firmly on me.

"You still want this?" he asked. "Because I'm planning to go into that new territory tonight."

I got wet just at the idea of it. He'd *planned* this. I could hardly contain myself. "Oh, I fucking want this. What are we—"

He pulled me into a kiss, rough and uncompromising. His tongue possessed my mouth and seized command. And as quickly as he'd taken my mouth with his, he drew away.

"Take everything off except your underwear, lie down on the bed, and put the blindfold on. Call me when you're ready."

He turned and stormed out of the room.

Okay. That was unexpected, but still kind of hot. My excited hands yanked off my clothes, and as I sat on the center of the bed, I pulled on the blindfold. The sensation was both foreign and familiar. Knowing the man who was on the other side of the blindfold was new. But not knowing what he was going to do to me, that wasn't. The excitement I'd had long ago when putting on a blindfold returned. My lust threatened to spiral out of control when I lay back on the bed.

"I'm ready," I said in a raised voice.

Footsteps approached, as did his heavy breathing. "I'm going to need those hands."

Yes. I held them up toward his voice. Something hit the

floor like a box, and then the distinct sound of a metal chain rang out. Handcuffs. They were cold and my skin burned against them. Once he had them secured around my wrists, Dominic pushed them into the mattress above my head.

"Those stay there unless I move them. Got it? It's dangerous if you move without warning."

"I understand." The anticipation made my voice tight.

He took a deep breath in and blew it out slowly, obviously anxious. "You remember the safe word?"

"Yes."

"Good. Open your mouth."

Was he going to put his cock inside? It'd been a solid week of blowjobs and nothing more. He'd had to stay really late at the office last night and was too tired to mess around, or so he said. I opened my mouth, expecting the fleshy head of his cock.

This was hard, and round, with a strap on either side. Dominic hadn't lied. The blindfold did come with more . . . it came with a ball-gag.

"I don't want you getting so loud the neighbors call the cops on us." I lifted my head as he did the buckle in the back to hold it in place. When it was done, his fingertips caressed over my cheek, tracing the edge of the strap. "We still okay?"

I nodded. I was ready to burst with this new level of restraint.

Something that felt like a tennis ball was set in my hands. "Since you can't use your safe word, if you want to stop, let go of the ball. Understand?" The rough voice rolled over me, my whole body aware of him.

I nodded again.

"Good." There was noise like he was rummaging in the

box. "One more and we're ready."

One more? Something large and square clamped down over both ears, and it was playing white noise. Static. Noise fucking canceling headphones. My breath came and went it sharp bursts through my nose.

He'd isolated me completely and locked me inside my body.

Dominic. Where was he? I couldn't move, see, speak, or hear. The hairs on the back of my arms stood on end. I needed to know where he was. Where he was going to start.

Soft lips trailed over my collarbone and I sighed in relief. The wait for him to touch me, even though it had only been seconds, felt like days. The warm mouth descended until it traced the curve of my breast. Then he licked. One long stroke from one nipple to the other, bringing me to full attention.

He'd asked me our first night in Japan if I could come like this, with just his mouth sucking at my tits. Tonight I most definitely could. He had my total submission, body and mind.

I wasn't going to come from his mouth teasing my sensitive nipples, because it carved a path lower. Just when he reached the top of my panties, the heat was gone.

It was me here, on my own with just my thoughts of him and my crushing desire for his touch. *Please.* I moaned into the silicone and bit down on the gag when fingers dipped beneath the waist of my panties, and something round edged its way inside. Round, and vibrating.

It was positioned right against my clit inside my panties. Oh my god, it felt good. I wanted to shift my hips against it, but obeyed what Dominic had told me about staying still.

He hadn't said who specifically it was dangerous for, and I worried more that I might hurt him than myself.

His hands pushed my knees apart, opening me to him while that vibrating ball my panties held in place filled me with bliss. So good, but not enough to push me over the edge. He trailed fingers down on the inside of my right thigh, past my bent knee, until they reached my ankle.

There was a twinge of something. Like he'd flicked me with his fingers. What was that about? His spread fingers were set against my ankle with a band up against my skin. I felt the band pull away, and . . .

Snap! It stung as the band hit my skin and I flinched. Instantly the vibrator pressed down and I groaned in satisfaction. Oh my god, that was amazing. It only lasted a few seconds, and the fingers with the band were back against my skin, an inch closer to my knee this time. His fingers hooked around the band and pulled it away.

I jerked at the bite on my flesh, and moaned when the vibrator ground against me.

Dominic continued this pattern, working his way up my leg. My thoughts began to fracture. I wanted the faint hint of pain the band's snap against my skin caused, because the pleasure that immediately followed was intense. But as he inched closer to my center, worry formed. Where, exactly, was this going to finish? The top of my thigh where my leg met my body? Or, further?

It was getting hard to hold still. Each round got a little more aggressive, both in pain and pleasure. It happened so fast, it was hard to keep them from bleeding into each other. I was gasping for breath and shaking when the band was placed at the hollow of my leg, just where the underwear ended.

I made a sharp noise as fire licked at me in the aftermath of the rubber band's strike. The vibrator rolled a circle on me, taking me right to the edge. Instead of sending me over, he pushed my knees closed and pulled the panties down my legs, taking the vibrator with it.

I longed to have his hands on me until he urged my knees back into the same position. I stopped breathing when the band pressed up against my clit. "No, wait," I said into the gag, although I'm sure he couldn't understand a goddamn thing. That was going to hurt way too much. His finger teased my clit as it slipped under the band and pulled it away.

I was shaking violently, ready to not just drop the tennis ball, but throw it across the goddamn room. One side of my headphones suddenly pulled away from my ear.

"It's okay, Payton. Trust me. Can you do that?"

I nodded slowly.

The headphone was put back in place. How the fuck did he have enough hands to do—

The band slapped against my swollen, aching skin and I screamed against the gag, only to start coming without warning. His tongue was on my skin, soothing the burn of the band.

Holy. Fucking. God.

Intense, deep waves washed through me, over and over, as I convulsed in orgasm. I could only imagine what I sounded like since all I could hear was static. Hopefully he could tell my moans were ecstasy and not pain. I think so. He continued to caress me with his tongue, working every last drop of the orgasm from my body.

I stilled as quickly as I could when I floated back into the present.

The warm mouth was gone and the bed shifted. On my stomach, he used a finger to trace a large circle. Then a line down my center. A diagonal to the line and back again. He'd spelled the letters O and K and now he traced a question mark.

I nodded quickly as an aftershock of that amazing climax rippled through.

The headphone pulled to the side.

"Again?" he asked.

I nodded vigorously, and heard him chuckle, but it died when the headphone snapped back into place.

He started above my left ankle this time, and it wasn't a rubber band. This was like a crop or a switch. Its crack against my skin was sharp and focused, and it stung harder after, but he'd turned up the intensity on the vibrator and teased me longer. His second strike was above my knee, and I inhaled sharply.

"Fuck," I tried to say, in both pain and pleasure. As the ache from the impact faded, an intense wave of bliss moved in and took its place. That tremor in my body was going to shake me to pieces when I felt the switch against my clit, preparing for the final strike. I couldn't breathe. *Oh shit, oh shit, oh shit . . .*

I screamed as the switch left and then snapped back against my flesh. I jerked hard and this time I didn't come. It was delayed until Dominic's tongue flicked my clit and he plunged a finger inside me, deep to my G-spot.

I bowed off the bed, unable to stay still as something beyond ecstasy took control. There was no thought. Only pleasure and heat, and him. Thrusting his finger and sucking me while I went out of my mind. I was floating above my body, weightless.

He put a hand on the center of my chest and urged me to lie back down, and once again, the hand traced the O around my bellybutton, followed by the K and his question mark. Goosebumps lifted off my skin. Everything tingled.

The headphone pulled away.

"Are you okay? Payton?" He sounded panicked, and hearing that ripped me from my subspace and back to reality.

I nodded. I would have smiled if I could. It had been intense.

There was a sigh of what was probably relief from him right before everything went silent again. He tugged at the chain between the handcuffs, bringing my arms down by my waist, and then a hand scooped under my shoulder, guiding me to sit up.

It was time to take a break, I guess.

Nope, wrong. He cupped my breast with a firm hand. Something small nipped and latched onto my erect nipple. It was cold and felt like metal, compressing my flesh between its jaws. Beneath my blindfold, my eyes blinked open and went wide. Nipple clamps. Jesus, was he going all in with the BDSM stuff? Not that I was complaining, but what else did he have planned for tonight?

The bite sharpened another degree and my shoulders straightened as he got right up on the edge of pain. Then, the bed moved as he sat on the other side and did the other breast. Again, adjusting the clamp until I gave him a signal that I'd reached my limit on the tension. The chain that dangled between the clamps hung heavy between my aching breasts.

The sharp knots of my nipples were so sensitive I could feel the touch of his warm breath over them. The gentle brush of his fingertips made me moan. I figured I'd like this stuff, but I had no idea how much I was going to like it. The inferno of need was building again.

The headphone came off my ear and was set to the side. "Get up on your knees," he commanded. "Turn and face the wall."

I bent my legs and slid them beneath me, rising up and turning with his hand on my shoulder. The chain swung and the sensation was a blurred line of pleasure and pain.

"Lean forward and put your hands on the headboard."

Dominic's hand skimmed down my arm and guided me to the wall. This position was awkward. I had the palm of one of my hands against the headboard and the tennis ball clutched in the other, and my back was arched as I bent forward, my ass in the air. The chain between the clamps was heavier in this position, too.

"Stay *exactly* like this."

I wanted the headphones gone so I could focus on that throaty, gravel voice I loved.

"Next time you count them out loud, but tonight you count in your head."

The headphone was put back in place and for a split second I thought about using my shoulder to knock them off my ears. No. If I did that, he was likely to stop, and I was way too into it. A warm hand settled in the small of my back and I felt his thigh against mine like he was kneeling to the side of me. What was I supposed to count?

A hand smacked my ass and I sort of laughed. He hadn't

spanked me any harder than he'd done the few times before. Given everything else we'd done tonight, this seemed so tame and playful.

That's because it was one. Two was less playful. Maybe laughing had been a bad idea. Three. Four. I sobered completely when I realized what was happening. As his spankings got harder, my body flinched and this made the chain sway, tugging painfully on my nipples. I had to hold still.

Five. Six. I swallowed hard as the skin on my ass began to burn. The slap of his open hand seared across my skin. Seven. I jumped on the eighth one, and the hand in the small of my back pressed down, commanding me to stay still. Nine. It stung, but I fought against it. I wanted to do this.

I bit down on the ball in my mouth as he smacked me so hard it took the last of my breath. Ten.

He moved on the bed and got behind me. His hands caressed the places he'd just spanked me. My ass had to be red, it felt like it was on fire, but it was a weirdly good pain. This touch now was soothing and erotic, and fingertips skated down through the crevice of my cheeks, holding me open.

I moaned when something wet touched me. It swirled and teased my asshole where it felt so fucking dirty and good. I don't know how he did it since he had both hands on my ass, but he gave a sharp tug to the chain and the clamps tightened when I tried to press back against his face. I corrected my position immediately, bracing myself on my shaking arms. I wasn't going to be able to support myself much longer like this.

His tongue dipped down and slipped into my pussy, then moved back up again, licking a straight line through my valley. I was going to burst into flames. Or maybe fall forward flat on my face. My arms and legs were jelly.

How was he so good at this? I'd never get bored with this man. He constantly surprised me. *Dominic.* I wanted him. I needed that connection to him like I'd never needed anything before. Even more than the orgasm that was rapidly approaching –

Oh, shit! My left arm went weak and I fell forward, ready to slam into the bed and crush my nipples under my weight where they'd surely explode in pain. Hands wrapped around my arms and stopped me, holding me in place.

What. The. *Fuck?* I jerked against them. Dominic's hands were on my hips.

These hands belonged to someone else.

chapter
NINETEEN

The hands tilted me upright onto my knees and were gone as the bed rocked. What the fuck was going on? Should I drop the ball I was holding? The headphones came off and I heard them thump to the carpet.

"I'll explain in a minute, but I need you to stay still. Okay?" Dominic said.

I nodded, though my brain twisted with confusion.

Two pairs of footsteps left the room. It was a lifetime before one pair returned. A hand brushed my breast, loosening the tension on the clamp. Shit, it fucking hurt. Then, he did the other, loosening it as well. Blood began to flow back to my nipples, and I sucked in a sharp breath. He had to take the clamps off in stages. His fingers caressed my clit, probably in an attempt to distract from the pain.

When that was done, the buckle on the gag was worked loose, and he pulled it away. I rolled my jaw around and wiped the drool from my lips. The gag had been interesting, but I was glad it was gone.

I waited for him to say something, but it was quiet.

"Who the fuck was that?" I asked.

"He's gone now."

"*He?*" Dominic had given me plenty of hints at his possessive nature. It was stunning that he'd allowed another man in the room.

"It's a long story. Let's hit the pause button on it and finish this first."

I felt dizzy from how I'd been ripped from the moment. I turned to face his voice. "I don't know how–"

"I told you not to move."

And I was right back under his control. He threw me belly-down on the bed and climbed over me, trapping me beneath him. Boxers still clung to his hips, but everywhere else his warm, bare skin pressed against me. I shifted so my handcuffed wrists weren't pinned under me, and when they came out, Dominic stretched them up with a firm hand, holding them against the sheets.

His uneven breath hovered close and rolled over my skin. His cock prodded between my legs. I moaned. Yeah, I didn't care about the guy, whoever he was, now. All I wanted was this connection.

"Do you want me?" Dominic whispered into the nape of my neck. "Do you want all of me?"

I shivered. "Yes."

He shed his boxers and used his knees to widen my legs. He lowered himself so the smooth skin of his chest pressed against my back. The naked tip of his cock touched me, and inched forward. I was quaking and wild.

"Oh, please," I cried. "Give it to me."

His cock sank inside and he gave a primal groan that was so sexy, my pussy clenched on him.

"Payton," he moaned.

He rocked his hips once. Then, a second time and I gasped. Sex with Dominic without a condom? It was like taking the restrictor plate off of my pleasure. I could feel everything. While his body was pleasing me below, his mouth was doing the same above. He pushed my hair out of the way and kissed my neck. He nibbled on my ear. His hands were over mine, lacing his fingers through my grip on the sheet.

I wasn't going to last long. "I'm already close," I warned.

"Come for me. Right now."

I shouldn't have said anything. I wanted to wait. I wanted him to hold me at that edge forever, but once the words tumbled from his mouth there was no stopping it. I would do anything for him.

My fists tightened around his fingers while I burst inside, heat spilling all over. It pumped through my veins like lava. As it rushed out of my center, it caused spasms. Coming with him deep inside sent me into oblivion.

"Mine," he whispered.

He'd drained my mind of anything else and only this thought remained. "Yours," I whispered back.

A sharp noise of surprise rang out, followed by silence. One of his large hands untangled from mine. It slipped beneath the band on the blindfold and pushed it up on my forehead, and then his palm held my cheek, my face turned to his.

It came out like a question instead of a command. "Kiss me."

I blinked against the brightly lit room and he came into focus. Those blue eyes searched my face. I was more than willing to obey his order. That spark between us surged when I claimed his mouth.

Instead of thrusting, he ground his hips into me. I bit down on his bottom lip gently. It made him do it again. And again.

I broke the kiss. "Let's do this all night."

Dominic gave a short half-laugh. "All night? Just like this?" His hips swiveled and I moaned. Then that cock slid almost all the way out and eased back inside. "You don't like that?" he teased.

It all felt better than anything I'd had, so I wasn't about to be picky.

The air in the room got hot and thick as he fucked me. It was a struggle to suck air into my lungs when Dominic found a rhythm that walked the line of agony and ecstasy. His hand cupping my face tightened and his forehead pressed against my temple as his orgasm approached. His heavy breathing, occasionally punctuated by groans, filled my ear.

"I'm gonna come."

"Come," I said. "Come for me. Right now."

His cock hardened to steel. The muscles in his upper body went rigid, locking into place as he went to the brink, and then over the edge. The deep, throaty moan was almost as sexy as the feeling of him releasing inside me. No boundaries holding him back. His climax lasted a lot longer than anything he'd had with me before, and I grinned listening to him fall apart. He stilled and his hurried breathing began to return to normal.

We lay like that, him inside me, holding my head in one hand, the other still tangled with my fingers, for a quiet moment. It was as if he didn't want to leave. Didn't want to end that connection, and I sure as shit didn't, either. Everything about tonight had been . . . spectacular. I couldn't find any other word to describe it.

He nuzzled me with his nose just by my earlobe. A soft, sweet gesture that disarmed me.

"Payton . . ." he whispered. "I love you."

The world tilted and threatened to throw me off. I couldn't breathe. He was crushing me. Too much.

I . . . I had to escape.

He was looking for me to answer back with those three words, but I couldn't find them. I could only find one.

"Jaguar."

Dominic slid out of me and backed off the bed. Heavy foot-steps pounded off, telling me he'd fled the room. *Fuck.* This was a disaster.

I hurled the blindfold off my head, annoyed that I couldn't get off the handcuffs. I was annoyed at everything. This stupid bed where I'd had the best sex of my life. My response to Dominic's confession. And I was annoyed at the man in the kitchen who'd just driven me face-first into an emotional wall.

I rolled over onto my back. His form darkened the doorway, a large blue bottle in one hand.

"Akira said I'm not supposed to leave you alone or you might experience sub-drop." His voice was nervous. "Can I come in?"

I scrambled to sit and pulled my knees up to my chest. "It's your bedroom."

"Please don't be like that." He watched me like I was an unpredictable, wild animal as he entered.

"What's that?" My handcuffs rattled as I pointed to the bottle. He set it down on the nightstand and picked up a key.

"Truth serum." He sat on the bed and undid the hand-cuffs. "We need to talk about why, after everything else, you would bust out the safe word then."

He tossed the handcuffs aside, unscrewed the bottle top, and handed it to me. It was freezing.

"Drink up."

His truth serum was vodka and I choked a few mouthfuls down. "Who's Akira?" It was an attempt to deflect. "The man who was here?"

"Yeah. He's a Master."

I blinked and took another sip of the vodka that burned all the way down my throat. A Master at domination. "You said you would explain. So, explain."

Dominic got into bed beside me, throwing the covers over his lap, and sat back against the headboard. "When you told me you wanted to try this, I started reading stuff on the internet and realized I was in, like, way over my head." His expression was serious. "I didn't want to hurt you, and everything I read said an inexperienced top can do a lot of damage. I needed to talk to someone, just to tell me where to start . . ." His cheeks flushed. "I found Akira through a message board. I met him last week during my lunch break, which was awkward as fuck, but, whatever. I told him what I needed help with."

I took another sip of the vodka, and when I was done, Dominic tugged the bottle from my grasp.

"He was cool with me being a *Gaijin*. He's taught other Doms and subs, and said I should train with someone in the room. And he offered."

"You weren't worried I was going to be pissed when I found out?"

He gave me a slight smile. "You, the exhibitionist? No, I wasn't. And you weren't supposed to find out, you know, not until after."

I ran a hand through my hair and leaned back against the headboard. That was when I noticed the welts on my legs. I stretched one leg out, then the other. There were faint pink marks on my right leg where he'd used the band, but my left? I could see the two red, raised lines of puffy skin. It was weird. I felt a rush of heat at the sight. I liked Dominic's marks on me.

He must have noticed what I was looking at.

"Do you want some ice, or Advil?" His voice was quiet and his eyes wouldn't meet mine. I liked an embarrassed Dominic, but I didn't like an ashamed Dominic at all.

"I'm fine. It doesn't even hurt." It wasn't a lie. The skin was irritated and hot, but not aching.

"Okay, that's good." He took a hesitant breath. "Can I be honest? I didn't think I was going to like it."

"What? Then, why did—?"

"Because you wanted to try it, and I wanted to give you . . . whatever you want."

That affected me much more than it should have. "Okay, so you didn't think you were going to like it. But, you did?"

He looked conflicted. "Yeah. I shouldn't."

"Why?"

The aqua eyes gave me a plain look. "I hit you."

"You *spanked* me. There's a difference. If you hit me, we wouldn't be having a conversation right now. You'd be dead." This whole thing was silly. "Don't feel guilty about it. It's good you liked it, because I *really* liked it, and I'm going to want to do it again."

His arm went around my shoulder and pulled me against him. I felt weirdly clingy and needy, so I wrapped an arm around his waist.

"How was he as a teacher?" I stalled some more, worried the next time we lapsed into silence he was going to start digging. "What was it like?"

"He was good. I was kind of nervous bringing him in here. I mean, he said he was going to be hands-off, but I was sure he was going to take one look at you and go crazy. I fucking do." Dominic's hand stroked faint circles on my arm. "Turned out he was way more focused on helping me than anything else. I think he liked the control."

That made plenty of sense, for a Master to want ultimate control over the scene.

"He warned me," Dominic said, "you couldn't hold that position, but I was distracted. Too busy thinking about what I wanted to do to you next."

It got quiet again. "So, I fell and he caught me. Then what happened?"

"He told me how to take off the clamps so it wouldn't hurt and to try to get back into the scene as quick as possible. Then, to stay with you afterward."

"But what was he like?"

Dominic's grip on me hardened. "I know you're avoiding it, but I told you, we have to talk about you using the safe word. That truth serum should start kicking in soon."

I tried to pull away but it wasn't allowed. "I told you, I don't do love."

"That's total bullshit, but tell me anyway why you think that."

My lips were starting to get numb from the vodka, and I was tired from what we'd just done. I was weak. "My family."

I felt his heart pick up the pace. "What about them?"

"We're not the hugging, emotional type. Growing up, my parents were strict. They didn't show affection or do anything to make me feel like they cared about me."

Dominic's face contorted into disbelief. "And that's why

you don't do love?"

"I'm just giving you the setup here, Dominic. Give me a fucking minute." God, I could not be more uncomfortable right now. "Once I hit high school, I was all confused by affection and attention from guys. I craved it. I, like, needed it. You understand what I'm saying?"

"Yeah." He sounded sad for me, but I didn't want his pity.

"My sophomore year at Northwestern, I met this guy named Ian. We hooked up at a party, and then again a week later. . . And suddenly we were dating." It didn't seem like Dominic was going to let me sit up, so I put my cheek against his chest. "I don't know how or why it happened, but I fell in love."

"Wait a minute—"

"Yeah," I said. "I lied to you about that." I let him digest it for a moment. "Ian was a total mindfuck. One day he'd tell me he loved me, and the next he'd blow me off. I always got over it and took him back. He said he loved me and I *needed* that." Just recalling it now made the old anger burn again.

"He went home to Texas during Christmas break, and I couldn't get ahold of him, like he fucking ceased to exist, and he comes back at the beginning of the spring semester acting like nothing happened. He just wanted to pick up right where we left off."

My brain was getting that hazy, tipsy feeling. Thank god. The words were coming easier now.

"I told him to knock that shit off. He said he loved me, and I was the only girl for him, and he told me all the lies guys say when they want to keep getting pussy."

Dominic's mouth dropped open. "Payton, that's not why—"

"I bought it all. There wasn't a shred of doubt in my mind, so when I found the engagement ring a week before spring break, I was so happy."

My statement hung in the air.

I would remember that moment forever, the shock and excitement as I opened that blue velvet box.

"Oh, shit." Dominic's voice was hushed. "The ring wasn't for you."

"Nope. He'd gotten his high school girlfriend pregnant over Christmas break. I had to hear about it from his roommate when Ian didn't come back to school. He never answered any of my calls."

A shift went through the body holding me. "Where's this fucker now?"

"It doesn't matter, and I don't fucking care. That week when I thought he was going to propose and instead he vanished? It destroyed me." The only person I thought truly loved me, abandoned me. "I don't do love. It's just a lie."

Dominic's hand curled under my chin and forced my eyes up. "No, it's not. I love you. That's real."

I stared into his eyes. Since Ian, I'd become the human lie detector, and I didn't see any tell that Dominic was lying, but my damaged heart refused to accept it.

"Please stop saying it."

"Goddamnit, you are the most frustrating girl . . . Okay, yeah, you had a really shitty experience a long time ago, but we're going to get past it." He'd said *we're*. Like this was his problem now, too?

And, what the hell? Did he not think I'd tried to get past it? There had been Joel, and a few others, and I'd felt nothing with any of them. In fact, before Dominic, my fucked up relationship with Joseph was the closest I'd gotten to love with a man. My manager certainly didn't love me, but I knew he at least cared about me.

Dominic pulled me into his lap and wrapped his warm arms tight around me. "Now that I put it out there, it's out. Get used to hearing me say it."

"Then get used to not hearing it back."

I didn't argue to try to stop him, because Dominic did whatever he wanted. His hands started at the base of my neck and slid up gently until he had my face cradled in his palms, him just a breath away. The pad of his thumb brushed over my lips, pausing at the center.

"I love you."

The thumb slipped away and was replaced by his kiss, the same one he'd given me at the club. He'd kissed me then as a man who'd waited a year to kiss, but this time it was worse. This was a kiss he'd waited his whole life to give. One that tasted like love.

My eyes stung and I turned away.

"Are you . . . crying?"

I blinked and glared at him. Whatever was going on with my eyes dried up. "No," I spat out. "I don't cry."

A short laugh came out of him. "You know, *saying* you don't do something? That doesn't actually make it true."

I rolled my eyes and crawled off of him. "You better watch yourself. Your truth serum made me sleepy and bitchy."

He turned off the light and curled up around me like he always did, but I felt him all around me now. Like he was tattooed to my skin.

"Thanks for staying," he said. I don't know if he meant

through the holidays, or the fact that I hadn't bolted from the apartment when the L word came out.

"You're welcome," I whispered back. "Merry Christmas."

Every morning before he left for work, it was the same. He'd take my face in his hands, brush his thumb over my lips and tell me he loved me. That thumb would slide out of the way just as he replaced it with his lips to kiss me goodbye.

It snowed my final week in Tokyo. The city was more beautiful with the fat snowflakes drifting down to melt on the neon. My ticket home was for Monday afternoon, and as the weekend approached, the familiar panic crept in. I didn't love this place. I'd gotten more homesick in my five weeks here than my entire semester in Amsterdam. But I didn't know how I was going to get on that goddamn plane.

He'd been late getting home this whole week, cutting deeper into our remaining time together.

"I was hoping we could go to Kyoto for the weekend. You want to?" Dominic asked over dinner on Thursday.

"Well, yeah." When else was I going to get the chance to go there? "What did you have in mind?"

"We could stay at a *Ryokan*. It's like a traditional inn so you get the full Japanese experience. I've wanted to stay at one, but it'd be weird to go by myself." Something suspicious flashed behind the aqua eyes.

"Okay, sure, but what's going on with you?"

"Maybe I made reservations for us already. There's a really good one that has an *onsen*. You know what that is?"

"Yeah, a hot spring." But the weird expression continued on his face. "That's not what's got you nervous, though."

He gave me a tight smile. "You're not going to like this next part." He leaned back in his seat across the dinner table from me, massaging a hand on the back of his neck, giving me a view of the bicep flexing under his T-shirt.

"Out with it."

"The place I booked, it's supposed to be really great."

Okay . . .?

"Because it's so *traditional*."

I wasn't sure what he was getting at, but he delivered the word with so much weight it made me nervous. He sighed, and locked eyes with me.

"The bad news is I changed your last name. The good news is it comes with jewelry."

My chair squealed as I pushed back from the table and shot up. He leaped to his feet, too.

"Calm down," he said. "It's just for show. They won't take an unmarried couple."

My heart slammed in my chest and I ripped my eyes away from him. He wanted me to pretend to be his wife. I didn't hear him come over. It was the thick arms that circled my waist that announced his presence.

"You're asking way too much." I said it quietly.

"It's a lot, I know." He pressed me against him so my face was buried against his T-shirt and I breathed in the scent of cedar and soap. "I'll make it worth it, I promise." A hand smoothed over the back of my head, angling me to look up at him. "I mean, if you fake marry me," he teased, "you get half my stuff in the fake divorce."

I pushed out a weak smile to mask the terror inside. Not terror at this idea of pretending. I'd always been a good actor. It was that the idea of actually marrying Dominic someday – it didn't make me feel empty inside like it had with Joel. Instead I stood in Dominic's arms and felt lightheaded.

"Okay, so say I do this. What makes you think," I whispered, "that I'd take your last name? That'd be moving back in the alphabet."

"Too late." He grinned and looked thrilled I'd sort of agreed to it. "I already registered us as Mr. and Mrs. Ward. But go ahead and tell me you don't *do* name changes. It'll be fun."

"Asshole."

He laughed and lifted me up, causing my legs to fold around him. He stormed toward the bedroom. "That's no way to talk to your fake husband, Mrs. Ward."

Shit. That sent tingles down my spine. "Maybe you should put something in my mouth to shut it up then." I slipped a hand between our bodies, rubbing him. "Like this."

He gave me a wicked, dark look. "I'll put that wherever I goddamn please."

Fuck. I might just love him after all.

TWENTY-ONE

Dominic only made it twenty minutes into our six-hour train ride before asking about the rings. He'd dropped a wad of yen on the table Friday morning, along with a ring made out of paper he'd taped together for sizing, and tasked me with picking them out.

I glared at him as I dug the box out of my purse. I'd gone into a jewelry store and bought two simple silver bands, one for each of us, then bought a gaudy cubic zirconium ring at one of the tourist shops. Trying the rings on had been difficult, but I didn't suffer the full-out meltdown until after. I'd sat in a coffee shop like a zombie for over an hour, weighing my options and forcing myself to face the fact that I was leaving Japan soon. Leaving him.

He couldn't go back to America. My half-joking request for him to come home with me had been met with a wall of silence and an unreadable look. Slowly his expression filled with concern. "To where we'd both be out of jobs?"

No, that wasn't an option for him. He had another year left on his contract.

I almost dropped the box with my sweaty hand. "Hope it fits, *darling*," I said.

Dominic ignored me. He took the larger of the two bands, and I followed its quick descent onto his finger. How could he be so comfortable with this?

"It fits. Your turn."

As I stared at the band on his left hand, my breath

caught. A sign that he belonged to someone. To me. It was sexy. Wait, no, I didn't like this. I grabbed my rings and shoved them on my finger, then balled my hand into a fist, dropping it out of view. I expected the ring to feel like it weighed a ton, but it didn't.

We watched out the window as we raced through the gorgeous countryside filled with cedar trees and rice paddies. Dominic's hand rested on my knee, and as we barreled through a tunnel, the light glinted on the new band on his third finger. My eyes were drawn to it like a moth to a flame. What was wrong with me?

It was late afternoon when we arrived in downtown Kyoto, and took a taxi that wound through the city that seemed just as sprawling as Tokyo and yet more intimate. There were temples everywhere, and less neon.

The exterior of the *Ryokan* was a two-story building with a wooden-carved gate. A woman greeted us at check-in, and escorted Mr. and Mrs. Ward to their guesthouse. We followed a path through a perfectly manicured winter garden, over a tiny red footbridge, and into our private bungalow.

My eyes went wide as she showed us the space after we'd removed our shoes. The interior was classic Japanese with the tan matted floor and paper doors. The back wall of the room was all glass with a view of our own private garden courtyard. In one corner, two narrow mattresses sat side by side on the floor. They were called futons here, not the fold-and-fucks from college that word typically brought to my mind.

A glassed-in room was located in the corner opposite the futons, the bamboo shades drawn up to give us a view of the large soaking tub. The woman explained in English that dinner would be served in our room at seven.

"This must have cost a fortune," I said to him after she'd gone. "This place is beautiful."

Dominic gave me a seductive smile. "Want to take a bath? We've got lots of time before dinner."

I followed him into the glass room, admiring the tile work over the tub. A traditional scene with Mt. Fuji and a blue wave cresting beneath Japanese characters. This place . . . it wasn't just beautiful, it was *romantic*.

"Dominic."

He'd yanked off his shirt, but my sharp tone made him freeze.

"I know what you're up to," I accused.

He returned to life and went to the tap, turning on the water that flooded the deep, rectangular tub that was the size of a four-man hot tub, and continued to ignore me.

My words were supposed to be strong, but they faltered. "It won't work."

I thought maybe he couldn't hear me over the running water, but he straightened and put his focus on me.

"What exactly am I up to?" He unbuttoned his pants and yanked them down, kicking them away so he was only in a pair of gray boxers.

"You brought me here to get me to say it back."

His gaze warmed until it was hot as a sauna in the room. The steam rising from the tub didn't help. I stood my ground as Dominic strolled up to me. There was no denial in his face. His eyes didn't leave mine as he lifted my sweater up over my head and cast it away.

"It won't work," I repeated, this time stronger.

Cold fingers unsnapped my jeans and tugged them off,

and he returned to stand over me. The intense gaze bore down, like he was looking for a way into my heart.

"I can't make you say you love me." He blinked and the aqua in his eyes darkened. They filled with determination. "But I can make you *feel* it."

I expected him to pull me against him and kiss me, but his attack was subtler. He turned, dropped his boxers to the floor, and stepped into the water. He came back around to face me and sank down onto the ledge seat in the tub.

I was aware I was fighting a losing battle. The hour in the coffee shop had been scary as hell, but well spent. Dominic had planned this trip to get the words from me, but I'd made plans of my own. I could make sacrifices to get what I wanted.

"I went to the Imperial Palace yesterday."

The only sound was the water splashing. The eyes fixed on me through the steam didn't blink.

He blew out a long breath. "How was it?"

"It was nice."

I undid my bra. It fell onto the floor silently. My heart raced and the blood rushed loudly in my ears. I hooked my thumbs under my lace panties and pulled them down. "I'm going to need a favor."

My shaky tone made his eyes go wide with alarm. "What?"

Oh, god, was I really doing this? I'd been flooded with relief when I'd made the hard decision yesterday, but I was still nervous. "I need you . . . to cancel my ticket."

His expression shifted from alarm, to relief, and to confusion faster than a snap of my fingers.

"You're giving me another week?"

"No."

His breathing picked up, faster each second. "Two weeks?"

"No."

He must have realized I'd said *cancel* and not *reschedule*. His expression slowly shifted now to one of guarded hope. "Are you . . . staying?"

It came from me as breathless as he looked to be. "Yes."

"Why?"

"For you."

I might have short-circuited his brain. His eyes drifted down to the water pooling around him and he blinked rapidly, as if unable to process it. I couldn't find the words he wanted to hear, but maybe with time I would. Plus, staying – that made a pretty big statement, didn't it? I disliked it here, but he couldn't go and being with him trumped everything else.

"Holy shit." His gaze snapped back to me. "Get the fuck over here."

Standing outside the tub, completely naked before him except for those rings, with his gaze on me and so full of love, I'd never felt more powerful. And even though I came running to him, it wasn't because of his command. It was the crushing need to be with him. I'd barely stepped into the water and he whirled me into his lap so I was straddling him. He buried a hand in the hair at the nape of my neck and yanked me down into his desperate kiss, the hot water splashing around us.

Time slowed down as his lips pressed against mine. My hands skimmed along his strong jaw and my fingers curled in his hair, trapping his head against the tile wall. My tongue dipped into his mouth. Heat and water closed in all around.

"We're going to flood the room," I gasped as his mouth trailed kisses down my neck. The water was still running and the deep tub was nearly full. Hands locked on my waist so we could glide through the water close to the tap. He fumbled an arm out and shut it off, and then that arm was back, crushing me against his wet skin.

I couldn't leave. Every time I imagined going back to my empty apartment in Chicago, I felt sick. It wasn't much of a plan, staying with him, but it was all I had. It had to be enough. He was better at planning than I was.

His hands splayed across my back while his mouth worked steadily lower to my breasts. The caress of his soft tongue on my nipple was an electric shock of acute desire. I didn't think I could be any more needy until that happened.

"Please," I whispered. I shifted in his lap, letting his hard cock slip between my folds. I didn't want foreplay. The throbbing ache for him was going to consume me.

Like the first time we'd been together, he paused just as he was positioned to take me. Those arms held me steady and his gaze kept me immobile. One of his hands drifted up through the water. He repeated his routine of cupping my face. The wet thumb brushed onto my lips.

"I love you."

He claimed my mouth and urged me down onto him at the same moment, and I sighed against the kiss. I was trembling. The emotions snaking through my veins were overwhelming.

His slow, gentle slide inside me burned with scorching pleasure. This was like that first time, only so much more. Not because he was sitting and I was on top. It was because what we were doing wasn't fucking. This was making love.

He'd given me a hint of it before, but now he had no need for restraint.

The ends of my hair skimmed the water and clung to me, and I clung to him. I clawed at his shoulder, wanting him closer. My forehead rested against his. The tremble in me grew and stole my breath.

"Payton." He moaned it in my ear when I went faster. "Slow. Make it last."

I wanted to, but couldn't. Each push of his cock claimed me over again, making me his. My hand slapped against the cold wall behind him, and I dragged it chattering down the tile. His left hand seized my breast and he sucked at the pert nipple just above the waterline. The ring on his hand. Oh, shit. I closed my eyes but the image was seared in my brain. How did I get so lucky? That he'd chosen me that night, and he'd chosen to give me all this.

His heart was pounding in his chest and I felt it mirroring mine. He approached the edge of his orgasm as I did, threatening to send us over. I'd never wanted anything as much as I did this man who pushed and tested me, but also wanted to give me anything I wanted. There was no demand to come for him. This moment was much deeper than our silly power play.

Yeah, he couldn't get the words out of me, but he was absolutely right. I *felt* it.

Dominic's hands drove me down on him in a final thrust that threw us both into oblivion. His quiet moan echoed off the tile. And me? The bliss was so out of this world I couldn't find oxygen. My mouth hung open and I barely made a sound. I closed my eyes and banded my arms so hard around his head, surely I suffocated him against my heaving chest.

The water rolled in waves, back and forth, diminishing with each pass, until it was smooth again.

"God, there aren't words," he said, muffled against my skin, "for how amazing that was."

"No," I panted, "there aren't."

I released his head and leaned back in his arms, still trying to catch my breath.

"You're serious about staying, right?"

I nodded and rose off of him, the water sloshing in the tub again as I sat beside him under his arm. "I'm going to need another favor, though."

"Just name it. Whatever you want. Anything."

I gave a pained smile. "I've probably got enough to cover another month of rent in Chicago, but that's it." I leaned my head back against the tile. "All my money's tied up in my car."

"How much is left on your lease?"

"Until April."

"We can figure out what to do after that, but I've got you covered until then."

I bit my lip. "I'll pay you back." Though I had no idea how.

His deep laugh filled the glass room. "Forget it. I don't want your money." I scowled, but that only made his grin wider. "Think of it this way, you're repurposing the money from the plane ticket, and I'll still be coming out ahead." His eyes gleamed. "Way fucking ahead."

When our fingertips were pruned and the water became cool, Dominic helped me out of the tub. We toweled off and he gestured to the two robes hanging beside the sink. One was a manly, deep blue, and the other a black and white floral print. Only they weren't robes.

"*Yukatas*," he said. "Or maybe kimonos. I can never tell the difference."

It was clear which one was mine, so I pulled on my bra and underwear, and slipped my arms into the sleeves of the soft fabric. Beneath it on the hook was a thin belt and a wide yellow sash. We had to watch a YouTube video on his iPad to figure out how to put them on properly. Of course the ultra-traditional inn would have WiFi. We had to help each other get dressed, and Dominic couldn't keep his hands off of me so it took forever.

"We look like stupid *Gaijins*," I laughed when it was done.

Even with my best effort, Dominic's was lopsided and looked ready to come undone any second. Not that I was complaining. Our host confirmed it when she delivered our dinner and did a double-take.

"You need to turn your obi to the back," she said, alarmed for me. "Wearing it in the front means you are a prostitute."

I couldn't contain my snort of amusement. "Wouldn't want anyone to mistake me for *that*."

Dominic didn't seem to find it as amusing as I did.

We ate the delicious meal at the low table in our kimonos, discussing the process of applying for a temporary visa. I'd gotten so good at using the chopsticks, I was able to snap mine around Dominic's when he leaned over to steal a bite out of my bowl.

"Get lost."

"Come on, Mrs. Ward." His playful smile was distracting. "Share with your husband."

"Okay, I'll fake share with my fake husband." I pushed his chopsticks away. "It's not my fault you already ate all of yours."

I couldn't stop him, though. His sticks snatched up a hunk of noodles and they disappeared into his mouth a half-second after. I shouldn't have been surprised. He always got what he wanted.

"Was that your plan all along?" I asked him abruptly. "Did you bring me here to get me to stay?"

His blue eyes widened. "No. I was going to ask for another week."

"And those three words."

His expression went serious. "Yeah. Look, I didn't think I had a prayer of getting you to stay another week, but I was gonna try." He set his chopsticks down and they tinged against the bowl. "You don't seem to hate it like I did when I first got here, but I know it's not easy for you." He took a deep breath. "You don't have to say those three words tonight. You already did."

"So, I'm off the hook, huh?"

He gave a sly smile. "For now."

TWENTY-TWO

TEN DAYS LATER

I'd spent hours at the US Embassy and gotten nowhere. The visa application was supposed to be submitted three months prior to the stay and filed from outside of Japan. My caseworker was fairly certain I was going to have to leave within ninety days of entry to Japan and go through the process properly.

Three months? No thanks.

But I was beginning to hate it here. The looks of disdain from strangers when it was clear I didn't speak Japanese, and the long, lonely hours when Dominic was stuck late at work. I didn't regret my life-changing decision to stay, but my resentment toward Chase Sports and the stupid contract they held over us grew thick.

I rode the train back to our apartment, my shoulders sagging in defeat about the visa. Dominic had joked that we could get married. "Hell, we already have rings," he'd said. The scary thing was I wasn't sure he was joking. Faced with the prospect of me leaving, he'd do whatever he had to. But it's not like he was a citizen of Japan, and getting married might only make the visa application process more difficult.

I texted him that I was in a bad mood and no way was I cooking tonight.

> If I'm bringing home dinner, you need to do something for me.

> Meet me at the door wearing those thigh-highs. Nothing else.

My pulse jumped and my mood improved in a single heartbeat.

> Agreed. Kimchi from that place by the konbini.

I spent the hour before he was supposed to get home shaving my legs, putting on makeup . . . doing anything I could to make myself look as fuckable as possible. I wanted him to come in the door, throw me over his shoulder, and slam me down on the bed. To fuck me so hard I'd forget about anything else.

I pulled on the black lacy garter belt, followed by the silky stockings. I hooked the garters to the lace trim at the top and adjusted the elastic. A quick inspection in the full-length mirror confirmed it. I looked hot. Get ready, Dominic Ward. Maybe tonight I'll finally give you those words you've been wanting to hear.

He hadn't pushed about that. Agreeing to stay with him indefinitely had made him so happy, I don't think he wanted to do a thing to screw that up. He still told me he loved me in the mornings before he left for work.

On Monday I asked him softly, "Why do you do that? Put your thumb here right when you say it?"

"Don't worry about it."

The pink in his cheeks was so subtle I almost missed it. "Tell me."

He exhaled slowly and looked resigned. "I do it so I can tell myself that's why you're not saying it back."

He put his thumb over my lips like that simple action was what kept me from saying it. My chest felt tight. Every time I didn't say it, I knew it hurt him, even if only a little. He knew what he was getting, though, I reminded myself. I'd get there. I just had to make sure when it came from my lips, it was the total truth. If it felt like a lie, it would crush us both.

I locked the door, so I had some warning before it swung open. At seven-thirty, the door thudded when he tried to open it and discovered it locked. I got into position. A curse word was muttered, in Japanese, which I always found hilarious from him. Metal slid into metal, the lock turned, and he pushed open the door.

"Holy shit." He dropped the plastic bag on the floor and kicked the door closed behind him.

I sat on the dining table, my legs spread wide and a hand touching my bare pussy.

He just stood there, his eyes glazed with lust. *Come on, come and get me, Dominic.* His gaze drifted down my body, over my naked tits, down the lace and silk that ended in black high heels. The gaze worked its way back up even slower.

But he stooped down and picked up the plastic bags. "Nice try, devil woman. We're eating dinner first." He moved to the kitchen cabinet and pulled down two bowls.

My mouth dropped open. "The fuck we are."

He walked the bowls and plastic bags toward the table

and set them down, and began to open cartons. I stood and put my hands on my hips, watching with disbelief as he dumped food into the bowls.

"Did you get hit in the head by a crane or something? You asked me to wait for you naked, and you want to fucking *eat dinner*?"

He chuckled and stuck a set of chopsticks upright in the food, and held the bowl out to me. "I have plans for this evening and you're going to need the energy."

My eyes went narrow but inside I got excited. I loved it when he made plans. I took the bowl from him. "What kind of plans?"

There was a faint smile on his lips but his expression was intense. Whatever it was, it was big.

I hurriedly pulled out a chair and sat at the table. Thick anticipation seeped into the room as we ate in almost complete silence, his gaze never leaving my curves. He finished his dinner but his expression announced he was still hungry. He fucked me with his eyes and my stomach clenched. I rose from the table. I took both of our bowls, then sauntered on my heels to deposit them in the sink, hoping he was watching the sway of my ass cheeks as I went.

"Bring the bottle of vodka back with you," he said.

"Don't you mean truth serum?" I yanked the bottle from the freezer and stalked toward him, unscrewing the cap.

"Not tonight. Inhibitions reducer."

"I don't need my inhibitions lowered." I took a long pull on the bottle and came to stand over him while he remained in his chair.

"It's not for your inhibitions." The vodka sloshed as he took the bottle and drank.

Wait, what the hell was he talking about? "If we're going to do something you're not comfortable with, maybe no booze."

He gave a tight smile. "Even if I got wasted, which I'm not going to do, you'd be fine. I just want to take my edge off."

The curiosity in me grew ten-fold. What did he have planned that he was nervous about? The bottle of vodka clunked on the table and his fingertips, chilled from the icy bottle, skimmed over my belly. I flinched at the cold, but melted into him.

His hands roamed over my skin, traveling behind me. His palms caressed my ass, his fingers digging into the round flesh, kneading me. His tongue skirted the top edge of my garter belt. The slow burn of anticipation ignited.

"Let's go in the bedroom," I whispered, anxious to get started.

The corner of his mouth lifted into a coy smile. "You don't get to dictate how tonight's gonna go. I've got a word for you that I hope you like. *Obey*."

The air left my body in a shuddering hiss. He was right, I did like the word, but I didn't want him clued in on that just yet. We could have some fun before he discovered it. I sank down on his lap, tugging the already loosened knot of his tie free. "Oh, really? You want me to obey you . . . Sir?"

He tried to hide it, but the words made an impact. His hands were below my garters and clenched on the bare flesh of my hips. The silk of his tie threaded around his collar, slipped quietly along the fabric as I pulled it free. Undressing him slower than I ever had, even though my mind was screaming to tear his clothes off.

I leaned in and dropped my head so my lips were just

by his ear and used the sexiest voice I had. "What happens if I don't obey?"

"You're going to want to try very hard, because you'll like the reward. Now sit back up on the table right here like you were when I came in."

I hadn't finished unbuttoning his shirt, but I abandoned the task and did what he told me. I wasn't sure who I was obeying right then, him or my lust. I seated myself and spread my legs wide. He slid his chair forward a few inches. Hands smoothed over my knees, running up my legs until they reached the elastic garter straps.

He hooked one under a finger and pulled it back, letting it snap harmlessly against my skin, but I jumped. The reminder of what he could do with a rubber band flashed through my mind and made my face warm.

He glanced at his watch before leaning in so his head was between my thighs, hovering just out of reach of pleasing me.

"Are we on a schedule?" I teased.

"Maybe I want to see how fast I can make this body come."

No time at all. A single command and I was sure I'd be a quivering mess. I swallowed a breath as his lips grazed me. I moaned when his tongue got into the mix. He stroked and swirled the tip over me, coaxing an orgasm to come close.

His mouth only stopped long enough to speak, and then resumed fucking me. "Can you obey, Payton? Can you be a good girl and do exactly what I tell you?"

I stared down at the top of his head and watched his tongue slide inside me. I groaned in satisfaction. "Yes, Sir."

He rewarded me with a frenzied flutter right on my clit, and I gasped. The need for release was ramping up big time—

There was a sharp knock on the front door and I jolted off of Dominic's mouth. He wiped his mouth with a hand, and as it fell away, it revealed a sinful smile beneath. Like he expected this knock.

"I forgot to mention we have company tonight," he said. His eyes were dark and focused. "Go answer the door."

I blinked back the fog of my impending orgasm and swayed. "What?" I was essentially naked. And, company?

"Are you going to do what I said?" he challenged, although it sounded like he was holding his breath.

It had to be Akira. Dominic knew hardly anyone else here, and last time he'd made plans like this, he'd been nervous. I climbed down from the table and onto my shaky legs, and marched to the door. I was excited to meet the man who had offered to help train Dominic, and the idea of another session tonight was unbelievably arousing.

I pulled the door open and gazed out into the hallway, my mouth forming the introduction to him, but my brain went blank.

Not a man. A woman.

chapter
TWENTY-THREE

The young woman looked regal and elegant. She was petite, waif-thin, and Japanese. Her long, black hair was pulled back into a high ponytail that trailed down her back. Her almond-shaped and shocked eyes blinked at my nakedness, and her gaze dropped immediately to the floor.

I took a hesitant step backward, stunned, and in my confusion I didn't notice *him* until he set a hand on her shoulder. There was no doubt in my mind who he was. He stood with perfect posture which made him seem impressively tall even though he was probably the same height as me without the heels.

Akira was older. Late forties, or maybe even fifty. Handsome, but serious and intimidating. His black hair was long, falling past his ears. This man had presence . . . and command. It forced me to stare at his feet, like it would be rude to look at him without permission. His black suit seemed to match his eyes, and the fabric looked expensive.

What the hell was going on?

Dominic's hand brushed my back and I jumped at his touch. He bowed respectfully and Akira did the same back. It seemed like there were introductions, and then the couple entered the apartment, shut the door, and removed their shoes.

"Payton," Dominic said. "This is Master Akira, and her name is Yuriko."

It was disorienting to be the only one without clothes

on. Sure, both men had seen me naked, and she was a woman, but the confusion over the situation left me feeling scattered. What was she here for?

I bowed to them, feeling like an idiot. Why hadn't I learned to do that properly? They returned the bow, their faces unchanged. Yuriko's gaze wandered up my body almost like she was curious.

"What's going on?" I tried to stay calm.

"He's training her to be his submissive and he needs our help." Dominic flushed. "Your help, actually."

"My help? With what?"

"He wants to push her soft limits. It'll be her final test before she becomes his."

I stood still as Akira peeled off his suitcoat and passed it to Yuriko, and Dominic showed her the tiny closet where we stored everything. Her jacket came off as well, revealing a slender body under a black wrap dress.

"Do either of them speak English?" I asked.

"No." A smile lurked under Dominic's lips. He'd be the only one in the room who could understand everything being said.

"What are her soft limits?"

Akira spoke and discussion broke out between the men. It left me to examine her closer. She looked about my age, maybe a little older. It was tough to say. Her skin was flawless porcelain. Her dark eyes examined me right back, like she was fascinated. Then Akira said something to her, and her attention snapped back to him. Her soft, innocent face went tense. As if whatever the plan was for this evening, she was just learning about it now.

I wasn't in the same boat as her. I knew even less.

Dominic said something and gestured to the table, and after a brief glance, Akira nodded. Abruptly Dominic was backing me toward it.

"What was all that about?" I asked.

My ass was cold on the tabletop as he sat me there. His face was a mixture of excitement and something else. Anxiety?

"She's never been with another woman before, but she wants to."

"That doesn't sound like a limit."

"It's not. We'll get to that in a second." Dominic's hands slipped around my waist. "Do you think she's beautiful?"

"Well, yeah."

"What would you say," his voice dropped to a hush, "if I told her she was allowed to touch you?"

I put my hands on his forearms and slowly ran them up until I could lace my fingers together behind his neck. This woman didn't seem to be able to take her eyes off of me. She *wanted* me. My pulse thumped steady and fast at the idea.

"Would you like that?" His voice was so fucking sexy when he whispered.

I nodded.

"What if I told her she could go down on you while we watched? Would you like that?"

I swallowed hard. I could barely breathe. "Yes."

"What if I told you . . . that you couldn't come during?"

It was like a needle dragging on a record. "What?"

"When he says go, she has ten minutes to try to make you come. If she fails, she's going to allow him to play with her virgin ass." He brushed his lips over mine. "He's hoping to push her limit, so I'm telling you not to come. Can you obey?"

Jesus, I was on fire already. It escaped my lips on a whisper. "Yes, Sir."

Dominic's kiss was aggressive and controlling. It lingered on my lips even after he was gone. He sat down on the chair at my side and uttered a short phrase in Japanese. Akira approached first, his gaze brushing over me, but there was nothing in his eyes to give me a clue what was going on behind them. He went to the other side of the table and sat opposite Dominic, then spoke.

Yuriko strolled up to the table like she had tons of time, assessing me. Maybe figuring out where to start.

"Did he tell—" I said to Dominic, hushed.

"No, not yet."

Yuriko stood a foot away from the edge of the table, just outside of my parted legs. Her long, delicate fingers skimmed along my thigh, over the sheer silk that covered my skin. A shy smile from her made my breath catch.

"Can I touch her?" I blurted out.

Dominic repeated my question to Akira.

"*Hai.*" One of the few Japanese words I understood. *Yes.*

She knew it was coming from Dominic's translation, but she still seemed bashful when I set my hand on her hip and urged her to come closer. I wanted to get this started as soon as possible. The quicker I made it through those ten minutes, the quicker I would get to my reward.

Her hand wandered, tentative. It crept up over the flare of my hip, along my waist, and up. Her knuckles brushed the underside of my breast and scurried away like she was embarrassed. Shit, if she was going to be this shy, this shouldn't be too hard.

I took her hand in mine and used it to cover my breast. It seemed to do the trick, because she massaged and explored. I could feel the men's heavy gazes on us, pressing us together. So I sat up straight and grabbed her ponytail, winding it into my fist, tugging her head back with force. It let everyone in the room know who was in charge.

Me.

Doing it exposed her slender, ivory neck, and I put my lips there. Her pulse was racing and her skin was soft. She smelled amazing, like jasmine. Yuriko gave a sharp cry of surprise, but a hot moan followed. Her hand on my breast pinched my nipple and I nipped at her neck in response.

"Hajimeru," Akira said.

It was as if he'd just cracked a whip. Dominic didn't need to translate that we'd begun. The submissive woman disappeared and a new Yuriko hovered over me. She shoved my shoulders back until I was flat on the dining table, the men staring down at me. Her mouth turned up in a devious smile, and she leaned over. Her lips found my nipple and she swirled her tongue on the flesh, startling me.

I gripped her head in my hands, holding her to me. It felt good, but listening to the effect on the men was even hotter. Dominic sucked in a deep, loud breath and my pussy clenched. He was going to enjoy the show I was about to put on.

Her mouth sucked at my sensitive, pebbled nipple, and both of her hands tightened on my breasts. She caressed me for a moment as if enjoying the experience, but didn't stay on my tits long. She was on a mission, after all. I moaned when her lips descended over my belly and arched my back into her trailing kisses. When she closed in on where I was wet, I once again wrapped her ponytail in my fist.

My head rolled toward Dominic as I sighed. Warm breath was between my legs. Then her tongue plunged inside and I stared at him through half-opened eyes, his face full of desire. He was already breathing hard. The tongue caressed up and flicked over my clit, drawing a moan.

"You like watching her lick my pussy?"

He shifted in his seat, adjusting himself. "Yeah, but that pussy's mine. It only comes for me, don't forget."

I gasped as her tongue moved over my flesh, faster now. My eyes closed and I tightened my grip on her hair. Okay, maybe this wasn't going to be a walk in the park. Flames of pleasure licked at me every time she did. I tugged on her hair, attempting to control. *Let's not get too good at that, Yuriko.*

Her head lifted away so she could say something. It was to Dominic, apparently. He came up out of the chair and seized my hands.

"Wait–" I cried, but he moved to the head of the table and stretched my arms out, pinning them to the tabletop. Uh, oh. His hands on me, him looming above with a hint of a smile on his lips . . . this shit just got fucking real.

Her hands had been on my knees, and now they skirted up my thighs, traveling closer to that mouth tasting me. One stopped there, but the other . . . A finger eased inside me. Out. In. Faster. Hotter. I gulped down a huge breath.

"Are you going to be good?" Dominic asked on a low voice.

"Yeah. How much longer?"

He shifted my wrists to one hand so he could look at the watch I'd given him. "You've got seven more minutes."

Oh, Christ. I kept my breathing steady and focused on

that. Not her soft tongue or the finger sliding in me. Her pace was slow but that was dangerous. It gave her room to work with. To build need inside me that could erupt with little or no warning. I glanced down at the dark head of hair moving between my legs. It was so erotic. This timid woman was desperate to bring me pleasure. I had to look away.

Dominic leaned down and kissed me, but I turned my head at the last second.

"No. I don't need any fucking help."

He grinned, but actually respected my boundary for once. He straightened and his gaze crept back to the woman whose tongue darted all the way inside me. Then, she fucking moaned. Akira exhaled loudly. He seemed to be enjoying the show. The way her pink tongue fluttered on my skin, her mouth shiny from my arousal. Oh, shit. I closed my eyes again, reminding myself not to watch.

"Hanmichi." Akira's voice rang out.

"Halfway," Dominic echoed. "Is it starting to get difficult?"

It was difficult about four minutes ago, but I didn't want anyone to know that. "I can handle it." It might have been more believable if I wasn't panting when I said it. A second finger pushed its way alongside the first, filling me with more acute need. I bit down on my bottom lip to quiet the moan.

"You are so fucking sexy like this," he said in that deep, rough voice. "All crazy and desperate to hold it together. It turns me on like you can't imagine."

"That shit is . . . Not. Helping." My eyes opened and sought relief somewhere that didn't make me think about him or the woman lashing me with her tongue where I was swollen and aching. I'd hoped looking at Akira might do the trick, but I was dead wrong. His gaze was on Yuriko, studying her, but he must have felt my eyes on him. His head turned slowly and he gave me the full intensity of his stare.

It was ruthless. Brutal.

The sudden desire to please him was crushing. I couldn't fail at this, because if I did, who knew what this man would do to me via Dominic? Akira looked like he knew a thousand ways to please and punish. I choked back a panicked, excited gasp.

"Three more minutes."

Akira repeated the warning to Yuriko and she let loose a sound of frustration. She used the fingers of one hand to spread me open to her hurried tongue, and continued to fuck me with her other hand, plunging deeper and deeper.

"Shit," I murmured under my breath. That felt really fucking good. I tried to shift away from her, but Akira didn't like that. His sharp tone was directed at Dominic.

"Don't cheat, devil woman."

"Give me back my hands," I pleaded. I needed to slow this train way the fuck down.

"Come on, you can do this. It doesn't feel as good as my cock, does it?"

What the fuck? Like I needed to think about that right now. I tugged at his hold on my wrists, but it just made his grip tighten. Oh, I was in trouble now. I couldn't stop the moans from rolling out of me, or my back from bowing off the table.

Prickly anticipation washed over my skin. I was getting close. Too close. She could sense it too. The urgent pace of those delicate fingers fucking me was dangerous. I willed my hips to stay still and not match her rhythm.

"Ninety seconds."

I started counting in my head. I pictured the numbers. She was as desperate as I was. Her hand abandoned my clit and crawled up to grab one of my tits, squeezing hard.

"Oh, god . . ."

I gulped down air. The fingers inside me retreated, and she used them to tap my clit. Short, sharp, and rapid taps, followed by hard and furious rubbing. She spoke to me directly, either begging or pleading.

"Shit, *oh shit* . . ." My body screamed for release. It demanded the rush of pleasure I was barely holding back. I just had a fingertip's grip on control on it.

"Thirty seconds, almost there." Dominic's voice was hurried and he spoke over Akira, who'd risen from his chair as we closed in on the deadline.

I wasn't going to make it. Her fingers pushed at just the right stop, stirring me into a meltdown. *No,* I told myself. *Just wait.* At some point my black pumps had fallen off, and now my heels scored down the table.

That hot mouth. She used both hands, one on the outside and one jammed what felt like three fingers deep inside me. I cried out with pleasure. No, no, no . . .

I was trembling and writhing, my forehead wrinkled in concentration. Everyone was talking at me, Dominic urging me to hold back, and I could only guess what Yuriko was asking me to do. Certainly everyone was watching. Payton McCreary wasn't the appetizer tonight. I was the motherfucking main course.

"Ten seconds." His hands coursed up my arms, sliding past my elbows. I held my breath. The weight of the orgasm was crushing and my heart wanted to burst out of my chest.

"Dominic," I cried. *Wait!*

A hand curled around the bottom of my chin and tilted it up to him. "Three . . . two . . . one. Come for me. Right now."

chapter
TWENTY-FOUR

I shattered. And I screamed, but it was silenced under Dominic's kiss as I came undone like I hadn't before. The sun had been liquefied and poured over my skin, followed by acute pleasure that burned and disconnected my brain. I lost all sensation except for the heat and satisfaction of his words. I'd pleased both men without touching them. That made the orgasm last longer. My back banged against the table when I flopped back down on it, returning lazily to reality one deep breath at a time, all the while kissing him. His command broke me into pieces, but that kiss put me back together.

When the kiss ended, Dominic and I both turned our attention to our Japanese friends. Yuriko was standing between my legs, one hand on my knee, but her fearful gaze was on her Master. Akira spoke a long sentence that forced her gaze downward.

"He said, you didn't try very hard, perhaps you wanted to fail. Take off your dress."

Yuriko's hands went to the knotted belt on her hip. As she undid it, her eyes flitted to Dominic's for a moment then on to mine. Once the time limit had passed, she'd retreated back into her submissive role, and now she looked shy. Nervous.

The dress fell open and dropped off her shoulders, exposing her lacy white bra and panties. She looked almost virginal, but maybe this was on purpose. Maybe Akira had commanded her to wear that.

She wasn't curvy, but had a beautiful, slender body. I was jealous of her long, thin legs, narrow hips, and her perfectly flat stomach. Her breasts weren't huge, but nicely proportional. Akira was a lucky man.

"Tell her that she's beautiful," I said to Dominic.

He paused.

"What is it? You don't think so?"

"No, I do. There's, like, six different ways to say everything in Japanese. It's all about context, so I'm trying to find the right way to say it without making her uncomfortable."

Words finally spilled from Dominic's mouth and Yuriko blushed. Then Akira grabbed a handful of her hair and shoved her forward so she was bent over on top of me, her face on my chest. Her head lifted and her startled gaze found mine. We both heard Akira's belt unbuckle, judging from her reaction. Holy shit, he didn't want to waste any time, huh? I turned my head to Dominic while my arms closed around her tight body.

There was discussion between the men and I didn't need the translation. When I lifted my head to peer at Akira over Yuriko, I saw him coil the belt in a fist, leaving the tail of it out as he stepped up behind her. He feathered the edge of the belt over her back, tracing patterns as he worked his way down. She shivered in my arms. Then her soft ponytail of hair spilled over me as she laid her ear down between my breasts, her eyes closed, her lips whispering something.

"She's saying, I need this, Master."

The belt slammed down on the table just outside my leg, making us both jump.

"He said, your needs are my concern, not yours."

His first lash was a gentle slap of leather against the

back of her panties. Like he was warming her up to it.

"*Ichi, Arigatō,*" she said. *One, thank you.*

I let out a sigh when she nuzzled between my breasts and her delicate hands cupped them. There was a louder slap of leather and she flinched.

"*Ni, Arigatō.*"

My hand wrapped around the back of her neck, stroking down the length of her spine. This time the leather whipped as it hit her and she gasped.

It was shocking to be under her while this happened. I could feel every crack of his belt against her through her soft body, but not feel the pain. At first I begin to wonder what that pain would feel like. And then as the lashes became more intense . . . I began to *want* it. But what about him?

Dominic had moved from the head of the table to my side, watching the scene play out. As Akira's blows increased, he spoke to Dominic. Like he was demonstrating. I got a tingling, anticipatory shudder at the thought. Those blue eyes studied the movements of Akira's hands as if determined to pick up every detail of the lesson.

The woman lying on me was moaning. Not in pain, but what looked and sounded like ecstasy. I brushed my fingers over the clasp of her bra and dared to look at Akira. I wanted the fabric gone so I could have all of her warm skin on mine.

His dark eyes were intense but it looked like he understood what I'd asked without words. "*Hai.*"

I undid the hook and pulled the straps off her shoulders. She rose up on her hands and pulled the bra off, showing me her round breasts and small, dark nipples that were already hard. She looked so sexy topless, I had to touch her. I crushed my hand to her heaving chest as she lay back down on me. Her skin was softer than silk.

"*Roku, Arigatō.*"

Yuriko had made it to six, barely jumping with each new strike. I was out of control and touching her firm tits wasn't enough anymore. My fingers walked down her back and to her hips, hooking under the top of her panties. Once again, I checked with her Master if this was allowed.

"*Hai.*"

I eased the lace down one side at a time, inch by inch, until her ass was completely uncovered. Since I was trapped beneath her on the table, I couldn't get them more than halfway down her thighs, so I left them bunched there.

She whimpered when the leather snapped against her bare flesh, but she thanked him, over and over again. I snaked a hand between our bodies to try to slip a finger inside her, but she was too far away. My fingertips barely brushed over the short patch of hair she had down there.

Akira's hand closed on her shoulder and pulled her upright. Whatever he said next made Dominic exhale loudly.

"I didn't understand the first part, but he wants her to play with you while he finishes punishing her."

I stayed right where I was on the table, but my breath caught. "I want your cock in me."

His chest rose and fell. Obviously Dominic wanted that. He'd finished unbuttoning his shirt at some point and it hung open, giving me a peek at the sculpture of muscle that he was. His hand went to his crotch and tried to smooth out his erection, adjusting himself. It was so fucking sexy.

Yuriko tugged her panties down the rest of the way, revealing the tiny landing strip of fuzz at the delta of her legs. Color flushed her face, but she didn't remain standing there.

She walked to the closet and dug items out of the bag she'd been carrying, bringing them back to the table.

A bottle of lube in one hand, a silver starter toy in the other. She set them beside me and placed her hands just outside my hips, her breasts swinging over me. Fuck, she looked gorgeous. I stroked a hand from one breast to the other, teasing her nipples.

She took one lash from his belt in that position before dipping her head down and tasting me again. I felt . . . wild. I was so far gone in enjoyment, I didn't notice much of what was going on around me. The men were talking again, but it wasn't for instruction.

The back of Dominic's hand brushed on my shoulder. "Slide over here."

He helped me move over so I was right at the side of the table, still on my back. Still getting teased by Yuriko's tongue that licked at just the right spot. Dominic undid his belt. Unbuttoned and unzipped his pants. The fabric slid down his legs and in a single breath, his boxers were tugged out of the way and his cock was out.

"Yes," I panted. I wrapped a firm grip on him, stroking from the tip all the way to the base.

"You want this? Open up."

He wasn't gentle when he shoved inside my mouth, and that was fine with me. I'd learned the taste of Dominic and now I craved it. I loved feeling him slide between my lips, his velvet skin on my tongue, the struggled breaths he took when I brought him to the brink. He set a hand on my jaw, controlling my pace.

There was a smack of leather against skin and the mouth sucking at my clit paused. Lips moved over my flesh as she spoke. *Ten, thank you.*

I sucked at Dominic and stared up at him. My heart was crashing in my chest. Abruptly the mouth on me was gone as Japanese came from Akira. Her knees thudded on the table as she climbed up, posing over me on her hands and knees. What was the plan now? She came close, watching as I hollowed out my cheeks. I pulled him out of my mouth with a loud pop, only to clench him in a hand.

Dominic shook his head in response to Akira's question. *"Īe."*

Another word I knew. *No.* I pumped him with my fist, smoothing my thumb over the tip and he groaned.

"What did he just ask you?" I said.

"If I wanted her to help you."

My hand paused. Really? He didn't want two women to go down on him at once? He wrapped his hand around mine and urged me to stroke him again.

"Doing that," he said, "might mean you'd have to do the same to him."

Oh. Yeah, that made sense. He didn't want to share me with another man. Yuriko let out a moan that stole my attention. The bottle of lube was gone from the table and the cap popped open. Her almond-shaped eyes peered down at me and she snared her bottom lip in her teeth. Akira was preparing to push that soft limit.

I kept one hand on Dominic, stroking and twisting, but my other hand reached up and slipped behind her neck, holding her head, trying to reassure. The lube clunked on the table and Akira snatched up the toy. Yuriko was trembling, but it didn't seem like she was going to say no. In fact, her face was unreadable. She might have been trembling from excitement.

"Relax," I whispered in a soothing voice, and Dominic echoed my words in Japanese. "You might not like it at first, but it'll feel good."

I couldn't see much other than the woman looming over me, but her head lowered until her forehead was in the crook of my neck and her breath hot on my shoulder. The line of her spine drew my gaze up to her cherry-red backside and further to her Master towering over us. Akira's dark look swept to me, then back to her ass that was presented in the air. He had a hand on the swell of one cheek, and his fingers dug in as his other arm moved. The silver toy began to disappear.

She murmured something as her shoulders tensed, but Dominic didn't translate. I didn't ask permission. My hand abandoned its hold on her neck and streamed down over her breasts and taut belly, all the way until it was buried in between her legs.

Yuriko gasped. More hurried words from her, followed by words from Akira. I glanced at Dominic. He was watching me, and the lust in his eyes made my mouth water. Sex clung in the air, stuck to my skin like sweat. I itched with need for Dominic like a junkie who'd gone too long without a fix.

Her skin was hot and wet, so my finger slipped into her easily. She sucked on my neck, and I didn't fight her when that mouth traveled a steady line upward. Over my jaw, onto my lips. Her kiss was sweet and pleasant, but not what I wanted right now. Dirty. Raw. That was what I wanted. I broke the kiss and fucked her with two fingers. And I could feel the toy in her ass as Akira worked it deeper.

"*Arigatō,*" she cried. He must have gotten it all the way in.

He said something back that sounded soft and like praise. My fingers pumped in and out of her pussy, and sometimes I'd pull them out and rub a circle on the nub just above. Yuriko seemed to like that. She made a quiet mewling sound. Was she going to stay quiet when she came?

Her breathing grew rapid and uneven, and I moved my hands in time with each other. One inside her, curling back in search of her G-spot, my other hand sliding along the length of Dominic's massive cock. The one I'd been without for what felt like a millennium.

Conversation seemed to be a struggle for Dominic, but I didn't think he was having a hard time understanding Akira. Yuriko was getting close to orgasm, and it was from what I was doing to her.

"She just asked," Dominic's hand stilled mine, probably because he was getting close, "for permission for something."

Akira's hands roved over her back like a sensual massage. Her breathing was rapid and crossed into a pant. I hurried my fingers, fumbling them over her flesh, wanting her to get that release she deserved.

Yes, Akira said.

The woman on me convulsed at the word and gave a tremendous sigh, her eyes shut tightly when the orgasm took her. I slowed my hand almost to a stop, but could feel her muscles clenching on my fingers. There was a rush of wetness between my thighs, but everywhere else burst into flames.

She lifted up on shaky arms as Akira's voice broke the quiet.

"He told her to get off the table and onto her knees." There was a short exchange, and she sucked in a breath.

"She wanted to know if he was going to take that out of her, but he said no. It pleases him."

She stepped down gingerly off the table with the toy still in her ass, and I was cold when her body was gone from mine. But then Dominic moved. He stepped out of the pants at his ankles, his gaze full of desire and unwavering from mine, and I was right back to being on fire again. Those clear blue eyes were exquisite. There were plenty of beautiful things in this foreign country, but none of them compared to him.

He stood between my legs and bent over me, setting his lips on mine as I arched to push my breasts against his bare chest, my fingertips weaving through his hair. I wrapped my silk-covered legs around his waist, urging him to take me. To own me, even though he already did.

"Hands up," he whispered with a smile when the kiss ended.

My knuckles skimmed across the smooth wood as I put my hands above my head, expecting him to link ours together. Instead, Japanese came from him, and a warm, large hand closed around my wrists. Akira's. I tilted my head back to look at him.

I swallowed a breath. His authoritarian stare was on me while the hand not holding my wrists was on Yuriko's ponytail, guiding her to suck him off. I ripped my gaze away. Watching her go down on him was hot, but those ruthless eyes would incinerate me. Could he feel my pulse racing under his firm grip?

Dominic's eyes weren't as ruthless, but there was power and dominance behind them as he straightened over me and set his thumb on my clit. I moaned in satisfaction when he pressed down, grinding the pad of his thumb where I was swollen and sensitive.

"Enough with the fooling around." I fought to keep my voice from sounding desperate. "I want my reward for being a good girl."

He grinned, a devious expression spreading across his face. "Yeah? You want it?"

The thumb stayed on my wet skin, toying with my clit, but his other hand clamped around his hard dick just under the head. And he pressed his cock into me. He guided his way until the tip was barely inside, the fist around him stopping it from going any further.

"Come for me. Right now."

I hadn't been all that close, and he was only an inch inside, but the thumb . . . and the connection . . . I was doomed.

"Yes, yes . . ." I cried, tipping over into a wave of sudden ecstasy.

I struggled against the hand holding me down, desperate to pull Dominic onto me and get him to plunge all the way inside, but Akira's hand was too strong. It made the orgasm intense.

"You want some more?"

I gasped for air. I lifted my head up over my heaving chest. Of course I fucking wanted more. He retreated and the fist moved down an inch. One fucking inch. "No, Dominic. More–"

My brain and body couldn't figure out who was in charge when he pushed inside me again, only a little deeper than the last time. His thumb stirred. I figured out who was in charge then. It was one hundred percent him.

"You're going to come on my cock," he said, "one goddamn inch at a time. Come for me, Payton. Right now."

But I'd just . . . It was too soon . . . Oh . . . oh . . . holy shit. I turned my head to the side to bury my face in my arm as I came. *Again.* Less than a minute between them. This one wasn't long but it was sharp as a knife and tore through me. I cried out a sob of pleasure.

"Yes," Dominic said. Even with my eyes shut, I could hear the smile in his words. "Yeah. Fuck, that feels so good when you're coming."

Akira's commanding voice rang out and drew me back into the moment.

"He said I should make you come again." Once more the cock began to slide out. His fist shifted back another inch.

"No." Panic filled my voice. Twice was shocking and a fluke. Plus that wasn't anywhere near enough time to recover. I couldn't catch my breath.

"Yes. This body is mine. It does exactly what I tell it to do." He inched forward. "I'm going to show you what you're capable of."

The thick cock pushed and I welcomed him even as I felt spent and exhausted. I held my breath when the fist pressed against the outside of my pussy, the rest of him sheathed inside. He was going to give me the command any second and I wasn't going to be able to do it. I shuddered on the tabletop, rattled against Akira's hold. *Oh god . . . oh god . . .*

Dominic's gaze was inescapable. "Come for me, right now."

I screamed as the pleasure rippled and crept prickling across my spine. Then his hand fell away and his hard cock drove deep, all the way into me. It sent me into euphoria, and everything went black.

TWENTY-FIVE

Warm lips skimmed over my cheek and my head turned, searching to get them on mine. A rough voice asked, "Where did you go?"

My eyes fluttered open. Dominic was only a breath away, his eyes hinted at his concern. I blinked to clear the fog from my head and pulled my lips back in a satisfied smile. "Kiss me," I said.

He lowered his head so there was no space between us. His mouth moved on mine in a sultry, passionate kiss that tasted like love. It was the best kind of kiss. Akira had released his hold on me, so my hands settled on Dominic's shoulders.

His cock was lodged inside me, and as we kissed, he began to move hesitantly. Slow, the way he liked it. The way he'd taught me to like it. Taught me to love it, really. He'd taught me to love all sorts of things in the two months I'd been with him.

Beneath him, I tried to return the pleasure he was so good at giving. I'd wanted to fuck him on this table, but instead I made love. It wasn't hot, it was incendiary. Akira had picked up the pace with Yuriko and was fucking her mouth aggressively, but I ignored that. All I wanted was my boyfriend. This man I *loved*. And as soon as I could tell him, I would. Just not right now, not when we weren't alone. I'd have to show him until then.

He groaned when I widened my legs and pulled him

in as deep as possible, then flexed my internal muscles, squeezing him. He rocked against me, gliding in and out, his pace quickening and his ragged breath loud in my ear. My nipples dragged over his chest as his thrusts grew intense. Not as intense as this connection between us, but maybe nothing else could be.

"Oh, god," I moaned. "Don't stop. Don't ever stop."

He silenced me under his powerful kiss, his hips pounding into me. Faster. And harder. On, and on. At some point, I think Akira came. There were a slew of hurried Japanese words, followed by quiet. The only sounds were Dominic's body slapping against mine and my moans.

Dominic made good on my request not to stop, I mean, it felt like it. Time stood still when we were together. His lips were persistent on my skin. If they weren't on my mouth, they were on my neck, feathering kisses there.

"Mine," he whispered.

There was no hesitation from me. "So fucking yours."

A shift went through his body like last time, only it was more pronounced. He was a flurry of action, burying his face in my breasts while his hips drove into me, endlessly repeating until his breath came and went in enormous gasps.

He came. Hard. And loud.

His moan sounded like it was created deep inside his throat, and his cock jerked with spasms, pulsing inside me and fading slowly. God, that felt so good. Each pulse sent a small wave of bliss up my legs. His heavy body collapsed on top of me while he struggled to regain his breath.

"Jesus." It was barely audible from him. "Did I ever tell you that you were worth the wait?"

"What?"

"A year without sex to get to you. I'd do it again in a heartbeat."

I laughed softly and kissed him. When it was over, he turned his head to the couple. Yuriko was slumped down on the couch with Akira kneeling between her legs, his mouth buried in her pussy. She had her eyes shut and both hands in his hair, tugging on it while soft words came from her. Like she was pleading.

Akira sat back from her and pulled something from his back pocket. A tiny black pouch. Yuriko bolted to sit upright, her eyes wide and fixed on it.

"He just told her that she's his."

Dominic and I watched him open the pouch and pull out the glittering strand of diamonds. I gasped. Not just at the decadent jewelry, but what that short necklace really was. A collar. She seemed to be gushing while Akira leaned forward and fastened it around her throat. The stones glittered when it was done.

Akira's smile shifted away to fill with lust, as if seeing his submissive collared was overwhelming. He bent back down and kissed her between her thighs like he was desperate.

Dominic said a whole bunch of things to them as he stood and withdrew from me, and his hand slipped under my shoulder, guiding me to sit up. I groaned. My muscles were stiff from spending too much time on the table. I'd say table sex was overrated, but not when it was with Dominic.

"I told them they can stay in the guest room if they want to. C'mon, let's go to bed." He helped me stand up, but grinned. "Unless you want to . . . watch them?"

It was so hot, seeing her heels rake down his back, begging him as she rode that tongue.

"I kind of do, but . . . I'm fucking exhausted."

He kissed my forehead. "Maybe we can talk them into a show some other time."

We lingered for another quiet moment before shuffling into the bedroom. He flipped on the lights and got into bed, his gaze following the descent of my garters. Once I was naked, I crawled onto my side of our bed, and the lights went out, immediately followed by his arm around me.

My pulse quickened in the darkness. Finally alone with him. My heart leaped up into my throat, blocking my ability to speak. I swallowed. My mouth was dry, too.

I'd only said it and meant it to one other man before. Why was I nervous about this? I certainly knew how he felt. *Stop this,* I commanded myself. Tell him. The blood rushed in my ears. Finally, I worked up the nerve.

I didn't realize that the arm on me was growing heavier until it was too late. Fuck. I'd spent too much time being an idiot, and now he was asleep. I drifted my fingertips over his cheek, seeing if he'd stir, but he was down for the count.

Tomorrow, Dominic.

The bed sank down and jostled me awake. Dominic was already dressed in his suit, his breath faintly smelling of coffee.

"What time is it?" I scrubbed a hand over my eyes and glanced at the clock. It was late. Way too late for me to get him back in the shower, or do much of anything. "Why the fuck didn't you wake me up?"

He gave me a sheepish look. "I figured you were tired. You slept through the alarm." His hand cupped my face and that thumb smoothed over to pause at the center of my lips. "I love you."

Warm lips were on mine, and gone a moment later as he stood and straightened his tie. I'd been on autopilot while not fully awake, and just realized I'd missed the opportunity to echo it back. His heavy footsteps carried him away from the bed and out the room.

I threw back the covers and darted after him into the living room. "Wait a minute."

He pulled on his coat and turned to look at me, the corner of his mouth lifting in a seductive smirk. "No, devil woman. I'm already going to have to hurry to catch the train. We don't have time."

It was because I was stark naked. I'd been too tired to pull on clothes after last night. Well, shit. I didn't want to do this naked and he was already late. He stared at me, ex-pectantly. I'd have to cover. So I put a hand on my hip and gave him a seductive smile right back. "You sure you don't have time?"

He shook his head and his expression was wanton. "Careful. Maybe I'll tell you to stay just like that all day and wait for me."

"Try it," I said, smug, "and see what happens."

"I dunno, you did a pretty good job obeying last night." The muscles low in my belly clenched. He glanced at his watch and turned serious. "I really gotta go, I'll see you later."

He slipped out the door. Now I stood in our empty apartment, disappointed. But determined. Maybe this was a good thing it hadn't happened this morning. It was bet-ter to wait until tonight, until we had lots of time to act on our feelings.

The day dragged. I spent it working out and researching a plan of action for the visa, then walked to the market
in the late afternoon and bought some food for dinner. The
problem with such a small kitchen and fridge meant you had
to shop about every day, but at least it kept everything fresh.

He wasn't as good about putting stuff away as I was.
When I returned, I dropped the groceries on the counter
and put them in their places, then tackled the rest of the
clutter he let accumulate. In such a small place, junk mail
piled up quickly and made me claustrophobic.

The opened letter in English caught my attention. The
Chase Sports logo in the corner was recognizable and I was
too interested not to take a peek. It felt like the only time I
saw written English anymore on paper was on the tourist
brochures that were riddled with grammatical errors.

There was a check attached to the letter. I scanned the
number of zeros at the end of it, and reminded myself of the
conversion to yen–

Holy shit. It wasn't in yen. There was a US dollar sym-
bol on this check. $100,000. The memo line of it read "Com-
mitment Bonus."

I had to read the letter three times before it sank in. I
pulled out my phone to text him, or call him, but instead I
stared at it in my frozen hand. What the fuck was going on?
Dread poured into my stomach, topped off with suspicion
and anger. I set the phone down and my vacant stare shifted
to the floor. I'd need to see his face when I confronted him
about this, and he should be home soon. I'd just have to
stew in these mixed emotions until then.

The sun set. The longer I waited, the angrier I got. I
couldn't think of any reasonable explanation for why he'd

kept me in the dark about this. My hands balled into fists. I needed to have an escape route planned if this discussion went the way I thought it might, but hoped it didn't. I packed my suitcase like a mindless robot. So much of what I'd bought while here wouldn't fit. Stuff he'd bought me. Clothes, shoes, silk kimonos . . . Those fake wedding rings would fit, but the fuck if I was taking them.

I rolled my suitcase out into the living space, sat on the couch, and watched the door. My knee bounced with impatience. My skin itched and was annoying. I needed him to get home. Now.

A lifetime later the door swung open and he strolled in, dropping a new stack of mail on the counter. He went rigid when he saw my packed suitcase, me perched beside it on the couch, my eyes burning.

"What's wrong? The visa—?"

"Tell me about the hundred thousand dollar check there." I pointed to the table where I'd set the check face up, just in case he needed a fucking reminder.

Dominic's gaze went hazy and shifted away from mine. It was clear he was struggling to put together in his head whatever he wanted to say. Probably assembling a lie.

"Say something," I demanded.

The blue-eyed gaze swept back to me and he looked defeated. "I hated it here. I couldn't do another year of it. After the first few months, I hoped it would get easier. It didn't, it got worse. So I put in a request to break my contract and go home, which was going to fuck everything up with my job. I mean, doing that? It was just a step away from quitting."

I stared at him. I didn't care about his job right now.

"My request got approved December third, but I had to

stay at least another month until the new hire was trained."

My hands balled into fists on my thighs. "That's weird." My voice was icy. "I don't remember you mentioning *any* of this."

This time I didn't find embarrassed Dominic quite so adorable. "I never thought it'd get approved, and you'd been here a week."

"So you got it approved. What the hell happened?"

He gave me a pained look. "You gave me more time, and I started to think I could tough it out. I was on the fence, but Chase was clear what they wanted. They offered me the commitment bonus if I agreed to fulfill my original contract."

"I don't understand." My blood boiled in my veins. "How could . . .?"

He raked a hand through his hair, visibly upset. "I didn't know what the fuck to do, all right? If I canceled my contract, I'd be going back to a job where I'd never get any-where, and the year of hell I put up with would have been for nothing." He began to pace the tiny living room and he looked like he was coming unhinged. "It's so much better with you here, and you kept agreeing to stay—"

I launched to my feet. "I didn't know there was this whole other option. You never said a goddamn word about it!"

He stopped and turned, and his expression was devas-tating. "I know. I kept putting it off because I didn't know what to do, and then too much time had gone by and I had to make the decision."

In the back of my mind a voice reminded me that I was the same, how I avoided until the last possible moment, but I was too angry to listen. "We could have gone home." The words burned in my throat. "When? When did you decide?"

His face didn't change and his expression was like a knife in my heart. "After New Year's."

Then, the knife twisted and the pain knocked the air clean from my lungs. He'd just lied to me. I couldn't see it in his face. His pupils didn't dilate, his eyes didn't drift up while he accessed the part of his brain that created lies. His breathing didn't change its cadence.

The only way I knew he was lying was from the date in the letter attached to the check. Three weeks ago he'd signed the re-commitment paperwork. He must have forgotten that was in there, but then again, he'd left the envelope out, forgotten, too.

"Don't lie to me," I snapped. "Fuck, I wish I'd never found it."

"I'm sorry. Please, I knew it was a mistake to keep it from you, but I didn't know how to fix it . . ." He approached me cautiously until he was only a foot away. "The idea of losing you? It scares the shit out of me. I'll do whatever I can to keep that from happening."

My heart thudded to a stop and died. My skin turned to stone. He'd lied to me, and I couldn't tell. He'd been lying to me for at least a month and I'd been oblivious. Which meant – Oh, god.

"You'll do anything. You'll say *anything* to get me to stay with you, including . . ." Suddenly I was right back in Ian's apartment, the blue velvet box in my hand. I wrapped a shaky hand around my suitcase, but Dominic's arms stopped me.

"No. I love you. Real, Payton."

I stared into his eyes. They looked the same as they always did, whether he was telling the truth or not.

"Why should I believe that? You've been lying to me since I got here."

"I didn't lie. Yeah, I left something out that I should have told you–"

"Still a lie in my book."

His hands had trapped my waist, and they tightened at this accusation. His jaw clenched. "Yeah? You want to talk about not saying things you should? I'm in love with you. You got any kind of response to that?"

I took in a sharp breath. No way were those words coming from me right now.

"Every time you don't answer, it's a fucking lie, and we both know it."

"This is about you," I struggled free from his hold, "and how you made a massive decision without telling me. Maybe I've decided to go home, and you don't get a say in that. How does that feel? You like it?"

Whoa, no. He definitely didn't. His gaze turned hard and dark.

"And how exactly are you planning on getting home?"

Holy shit.

TWENTY-SIX

I'd never considered he wouldn't let me leave, which had been stupid on my part. He'd just said he'd do anything to keep me here. But still, I was shocked he'd resort to a level that low.

"You owe me a plane ticket." My voice came out uneven. I started to panic, feeling pinned down. Captive.

"I do, but we've got to talk about this."

"You had two months to talk." And he hadn't. Maybe he never would have. "Were you even going to tell me?"

He took a deep breath. "Yeah."

Well, that was less than convincing. Once again I wrapped my hand around my suitcase handle. "I want my fucking ticket, now."

"Payton, c'mon, I'm sorry. Can you stop with the suitcase?" He wrenched my hand off of it, and then wouldn't release me. "You can't just leave."

"The hell I can't." I was breathing so hard, I started to get lightheaded. The hurt of it all was too great. I felt trapped, and his hand around mine made it worse. "Let go of me, go to your computer, and start looking at flight times."

His shoulders rose and then fell, and the expression on his face turned unreadable. "No." It came out normal, but I saw his Adam's apple dip as he swallowed hard. Blue eyes examined my reaction, waiting anxiously for my response.

This was it. He'd pushed me before, but I couldn't bend any further to him. This wasn't bending, it was breaking. If

I didn't push back, I'd never be able to draw another line again. He knew I didn't have the money or the credit limit on my credit cards to afford a ticket.

I yanked my hand free from his grasp and dug my phone out, doing the time change in my head. Christ, it was just after five in the morning there.

"What are you doing?" he asked, but I ignored him and dialed.

Logan answered on the third ring, sounding out of breath. He was a marathoner, so hopefully I'd caught him while he was on a training run. "Payton? What's going on?"

"I need a really big favor," I said, locking my gaze on Dominic. "I need you to sell my car."

"*What?*" both men asked at the same time.

"Dominic won't pay for me to come home."

That was as far as I got before Dominic tore the phone out of my hand and put it to his ear. "Evie, wait a minute—"

Dominic's eyes went wider when he realized whom I was talking to. The reality was that Evie had never bought or sold a car, and she knew shit about mine. If I asked her to do this, she'd go straight to Logan for help, so this saved time. Plus, Logan was more administrative than Evie anyway.

I stood silent as Dominic appeared to get an earful from Logan.

"She's upset because I screwed up," he said into the phone, "but she doesn't need to—" He focused on me. "You don't need to sell your car. If you really want to leave me that bad," he pulled out his wallet and plunked it down on the table, "go ahead."

I stared at the black square of leather while I heard Dominic mutter a goodbye and hang up. My phone was set with a thud beside his wallet. My bones hurt. My eyes felt like they had acid in them.

"I don't want to go," I said, "but I can't stay here." In less than a month I was going to have to leave Japan anyway.

"Payton, I can't leave."

I shrugged, but inside I felt like I was cracking. Breaking into a thousand jagged pieces. "*You* made that choice."

"Don't do this, please." His voice was so desperate, it was terrifying. "I love you. I'm sorry. I love you so much . . . How can you just walk away from that?"

My eyes filled with more acid, and it spilled over my eyelashes. Tears. He'd made me fucking cry—the first time since that deathly silent spring break my sophomore year. I swiped at my cheeks and reached for his wallet, but suddenly Dominic's arms were around me. His lips slammed into mine. *No.* I turned my head away, breaking the kiss.

"I'm sorry," he whispered. "We belong together, and . . . I can prove it."

Because I was pressed up against him, I could feel how fast his heart was banging in his chest. I put my hands on his shoulders to ease him away.

"Come for me," he said, his voice hushed and unsure. "Right now."

"What? No," I gasped. What the fuck was this? That was the absolute last thing I wanted. But my body had a hard time fighting two months of training, and I was filled with horror when the first wave of pleasure began.

"No!" I gasped again, this time for myself but it was too late. It was happening whether I wanted it or not. I shut my eyes, determined not to look at him, willing my traitorous body to stop. Futile. The heat spread like fire through gaso-

line and I shuddered. Since I had limited control, I did the
only thing I had left. I dug my fingernails into his shoulders,
biting them into his flesh.

I heard him make a noise of discomfort while I came.
My body bucked in his hold, and thankfully the damn thing
went away as quick as it had arrived, but it left me reeling.
My eyes flew open and I gave him the darkest, angriest look
I had. The one that said, "Drop dead, motherfucker."

"How could you?" I shoved him away and once the orgasm had completely left my body, it was replaced with fury.
He'd used that command on me like a weapon, flexing his
control. When I first arrived here, Dominic had said he was
going to own me, and I'd never felt more owned than I did
right now.

He'd made me a slave.

"This is over." I snatched up my phone in a shaky hand.
"I'm going to the airport. Text me with the flight details, and
then delete my number from your phone."

"Fuck, I'm sorry! Wait, please—"

Not a chance. I grabbed my suitcase and stormed
out the door, slamming it shut. He had enough sense not
to chase after me, which was good because I would have
stopped him any way possible.

I sat at the bar in Tokyo airport's first class lounge, staring at the three cubes of ice in my rum and Coke. I'd had two
already, and my thoughts were fuzzy and distracted. He'd
bought me a first-class ticket home. Was it supposed to be
a gesture? Part of an apology? It didn't make a statement if
that was his plan. We were both aware how much money

he'd come into recently.

That fucking check, with all its zeros and the months of lies that went with it.

"Excuse me, miss, do you speak English?"

I turned in my seat to face the male voice. Older, maybe mid-forties. Friendly eyes and a crooked nose, packaged in a suit. British, maybe?

"Yeah," I said. "I don't know how to speak anything else."

"Ah." His lips pulled back, revealing a matching crooked smile. "American." He made a face. "I meant, you sound American. I didn't mean to imply that Americans—"

I waved a hand. "I got it." Then I blinked with annoyance when he sat beside me without an invitation. I wanted to be alone.

"Are you on the flight to Heathrow?" He had a pleasant expression on his face, but it wasn't working for me.

I shook my head and took a big sip of my drink. "Chicago."

The man glanced at the monitor behind the bar. "You've gotten here early."

"I needed to get a head start on the liquid courage."

"Nervous flier? Me, too." He signaled the bartender. "I'm Simon." He probably thought he was charming and seductive.

I sighed. "Okay, Simon. Can I be honest with you?" God, two months with Dominic had taken its toll. I sounded like him now.

Simon nodded and looked curious about what I was about to say.

"I'm going to save you the effort. If you're hitting on me, it's not going to work."

The curious expression froze on his face. "Why not?"

"I'm not interested." I finished my drink and pushed the glass away with my fingertips. "Not in anyone right now, and definitely not a married man." My gaze dropped down to his hand on the bar, where the worn impression of a ring was obvious on his bare third finger.

His hand drew away as the pleasant smile faded to nothing. "I'm newly divorced."

My gaze sharpened on his shifting eyes, and I gave a short, bitter laugh. "Okay, newly divorced, and a fucking liar. So not interested."

Simon gave me a sour look and wandered away. I still had the ability to read liars . . . just not Dominic. I dug my phone out and stared at his text messages again. The flight information first, then:

> Text me when you land
> so I know you made it
> in safe.

That was it. No pleading, no more apologies, and there was terrible finality that made me sick. I'm sure he was pissed I'd walked out. Whether or not I walked away for good was up to him. I needed time and space. It just sucked how much space was about to be between us.

I did fine on takeoff, but thirteen hours is a long-ass time not to think about what had happened, and the Asian man sitting next to me looked mortified when I spent twenty minutes crying silently turned toward the window. I couldn't help it. I was exhausted and Dominic had broken the wall I'd built around this part of my feelings.

The nice thing about first class was I drank myself to

sleep, and the seats were pretty comfortable. It was six in the morning when I landed at O'Hare, and after customs and immigration, I was on the train toward my apartment in the thick of rush hour. It was loud, and dirty, more than I'd ever noticed before.

> I'm on the train leaving O'Hare.

> Okay, thanks for letting me know.

Dominic's emotionless text was unnerving. I spent the remainder of the ride overanalyzing it. When I got home, I slept in my bed – my first time sleeping alone in more than two months – and I hated it.

My intercom buzzed and woke me at noon. It was Logan, which immediately made me suspicious. I'd texted Evie this morning and made arrangements to have dinner with them when they got off work.

"Did Dominic send you?" I asked into the call box.

"I came to return your car."

Oh. I buzzed him up and pulled on a sweater and jeans.

It didn't register that he hadn't answered me about Dominic until I opened the door and was greeted with flowers.

"I'm sure you know who these are from," Logan said, lingering in the hallway. "Can I come in?"

I motioned for him to do so, but gave him a guarded look. "What a cliché. He shouldn't have asked you to do that."

"He didn't. I offered."

Logan evaluated the room and sat the vase of red roses on my kitchen counter. They were beautiful, but I refused to show my appreciation. A first-class ticket hadn't fazed me, so a dozen roses weren't going to either.

"Dominic told me what happened."

My neck burned hot and I clenched my teeth. "Oh, did he?"

Logan's face was serious. "All of it, and I mean, *all* of it. He knows how bad he screwed up."

I didn't know what to say. I picked up the flowers and moved them to the center of my kitchen table. "That conversation had to be awkward."

"Payton, he's a fucking mess."

"Good," I snapped. "Me, too."

Logan's face softened. "Look, I've been where he is. I kept secrets from Evie and it was the dumbest thing I ever did. I almost lost her."

"I remember." In fact, I'd been one of the people pushing her to forgive him.

He put his hands on his hips. "It was . . . really hard when she asked for space, but it helped her find a way to forgive me." Logan's stare bore down. "So I told Dominic to give you space. And I know it's none of my business, but do you think you might be able to, with some time?"

"Forgive him?" There was the $100,000 question, wasn't it? "I don't know."

Logan pressed his lips together and nodded. Then he pulled a set of keys from his pocket and set them on the counter. "I got your car up into the triple digits on the Stevenson."

My jaw fell. "You better be fucking joking." It was impossible to tell with him sometimes.

The corner of his mouth lifted in a smirk and his joke

helped ease some of the tension from my weary body.

He glanced at his phone. "I should probably head back to work. Evie said we're meeting for dinner tonight?"

"Yeah." I took the keys and put them in my purse. "Thanks for your help."

"Hey, anytime you want me to drive your car, I'm available."

I followed him to the door, and as he stepped through it, the words tumbled from my mouth. "I want to."

He paused. "What?"

"I *want* to forgive him. I just don't know if I can."

He looked startled, but it shifted to a pleased smile. "It always seemed to me that you, Payton, can get whatever you want."

On Thursday I met Joseph for lunch. He had something he wanted to discuss, but didn't want to do it over the phone. Maybe he wanted to apologize in person, but it wasn't necessary. I knew it wasn't personal.

"Where do you want to eat?" he'd asked.

"Anywhere that's not Asian."

So we picked a Mexican place near my apartment where the décor was a bit over the top, but the food was great. When I came in, Joseph was already seated at a table, wearing a sweater over a tie and dress shirt. He always looked professional, but today he looked . . . odd. Academic.

His dark eyes went large as he evaluated me. "You look different."

I sat at the table. "Yeah, I know. I've been out of town for a while, and the earliest appointment I could get at the salon is tomorrow." My hair color needed some serious help. But Joseph continued to look at me, confused. It was kind of annoying. "What?"

"You look older. And, honey, I don't mean it in a bad way."

Now I was really annoyed. "It's been two months, not two years."

Joseph's eyes warmed. "I'm sorry about how I handled that night. I didn't want to lose you, and lost control myself."

I let out a breath. "You didn't make him pay. I mean, more than the club's cut. Why?"

There was surprise in his eyes. "You said what it would do to you, how it would make you feel. Payton, I've always given you what you needed, when I could."

"Why?"

"I don't know. I like doing it. You and I are a lot alike."

It was at this moment I realized he looked different too. Not just the clothes, but faint, dark circles hung under his eyes. He looked . . . exhausted.

Joseph wrapped a hand around his margarita. "Can I ask where you went?"

"Tokyo." That stunned him. *Get ready, Joseph, here comes the mother of all surprises.* "I went with the guy from that night at the club. He lives there."

He froze.

"Crazy, huh?" I continued.

Slowly Joseph returned to life. "You're certainly not predictable. So, you're back. Are you and him–?"

I inhaled deeply and blew it out. "I don't know what we are."

Since arriving in the States, I hadn't heard from Dominic until this morning. I didn't sleep well without him. I lay

in bed, stared at the sunrise and wondered what he was doing on the other side of the earth. I was still so angry, but
fuck it. I pulled my phone off the charger.

> I'm still pissed at you.

You've got every right
to be. I'm so sorry.

Can I call you?

> No.

Can I be honest?

I didn't delete your
number. That's the only
thing I'm not sorry about.

Today was the first day I felt a little better. I told myself
it was because I'd completely recovered from the jet lag, but
it was bullshit. It was from opening the door to Dominic,
just a tiny bit.

Now I stared at Joseph and began to wonder about his
motivations. "Why did you want to get together? To see if I'd
come back to work?"

His eyebrows lifted in what seemed to be curiosity.
"Would you?"

"No."

"And if Mr. Red wanted to work out an arrangement,
would you be interested in that?"

My heart beat faster with anxiety. I hadn't thought
about Mr. Red at all, and doing so now only made my disdain for him more intense. "What kind of arrangement?"

"One that would make you exclusive to him. He wants you bad. As in, he'd pay for *everything*, bad. Car. Apartment. He's loaded up to his eyeballs."

"He wants me to be his on-call whore." I shuddered. "I don't care how much money he has, or how broke I'm about to be, a thousand times no."

Surely Joseph would make some percentage or land a fee if he could broker this arrangement, but he didn't look disappointed about my outright rejection. Instead his lips curled back in a bright smile.

"Then, I'd like to offer you a job."

Had he gotten stupid in the past two months? "I told you, I'm not going back to the club."

His smile was devious. "But what if it was to take over for me?"

My glass slipped from my fingers and thumped loudly on the table. "What? Where are you going?"

"I have some personal stuff to take care of. I need some time off."

My brain raced with thoughts but my voice went skeptical. "You want me to fill in for you?"

"You and I both know you can do it. Next to me, you're the one who knows the most about the club, and I trust you. It's not like what I do is all that hard. The place practically runs itself, but you've seen me handle the sticky situations."

Me running the club. The thought gave me a rush of power. And the money . . . "How much would I pull down?"

He laughed. "Probably more than you made in the room. Are you interested?"

"Fuck yeah, I'm interested." I was way more than just interested.

He detailed it all out then. I'd train and shadow him this weekend, and next weekend I would take over as manager. I spent the rest of the day at the club with him, learning how the monitor system worked and the cash-out process. It was weird to be back at the club, and I forced myself not to think about how I left.

A daily morning routine began to develop with my texts to Dominic.

I'm still pissed at you.

I know. I deserve it.

Can I call you?

No.

I refused to go over to Evie and Logan's place, but the reminders of Dominic were everywhere. The first time I got into my car, I couldn't enjoy the feeling of the steering wheel in my hands. All I could do was think about the man who had sat in the passenger seat last time I'd driven.

Thursday morning I woke from my restless sleep in my big, empty bed.

I'm still pissed at you, but that doesn't mean I don't miss you.

I miss you so much. Can I call you?

No.

Maybe tomorrow.

That night, I sat down and took a hard look at my finances. If I could make around ten grand during my weekend managing, which should be easy, I'd have enough breathing room to last to the end of my lease.

Or enough for a ticket back to Tokyo. I pushed the thought away.

On Friday I woke at four-thirty in the morning, my internal alarm clock ringing.

> I'm still mad.

> Can I call you?

His response was fast, as if he'd been waiting for me. I filled my lungs with air, then typed out the response I knew he'd interpret as consent.

> It'll be expensive.

Thirty seconds later, my phone rang.

"Hey," I said, my throat tight.

There was a sigh on the other end, one that sounded like relief. "Hey. How are you?"

I closed my eyes and my hand tightened on the phone. It'd been eleven and a half days since I'd last heard that rough voice. There were a million different responses I could have given him, but went with the safest. "I'm tired. It's really early here."

"I know. You didn't have to get up. I mean, when you're ready to talk, I'm ready. Whenever."

"Okay," I said. "Talk."

"I'm sorry. I can't say I'm sorry enough that I didn't tell you. I lose my shit around you."

"The Payton effect?" I groaned. "Seriously, this is your excuse? Your idiot decision-making is *my* fault?"

"Yeah, the Payton effect. You don't know what you do to me. You're all I think about. When I'm with you, I don't know, it's like everything else doesn't matter. It's only you.

I can't focus. And when you're not here? I can't fucking breathe." His voice dropped low and hesitant. "I wanted you to feel the same way about me, and I think that's part of why I put off making a decision, maybe subconsciously."

"What?"

"You're smart, and gorgeous, and confident . . . in Chicago? Some better guy is going to come along and steal you away. I wanted you in Japan so I didn't have any competition. I'm fucking weak." His voice was heavy with guilt.

Holy shit. "Are you insane? I mean, fucking insane? Who's going to compete with you?" There was silence on the other end of the line. "That's right. Nobody. Nobody who pushes me, and ignores my rules like a giant pain in the ass . . . and I mean *all* of my rules, including the one about love."

There was a sharp noise of surprise.

"But you fucked up. Believe me when I tell you I don't *do* lies. Test that rule again, and we're done. As in, forever. And that," I began to shake uncontrollably, "that would destroy me."

"Me too. I won't lie to you again, I promise. Never again."

"Good." There was a tightness in my chest I hadn't noticed until now, as it began to ease.

"Payton," His voice was strong. "I love you. Real." He exhaled into the phone. "Always real."

I wouldn't say those three words for the first time through the phone when he was on the other side of the world, so I gave him three different ones. "It better be." They were meant to be confident, but came from me shaky. Desperate.

I turned onto my side on the bed, and hearing his voice

in my darkened bedroom, I could pretend he was beside me. Maybe I'd finally be able to find sleep when we hung up.

And I'd need sleep.

Tonight I was going to make enough money to get my ass back to Tokyo, determined to get rid of all the unspoken things between us once and for all.

I sat in my front seat, put on a final coat of mascara, and ran through the schedule once more in my head. I'd parked out front of the club at nine – an hour before the girls would arrive. When I stepped out and locked the car, I tugged at my coat. Beneath, I wore my black pants, a royal blue top with a fitted black tux jacket over it, and high heels. My sexed-up version of professional.

Julius was waiting for me at the front door, a huge smile on his face.

"You happy to see me again?"

I grinned as I unlocked the door and stepped inside. "Of course. You weren't working last weekend."

I went room to room, flipping on lights and confirming setup.

Joseph's chair was comfortable when I sat in it and booted up his computer, hooked my earpiece in, then turned on the monitors and ensured the drives were recording. Joseph was right, the place did run itself. The girls arrived and checked in, and once I finished pairing sales assistants with the girls, I scanned the member appointment list.

"Tara?" I asked into the comm system. "Mr. Red's on the schedule."

"He does Claudia. She won't see anyone after him."

I marked a line through Claudia's name. I was more than a little curious to see Mr. Red's face. Most of the schedule was booked. "Whose girl is willing to take an unannounced guest?"

When there were no immediate takers, Tara joked, "How about you, Payton? Room Six is open."

There were some friendly laughs from my former coworkers, but I scowled. "No."

"Rachel says she's up for it," a female voice said through the earpiece.

"Okay, thanks. Let's go ahead and get into position. Julius?"

"Yeah, girl?"

"Can you show our first client in?"

Mr. Red showed up just after midnight. He checked in with Julius, had a glass of whiskey at the bar, and then Marquis escorted him to Room Two. I watched it all unfold on the monitors. Mr. Red's real name was Rosso, the Italian word for red. He was a media mogul who controlled half a dozen cable networks, and had one of those name-brand personalities, like Trump, or Cuban. Ironically, I'd worked for him before I came to the club. That job I hated, the one that had driven me here? Rosso owned the company.

Black Friday, when I called in and asked to be put on the schedule, Joseph had asked if I wanted to see Mr. Red. How fucking different would my life be if I'd said yes? Dominic would have been escorted into someone else's room and we'd never have met.

Tara wandered into the office shortly after the deal had

been struck and sat at the monitors beside me, her eyes on the flickering screens. Mr. Rosso had dropped five grand on Claudia. I'd never taken less than seven from him. I watched the screen as he pulled his cock out and shoved it in Claudia's mouth, face-fucking her on the table. I had the strange déjà vu feeling of wanting it to be over, even though I wasn't the one servicing him.

My phone buzzed on the desktop and I glanced at the screen. Dominic?

"Hey," he said, his voice curious when I answered. "Where are you?"

"I'm working, why?"

There was a long pause. "Working where?"

I hadn't told him about what I was doing because I didn't want him to know I'd have enough money to purchase a plane ticket. The goal had been to surprise him. I sighed. "I'm at the club."

"You're . . . *where?*" It didn't come out angry, it came out horrified.

Wait, did he think I meant I was working as one of the girls? My face heated with annoyance. Yeah, I hadn't actually said the words out loud, but he knew I loved him, right? That I belonged to him, and wouldn't even consider . . .

"Dominic, wait, it's not like that."

"How exactly is it like?" Now there was anger in his voice.

Oh. So, I guess he did think I was seeing clients again. My stunned, hurt silence probably didn't help.

"Did you take any offers tonight?"

The hurt was burned up and replaced with rage. It flooded in my veins and overpowered my brain. "Nope, not yet."

He exhaled in a burst. This was a lie by omission and I

let it hang for a moment because the bitch inside me wanted to see how much he liked it when the tables were turned.

"Then again," I added, "my price has gone way up. No one can afford me."

"I can."

I gave a bitter laugh. "Okay, stop by and make an offer."

It was deadly silent on the other end of the line, until his deep voice rumbled. "I'll be there in twenty minutes."

TWENTY-EIGHT

I tried to call him back, but Dominic didn't answer, not my calls, or my texts. My heart pounded. He was here in the States? What the hell was going on? I fidgeted in my seat, not sure what to do. Was he really coming to the club and planning to make an offer?

"You okay?" Tara asked.

No. Not at all. I was still angry and hurt, but the excitement that Dominic was on the same continent as me trumped that. "Yeah, I'm okay," I lied.

She gave me a skeptical look, but her focus returned to the monitors. My brain refused to acknowledge what was happening on the screen with the two writhing bodies on it. My attention was painted on the front entry camera.

I'd barely been able to breathe while waiting, but fifteen minutes later when Dominic stepped inside, my lungs quit working altogether. Even on the grainy black and white screen, I could see every detail. He looked exhausted, but it was masked with anger and pain.

"Oh, hell no," Marquis snapped immediately. "You on the blacklist."

"Wait!" I all but screamed it into the comm. "Marquis, wait a minute."

"Payton McCreary," Dominic said, his voice filtering through the speaker. "I'm going to see her right fucking now."

Marquis smiled and it was disturbing. Dominic wasn't small – he was cut and lean, but Marquis was a mountain of muscle and aggression. He liked to fight, and he looked thrilled that this white-boy might challenge him.

"Don't know no one by that name," Marquis lied.

Dominic's hands balled into fists. "Paige."

"She ain't seeing clients no more."

"She'll see me."

Marquis turned and looked up at the camera, like he was looking directly at me. "What you want me to do about this?"

My voice was breathy. "Put him in holding room B."

I glanced at the other monitors. Only Claudia was still on. Rosso wasn't going to be a safety issue, but Tara was still watching just in case.

"Julius, where are you?" I said, pushing back from the desk and standing.

"Just left the payment room."

"Meet me at Room Six in one minute." My focus locked on Tara, and her gaze followed me as I gestured to the screen. "Can you give me updates on this?"

Her eyes went wide as she realized what was happening. "Holy shit, you're going to take the blacklist walk-in?" She peered closer to the monitor. "Wow, he's fucking hot. I can do him."

Like I needed to add jealousy to the list of emotions swirling inside me. "I know he's hot. That's my boyfriend."

I heard her surprised gasp as I hurried across the hall to the changing room, stripping off my clothes. My hands clawed at fabric, flinging my bra and underwear into a heap, and I yanked on one of the silk robes, repositioning the earpiece and comm pack. I thought only about this task, about getting down the stairs and into the room, and not how it was going to play out once that happened.

"What's going on?" Julius asked me as I rushed to the door of Room Six. His gaze passed over my robe.

"I need your help." I tugged at his arm, pushed at the door, and turned on the light.

He froze. "Not supposed to go into the rooms."

"Tonight you can. I'm the boss."

He followed me inside but looked at the room like he was sure it was going to explode at any second. "What do you need help with?"

I scrambled to pull out the blindfold and the straps from the cabinets beneath the table. Julius was so cautious, I knew I couldn't ask or he'd tell me no. I undid the sash on my robe and slipped it off, casting it onto the white chair.

"What–?" His eyes went as large as bowling balls. His gaze flitted down over my naked body and settled at my feet.

I moved as quickly as possible, pulling the blindfold on, and tucking the comm pack in one fist so I could push the *talk* button if needed. My back slammed against the cushion-top. "Strap me down."

There were no footsteps closer, and I imagined him staring at that same spot on the ground.

"Please. I can't ask Tara, and I sure as shit won't ask Marquis."

Still nothing.

"I'll give you two hundred dollars, but you gotta do it right now."

There you go. A smile tweaked on my lips as he moved closer. His hand closed on my wrist, wrapping the Velcro closed.

"Are you looking?" I teased.

"Nah." He moved and did my other wrist. "But if I was, I'd say, damn, girl. You fucking sexy."

"Thanks," I grinned, and then sobered a little. "Send the man in holding room B in here."

His heavy footfalls got quieter and I heard the door swing shut, leaving me alone with my racing thoughts. Why hadn't Dominic told me he was in Chicago, and how long had he been here? Deep down, part of me was thrilled he'd come. For me.

My pulse raced when the door creaked open and someone entered. The door slammed shut and I jumped at the boom.

"Fuck," Dominic said. "Tell me I'm the only man who's been in this room."

Technically Julius . . . "You're the only client who's been in here. I had them put you in the holding room so I could give you what you wanted."

"What I wanted?"

The longer he remained motionless, the angrier I got. "Yeah, a whore. You think that's what I am, right? That I would fuck someone else, like you mean nothing to me. When the hell did you get to Chicago?"

"My flight landed at ten, and I went straight to your place."

My thoughts scrambled. "Why?"

"For you. You're here, and I want to be with you." Finally, it sounded like he took one step forward. Then, another, and the rough voice grew louder. "But I don't understand why you're *here*."

I gasped. "Because I'm managing the club tonight. Five minutes ago I was upstairs, dressed and sitting behind a computer." It was then I realized what a stupid plan this had been. I was blindfolded and restrained when I wanted desperately to see him. "Take off my blindfold."

There was hesitation. "You were managing? Why?"

"Because Joseph asked me to." I didn't want to lie. No more unspoken things between us. "Because I wanted enough money to buy a plane ticket to Tokyo."

It sounded like he stopped breathing. "What?"

"I was under the impression you couldn't leave, you know. But here you are. Can you undo my straps?"

There was no noise so I didn't think he was moving. "I told Chase I had an emergency, and they gave me off until Wednesday." His voice wavered. "The plan is I go back if you want me gone. But if you want me to stay . . . I'll stay."

"What about your job?"

"Fuck it. You're all I care about." His words were like warmth, wrapping all around me. It was annoying I couldn't see his face or those aqua eyes. "So . . . the question is, why were you coming back to Tokyo?"

Because I loved him, but once again, the nervous flutter in my stomach crept into my throat and made the words difficult. "Come on," I stalled, "surely you know the answer to that."

"I'd like to hear it. And don't call me Shirley."

My pulse raced. I squirmed against the straps. "Get these off me first."

"No, no, no. Things are going to go differently than the last time we were here."

Uh oh. The determined timbre of his voice was sexy as fuck. Suddenly those straps weren't quite as binding.

"There's no list." His words were low and seductive. "How am I supposed to know what you're offering?"

I bit down on my bottom lip, attempted to keep my breathing steady and to sound confident. "Maybe . . . I'm offering everything."

His hurried breathing said he was standing right over me. "Everything? What does *everything* run these days?"

"I don't know. A hundred grand."

His hot breath washed over my skin. He was hovering what seemed to be only an inch from my lips. "Will you take a check?"

"I'd prefer it in yen. But I don't want your money." My pulse raced a million miles an hour. "Just you."

The coarse skin of his palm heated my cheek and that thumb slid over my lips. "I love you."

As that thumb brushed away, it brushed all my unease away with it. I wasn't scared or nervous or shy.

"I love you, Dominic."

I melted beneath his kiss that was a thousand times better than any orgasm, more passionate than any time we'd been together. His kiss dripped with love, commitment, and the promise of more. I trembled beneath his lips, in his hands. *Dear god, don't let this kiss stop.* The straps cracked and went taut against my attempt to seize Dominic's head when his lips left mine.

Last time I'd worried he might kiss me a second time, and now I was worried he might not.

"Where are you going?" I cried. And . . . what the hell was he doing? His hand was on mine. "I'm not interested in your sexy hand-holding right now."

His kiss had left me disoriented, and it took a full five seconds to comprehend what was happening. I couldn't stop him with the straps. My left hand stayed immobile while the ring descended onto my finger.

"What the fuck do you think you're doing?" I demanded.

"You said you were offering everything." His lips brushed over mine. "Go ahead and tell me you don't do marriage."

Holy. Shit.

That gaudy, fake ring rested comfortably there on my finger. I trembled, but not in fear. It was with excitement and something else, something new. And it intensified when I considered giving him a real answer. Was this feeling . . . was this happiness?

I'd always been adventurous, up for whatever. And marrying Dominic would be the ultimate adventure.

"I don't do marriage." I could barely hear myself over the heartbeat pounding in my ears. "I don't do talking, or sleeping, or love," I whispered. "Not with anyone . . . but you."

The mattress shifted as he climbed on top of the table, on top of me. I didn't know how long we made out. It was the most innocent thing I'd ever done here at the club and easily the hottest. His slow, sensual mouth met mine, teasing me with his tongue and teeth. I whimpered as he mouthed kisses down the side of my neck, to the hollow at the base of my throat.

"Payton," Tara's voice said in my earpiece, "Mr. Red just finished."

I pressed the *talk* button. "Julius to Room Four."

"What was that?" Dominic's voice rumbled.

"Nothing, work stuff." I sighed as his hands closed on my breasts. I arched into his caress, but his fingers danced lightly, like he was staying just out of reach. "You fucking proposed with a fake ring, don't tease me, too."

He chuckled. "I took that fake one to the jeweler for sizing. I don't know what he did with it."

My brain blanked. The ring I was wearing, "It's real?"

"Yes. Real."

"Is it big?"

His hips moved, pressing his hard-on against me. "It's huge."

I giggled at his silly innuendo. "I know that's huge. Take off my blindfold."

"I told you, things are going to go differently this time. You don't get to be in charge. I learned that lesson the hard way."

His mouth skimmed over my nipple and I moaned. "Please?"

"Do you want me to, uh, turn the cameras off?" Tara asked, her voice breathless.

The corner of my mouth curled in a smile. Tara was one dirty girl. Similar to me, she liked both men and women, but unlike me, I think she liked women more. She loved to watch, too. Of course I didn't have any problem with her watching. Hell, she could come down and get a front row.

The blindfold slipped up and away. I smiled up at him, almost shy. Like I was looking at him with new eyes now that everything was out in the open.

"Hi," I whispered.

"Hi. If you don't like it," his gaze went up to my hand, "we can go back and pick something else out."

"Holy fuck, Dominic."

The ring was huge. The size other women would say, "that's too much for me" but you'd wonder if secretly they were jealous. An enormous round solitaire ringed with smaller diamonds that descended down the band.

"It's beautiful."

He gave me a sly grin. "You're going to take it off as soon as I undo the straps, aren't you?"

Was he fucking crazy? I shook my head. "The only way it's coming off is if you pry it from my cold, dead hand."

His mouth covered mine as his fingers walked over my skin, traveling lower toward the juncture of my thighs.

"Are we going to fuck on this table?" I asked.

His fingers slipped down to touch me, slow and hot. "Do you want to?"

"Undo my straps."

"Not a chance." His touch set me on fire. "We're going to do this slow this time."

I stared at the aqua eyes and grinned. He thought he was in control just because he had me strapped down to the table? I punched the *talk* button.

"Tara to Room Six."

chapter
TWENTY-NINE

Dominic was oblivious to the door opening because he was going down on me. His tongue grazed my clit and then his mouth seized on it, sucking. I moaned and watched him through half-closed eyes. Fuck, that felt good.

"Yeah, right there," I whispered.

Tara took a quiet step into the room, wearing only the silk robe, her face flushed as she watched him fuck me with his mouth. Her long, bottle-blonde hair hung straight to her shoulders. She was Barbie-pretty. Big tits, small waist, and curvy hips. I was curious what he'd think of her.

His finger pushed inside me, working together with his mouth to pull the orgasm from me.

"I want these straps off."

"Pretty sure I said no."

"Maybe I'm not talking to you."

He froze. "What?"

Her robe came off at that moment, and the blur of motion drew his gaze. Dominic bolted upright, his hand tensing on my thigh. His head snapped to me. *Oh my god!* Adorable, embarrassed Dominic. I felt like I hadn't seen him in forever.

I had a smug smile on my lips as she stepped to the table and undid my straps. He didn't stop her. He was too stunned and trying not to look at her. She was beautiful. Her tits were round and firm, her nipples were a pale pink that matched her lips. The soft line of her body drew my gaze down to her bare slit, and further to her legs. Shit. Tara gave me a run for my money on the best legs at this club.

"Dominic, this is Tara. Just so you know, she offered to do you when you came in."

She laughed, her eyes shining. I sat up, yanked out my earpiece, and reached for Dominic, hooking a hand around the back of his neck and pulling him into a kiss. He was hesitant, thrown off-balance.

"Do you want to fool around with her?" I whispered. "Like, together?"

My fingers curled under the hem of his T-shirt and pushed it up, gathering it until I could yank it over his head and pull it off. His gorgeous chest wasn't moving. Once again, I didn't think he was breathing. "Are you going into shock?"

"Maybe."

I climbed off the table. "Sit down." He had been up for god knew how long, he was probably exhausted. So he sat reluctantly on the table, one hand on my hip, his focus on me.

"We should talk about this," he said, worry pooling in his eyes.

"I didn't know you were into girls," Tara said, a pleased and anticipatory expression on her face.

"I'm still kind of new to it." I put my hands on Dominic's shoulders and urged him to lie back on the table. "You'll be my third."

"Payton," he said, his voice serious.

I climbed on top of him, straddling his hips. "Don't you want to watch me go down on her while you're fucking me?"

He gave a sexy groan and I could feel his cock twitch all the way through his jeans. "Yeah, but you want that?"

"Fuck yeah." Hands tangled in my hair and yanked me down into his brutal, raw kiss. My hands wrapped around his wrists and slowly pressed them back. Further until he let me pin his wrists to the leather.

"Tara, a little help?"

She picked up the strap and closed the Velcro around his wrist, then strolled to the other side of the table, her tits bouncing as she went.

"Wait a minute," he said, realizing too late what was happening. With the one hand bound, I latched both of mine on his free wrist, holding him while he began to resist. She was fast though, and a moment later he was bound. The straps went taut as he struggled, and his eyes went white.

"Do you remember the safe word?" I teased. His nod was just there, buried under his shock. God, this was fucking sexy. I climbed off of the table and went to Tara, his head turning to watch us.

A playful smile tugged on her lips. "I wish I'd known sooner," she said. "I think you're gorgeous."

Her mouth was on mine, her lips demanding I kiss her back while her hands slipped around my waist, sliding lower to grab my ass. It brought our bodies together and her firm breasts pressed against mine. Her kiss was seductive, but it didn't compare to the one of the man watching. When it ended, I whispered in her ear what I wanted to do.

His gaze followed every step I took around the table so she was on one side and I was on the other. My finger-tips trailed down the center of his chest, flowing over the notches of his abs, to the snap of his jeans. I popped it open. His chest rose and fell rapidly, his breath unsteady when I inched the zipper down, and tugged his jeans over his hips. I was excited to have him back in my hands. My mouth.

"Get ready to be jealous," I said to Tara. She smirked

right back at me.

"Shit," he groaned. I dug his thick cock out of his boxers and pushed them down out of my way.

"I am jealous," she said, pointing to the ring on my hand that clenched around him. "His cock's big, too."

She watched as I stroked him, her gaze fixed on the hand sliding up and down the length. She didn't last long. Her hand clamped at the base and squeezed, and the body beneath our grips shuddered.

His head lifted and Dominic watched us both lower in, his expression frozen. "Shit, are you two gonna . . .?"

"Yeah," I said. "We are."

And together, we licked him. There was a snap from the restraints as he bucked against them. He exhaled loudly. Oh my god, was he trembling? I swirled my tongue on the tip of his cock, drawing a moan that rumbled up from his chest. Desire burned across my skin. I drew up, put my hand on the back of her head, and guided her to take him inside her mouth.

"Fuck, *fuck*."

"You like that?" I asked her in a seductive voice. Dominic stared down while her head bobbed on him. "You like sucking my boyfriend's fat cock?"

"Fiancé," he corrected, although it sounded like he was struggling for air. *Fiancé*. There was a label I never thought I'd like, but of course, I was wrong. Tara pulled off of him and held his dick for me, giving me a turn. His warm, damp flesh parted my lips and slid back into my throat.

I pumped on him, sliding up and down in leisurely strokes, swirling my tongue. On the table, he moved under my mouth, writhing. Air was swallowed in huge gasps when

Tara and I returned to sharing him. Our tongues met wandering over his cock.

"Holy shit . . . holy shit . . . Payton."

When I rose up and turned to face him, Tara took over sucking him. His face was like that first time in the room. Tortured agony.

"Don't make him come," I warned her, then set my focus on him. "I like you like this," I whispered, echoing his words from that night with Akira and Yuriko, "trying to hold it together. It turns me on like you can't believe."

He moaned, his blue eyes slamming shut.

My hands bristled on his unshaven jaw when I cupped his face and brought my lips to his warm, trembling ones. My fingers crept back behind his neck and into his thick hair. I clenched a fistful and yanked his head back, lifting his chin up so I could drag my tongue down his neck. "You want to fuck me? Say it."

I could just hear it over the sounds of her sucking his cock. "I want to fuck you."

I nipped at his soft flesh. "You want me to lick her pussy? Say please."

It came from both of them, desperate. "Please."

Velcro ripped open as I undid one wrist. That was all I needed to do, he did the other immediately. Fuck, that was a mistake. When he was free, he stood from the table, yanked the pants and boxers the rest of the way down his legs, and shot me a predatory look.

"I told you I was going to be in charge."

He spun me in his hands and shoved me so I was belly down on the table. I pushed up on my arms, but the slap of his hand against my ass made me collapse forward. It was shocking to swing from dominant to submissive so quickly, but a rush. One I felt deep inside.

"Count." His dark order make me ache and eager.

"One, *Arigatō*."

"In English." His rough voice filled my ears. Tara watched from the other side of the table, like she wasn't really sure what to do, but intrigued.

His second spanking stung and left my flesh hot.

"Two, thank you."

It turned me on so much that my desire ran down between my legs. I blinked and was upright, my back against his chest. His hands slid all over naked curves, his lips drawing a line of kisses down my neck. Oh, he wasn't playing fair. I shivered from his hot breath and his indecent mouth.

"Tell your friend," he said, "to get on the table."

I blinked my lust-heavy eyes at her. "Tara—"

That was all she needed to hear. The leather squeaked when she sat and flopped down on her back. I moved between her legs and let my hands slip over her smooth skin. I tweaked her nipple, getting her to cry out with satisfaction, and skimmed my fingers lower.

"Your pussy's so wet," I said. Her flesh was slick and lush, and my thumb brushed over her swollen clit. More cries of desperation from her. Her hands gathered her hair up and spread it out behind her like a curtain of blonde silk. As if she were settling in, preparing for the pleasure I was about to give her.

Dominic kept a hand wrapped on his cock, squeezing. The thick, flexed bicep was mouth-watering. I needed him. I needed the connection to him now.

"Fuck me," I demanded.

He moved behind me, a hand on my waist. The other cracked on my ass so hard it stole my breath. His aggressive voice flashed lust straight into me. "Don't tell me what to do."

"Fuck," I swore under my breath. "Three, thank you."

His hands were on my hips now, his hard cock positioned to drive into me. My head fell down between Tara's bent knees and, as I tasted her for the first time, his cock began to intrude.

She whimpered. I let my tongue explore, but paused to catch my breath as Dominic slid deep inside, all the way to the hilt. My eyes slammed shut. That electricity between us, would it last our entire lives? I was excited to find out.

"Goddamn. Do you feel how hard I am inside you?"

"Yes," I moaned. "It feels so fucking good." The pleasure he gave me was unreal. My tongue fluttered over her clit, and it made Tara's chest lift off the tabletop.

"Put your tongue inside her."

When I did, his fingers curled on my flesh and he began to fuck me. Holy god, just one long thrust of that hard dick made everything tingle. The woman beneath me cried out and she fisted her hands in my hair.

"Yes, fuck me with that mouth, yes . . . yes . . ."

I sucked at the button of flesh and her body shuddered in response. The taste of her coated my lips, my mouth, my chin. It rolled down my throat. Behind me, Dominic established his pace. Steady and deep, but of course, slow.

"You dirty, little slut," he teased. "You like her pussy? Does she taste good?"

I shook her hold off of me and turned over my shoulder to look at him, her juices wet on my lips. "Kiss me and find out."

His eyes hooded with lust. He bent and his mouth collided with mine, his tongue probing and tasting. The moan from him brought my orgasm closer. My muscles clenched, choking the cock inside me, and Dominic broke the kiss, hissing through his teeth.

"Don't do that, devil woman."

"What, this?" I flexed my muscles again and he groaned. A hand shoved my head back between her legs, forcing my mouth against her quaking skin. I latched onto her, the smell of her thick and sexy. Hands threaded through my hair once again. Her hands.

The orgasm inched closed, creeping until the need was too great to think about anything else. Not her moaning. Not his building thrusts. Only the fire that needed relief.

"Don't stop," she gasped. "I'm gonna come all over that face."

He exhaled, giving a noise of approval. Hips beat his cock inside me, marking me over and over again, his tempo as fast as the heartbeat pounding in my ears. Pinpricks danced over my body, signaling the climax was about to take me. I made my final push to try to get her there before I lost control. This orgasm was going to be massive and threatened to make movement impossible. I sank two fingers into her hot channel, and it gripped at me like a vise.

"*Fuck!*" she screamed. It looked like ecstasy rolled through her. Her body went rigid for a moment, followed by uncontrolled jerks that gave me satisfaction. Thank god I was about to come too, or I might have been jealous.

I waited for his command as she seized, the hands tensing in my hair and then falling away. But Dominic was silent. Just the sound of his strangled breathing came from him.

"Tell me to come," I said. It was supposed to be an order, although I begged it.

"No. I'm never going to do that again." Another lesson he probably thought he'd learned the hard way with me. Two for him, but I'd learned three.

Don't tease him.

Don't give him boundaries.

Don't think you get a choice in who you love. All of my struggle against falling for him had been pointless. I was his, and he was mine. My body had known it from the moment his hand brushed my fingers our first night together, cluing me in with those unexpected sparks.

"I love you," I said. "Oh my god, I love you." Declaring it once again was the last piece to push me over the edge, sending me into that never-ending pleasure that only he could give me. His hoarse cry repeated those three words back, and he followed my orgasm with his own.

A sweaty, heaving chest pressed against me and the heart trapped inside was pounding like it wanted to break free from its cage. Which would be okay, since he had mine as a backup.

I turned my head to the side, my gaze fixed on those striking eyes.

"Mine," I whispered to him.

"Yours. Forever."

chapter
THIRTY

I stopped viewing Chase Sports as the enemy when they helped secure my visa. Sure, they dominated Dominic's time, and he hated his shitty office and repetitive work, but it was temporary. We'd be home in four months.

Four more months in Tokyo I could deal with. It was late summer now, and the cherry blossoms were beautiful. Romantic. One of the things I was sure I'd miss when we returned to Chicago. But there was plenty I wouldn't miss too. We'd always be treated as foreigners – second-class citizens, by everyone except for Akira and Yuriko. I didn't fault the Japanese for it. It was just the culture.

It was early Tuesday morning in Tokyo when I called Evie on Skype.

"Hey!" she said, her warm eyes smiling. "Your flight still on time?"

"Yeah." I took a sip of my drink that was more vodka than orange juice and received a knowing smile from her. "I'm going to wake Dominic up in a few minutes and then we're on our way to the airport."

Her and Logan's wedding was Saturday, and Dominic had gotten ten days of vacation approved for it. I hated being so far away and a crappy maid of honor to her, but Evie handled it gracefully. She wanted us to be happy, and this annoying living situation was something both Logan and she dealt with. They understood it was necessary, plus they got a pretty sweet apartment out of the deal.

At least I'd be in Chicago early enough to throw an epic bachelorette party and give Evie plenty of time to recover before the big day. Dominic had mentioned he had a similar plan for Logan.

"I can't wait to see you guys, you know, all life-sized," she said.

I chuckled. "I'm right there with you." The webcam was getting old. Four more months, I reminded myself. "I was just calling to let you know your wedding week officially starts as soon as my plane lands." I held up my drink. "I've already started, but I'll text you when to start doing shots."

She laughed. "Wedding week? Logan's mom has already turned this into wedding month. But okay, I'll have a bottle of tequila at the ready—"

"Where the fuck's my morning blowjob?" came from the doorway to our bedroom. I looked over to see Dominic standing there, his hand disappearing into his boxers. He thought this was Meredith since we'd started talking regularly on the weekends. Dominic loved to make his sister uncomfortable with his now-famous catchphrase.

"Wow," Evie said, an eyebrow raised.

"I gotta run."

"Yeah, sounds like it," she teased, her eyes sparkling. "Have a safe flight."

"See you soon." I shut the laptop and set my eyes on him.

He sauntered over and dropped down beside me on the couch. "Was that Evie?"

"Yeah."

He nuzzled into my neck.

"We need to get a move on," I said.

One of his hands fumbled for my breasts, oblivious that I wasn't reciprocating. His other hand found mine and put it on his boxers, like I needed guidance.

"We're going to be late, and you told me that word doesn't exist here."

He continued to ignore me and his wicked mouth ghosted kisses on my skin. Dominic knew exactly what he was doing and how to turn me on. He'd learned every inch of my body in the ten months we'd been together, but there was more to it than just that. We'd fallen deeper in love than I could have imagined, and the connection between us was so hot I could barely catch my breath around him.

"Okay, seriously," I said, trying to break free from his seduction. "Didn't you get enough last night?"

His eyes glazed with lust. Yeah, bringing that up hadn't been the best idea, because now we were *both* thinking about how insane it had been. Yuriko and Akira had come over to play.

We didn't see our Japanese friends that often. Between all of our jobs, including mine where I taught English, it was hard to get schedules to align. They'd arrived late and we'd gone immediately into the master bedroom. There was a hierarchy within our group, but last night it had shifted slightly. I'd stood over Yuriko with the crop in my hand, punishing her under Akira's instructions while my fiancé translated. The memory of Dominic's sexy words in my ear while his hands stroked inside my panties made me burn hot. Then the memory of the rush of power and the satisfaction on Yuriko's face cranked the temperature up to an unbearable level.

"Shit, now I'm all turned on," I groaned, "and we've got a thirteen hour flight."

Dominic pulled me onto his lap so I was straddling him. "What are you whining about?" He grinned widely. "You don't do slow, so let's do fast." He ground his hips up into me. "And hard." His mouth crashed against mine as his hands tore at my clothes. "I bet I can get you to come twice in the next ten minutes. I'll even let you decide how."

My body shuddered as I thought of all the ways he could do it. "You know, I fucking love you."

"You fucking love me, or you love fucking me?" His voice rasped as he yanked my shirt over my head and tugged my bra down.

"Yes."

He glanced at my half-empty breakfast cocktail and faked seriousness. "I hope that's not just the booze talking."

"Real, Dominic." I laughed. "Always real."

Always.

THANK YOU

To my husband. I am the luckiest girl in the world to be loved by you, and I promise to never forget that. Thank you for forever.

To my beta reader Robin Bateman. You are awesome on so many levels, it isn't even funny.

To my editor Lori Whitwam. Some day I'll figure out when to use lie vs. lay, and stop saying 'that' when referring to people. Thanks for sticking with me, and I can't wait to work together again.

To my publicist Neda Amini for twisting arms to get people to read a brand-new author who you believed in.

IF YOU ENJOYED THE BOOK

What had originally started as a novella and bloomed into a full-length novel, then a series, has been an absolute joy to write—one I could not stop, much like a drug. Thank you so much for taking the time to read Payton's story. If you enjoyed it, would you be so kind as to let other readers know via an Amazon review or on Goodreads? Just a few words can help an author tremendously, and are *always* appreciated!

THREE *simple* RULES

BOOK ONE IN THE BLINDFOLD CLUB SERIES

"Three Simple Rules is a smoking hot read that will have you hooked from the first page. Nikki Sloane is a hot new erotic author to watch for."

-The SubClub Books

"Get ready to be hot and bothered because Nikki Sloane creates the perfect erotic storm and you will love getting caught up in it!"

-Agents of Romance

"Hot, sexy, steamy, and so much more, Nikki delivers a story that will keep you begging for more!"

-Bella from PBC

"Undeniably explosive, flirty, and addictive... We were hooked!"

-The Rock Stars of Romance

"A slick, captivating, and incredibly sexy book. Sloane injects humor and depth into a compelling story, and ensures readers will be back for more."

-SM Book Obsessions

THREE *little* MISTAKES

"My club began to dominate my focus. So dark and illegal, the smell of it didn't wash off for days.

And I fucking *loved* it."

Joseph
owner of the
Blindfold Club

Get to know him
Summer 2015

ABOUT THE AUTHOR

Nikki Sloane fell into graphic design after her careers as a waitress, a screenwriter, and a ballroom dance instructor fell through. For eight years she worked for a design firm in that extremely tall, black, and tiered building in Chicago that went through an unfortunate name change during her time there. Now she lives in Kentucky and manages a team of graphic artists. She is married and has two sons, writes both romantic suspense and dirty books, and couldn't be any happier.

Find her on the web: www.NikkiSloane.com

Contact her on Twitter: @AuthorNSloane

Send her an email: authornikkisloane@gmail.com

Made in the USA
Columbia, SC
22 July 2021